THE LEGEND OF NIMWAY HALL

1750: JACQUELINE

2

STEPHANIE LAURENS

THE LEGEND OF NIMWAY HALL 1750:
JACQUELINE

#1 New York Times bestselling author Stephanie Laurens brings you the opening story in a series of romances touched by magic as old as time.

A gentleman fleeing the bonds of loveless marriage and a lady in desperate need of a champion join forces to defend an ancient legacy.

Jacqueline Tregarth, lady and guardian of Nimway Hall, is devoted to protecting her people, the Hall, the estate's wood, and its farms. She yearns for a husband to help her meet the challenges, but all those seeking her hand are interested only in controlling her lands. With the estate's stream running dry and summer looming, she sets men digging to reopen an old spring. Her workers discover a dirt-encrusted ornament buried at the spot; once removed, water flows and fills the old lake—and Jacqueline realizes the ornament is some kind of ancient orb.

Meanwhile, Lord Richard Devries, overly-eligible darling of the ton, fights free of kidnappers seeking to force him to offer for some lady's hand. But on escaping into the countryside, he gets lost in Balesboro Wood and stumbles on a covert scheme to divert a stream. Later, he finds his way to Nimway Hall, where the household is celebrating a spring running again.

Richard is welcomed and meets the fascinating Miss Tregarth. That his youthful hostess is disinclined to bat her lashes at him piques his inter-est, yet after his recent experiences, he feels safe in her company—for him, an unusual and comforting experience. Indeed, everything about Nimway Hall is calming and soothing.

Then Richard makes the connection between what he saw in the wood and the Hall's recent water shortage and leads Jacqueline and her men to the diversion in the wood. Subsequently, he learns of the various men pursuing Jacqueline, and recognizes the danger to her and to the Hall. Although self-protective instinct presses him to travel on, his lamed horse has yet to recover, and despite all inner warnings, Richard feels compelled to step into the role of a supportive protector.

Aided and abetted by the household, the estate community, Balesboro Wood, and the ancient orb, propinquity works its magic, seducing Richard with a role into which he and his talents fit perfectly, and tempting Jacqueline to hope that her champion has finally found his way to her side. If the tales told of those snared by Balesboro Wood and sent to the Hall are true, then…

Yet true love never runs smoothly, and both Richard and Jacqueline must search within, embrace their destinies, and find the courage to seize their heart's one true desire—all just in time to foil a dastardly plan that would wreck all they and the Hall's people hold dear.

First in series. A historical novel of 73,000 words interweaving romance, mystery, and magic.

PRAISE FOR THE WORKS OF STEPHANIE LAURENS

Praise for the works of Stephanie Laurens

"Stephanie Laurens' heroines are marvelous tributes to Georgette Heyer: feisty and strong." *Cathy Kelly*

"Stephanie Laurens never fails to entertain and charm her readers with vibrant plots, snappy dialogue, and unforgettable characters." *Historical Romance Reviews*

"Stephanie Laurens plays into readers' fantasies like a master and claims their hearts time and again." *Romantic Times Magazine*

Praise for The Legend of Nimway Hall – 1750: Jacqueline

"A romance fueled by more than one kind of magic, *The Legend of Nimway Hall (1750: Jacqueline)* is an utterly spellbinding tale." *Angela M., Copy Editor, Red Adept Editing*

"Mystical, historical, and entirely romantic, *The Legend of Nimway Hall (1750: Jacqueline)* will draw you in and captivate you as only a true love story can. Never has there been a more perfect pair than Jacqueline and

Richard. Their tale is one for the ages." *Amanda K., Proofreader, Red Adept Editing*

"Stephanie Laurens gives another delightful tour of the eighteenth-century English countryside, manners, mysteries, magic, mirth, and all." *Kim H., Proofreader, Red Adept Editing*

OTHER TITLES BY STEPHANIE LAURENS

A Fine Passion

To Distraction

Beyond Seduction

The Edge of Desire

Mastered by Love

Black Cobra Quartet

The Untamed Bride

The Elusive Bride

The Brazen Bride

The Reckless Bride

The Adventurers Quartet

The Lady's Command

A Buccaneer at Heart

The Daredevil Snared

Lord of the Privateers

The Cavanaughs

The Designs of Lord Randolph Cavanaugh (April 24, 2018)

Other Novels

The Lady Risks All

The Legend of Nimway Hall – 1750: Jacqueline

Medieval (As M.S.Laurens)

Desire's Prize

Novellas

Melting Ice – from the anthologies *Rough Around the Edges* and *Scandalous Brides*

Rose in Bloom – from the anthology *Scottish Brides*

Scandalous Lord Dere – from the anthology *Secrets of a Perfect Night*

Lost and Found – from the anthology *Hero, Come Back*

The Fall of Rogue Gerrard – from the anthology *It Happened One Night*

The Seduction of Sebastian Trantor – from the anthology *It Happened One Season*

Short Stories

The Wedding Planner – from the anthology *Royal Weddings*

A Return Engagement – from the anthology *Royal Bridesmaids*

UK-Style Regency Romances

Tangled Reins

Four in Hand

Impetuous Innocent

Fair Juno

The Reasons for Marriage

A Lady of Expectations An Unwilling Conquest

A Comfortable Wife

THE LEGEND OF NIMWAY HALL 1750:
JACQUELINE

THE LEGEND OF NIMWAY HALL

1750: JACQUELINE

Copyright © 2018 by Savdek Management Proprietary Limited

ISBN: 978-1-925559-09-5

Cover design by Savdek Management Pty. Ltd.

Savdek Management Proprietary Limited, Melbourne, Australia.

www.stephanielaurens.com

Email: admin@stephanielaurens.com

The name Stephanie Laurens is a registered trademark of Savdek Management Proprietary Ltd.

❀ Created with Vellum

THE LEGEND OF NIMWAY HALL

A love invested with mystery and magic sends ripples through the ages.

Long ago in a cave obscured by the mists of time, Nimue, a powerful sorceress and Merlin's beloved, took the energy of their passion and wove it into a potent love spell. Intending the spell to honor their love and enshrine it in immortality, she merged the spell into the large moonstone in the headpiece of Merlin's staff. Thus, when Merlin was far from her, he still carried the aura of their love with him and, so they both believed, the moonstone would act as a catalyst for true love, inciting and encouraging love to blossom in the hearts of those frequently in the presence of the stone.

Sadly, despite all their power, neither Merlin nor Nimue foresaw the heart of Lancelot. A minor adept, he sensed both the presence of the spell in the moonstone and the spell's immense power. Driven by his own desires, Lancelot stole the headpiece and used the moonstone's power to sway Guinevere to his side.

Furious that the spell crafted from the pure love of his and his beloved's hearts had been misused, Merlin smote Lancelot and seized back the headpiece. To protect it forevermore, Merlin laid upon the stone a web of control that restricted its power. Henceforth, it could act only in response to a genuine need for true love and only when that need impacted one of his and Nimue's blood, no matter how distant.

Ultimately, Merlin sent the headpiece back to Nimue for safekeeping. As the Lady of the Lake, at that time, she lived in a cottage on an island surrounded by swiftly flowing streams, and it was in her power to see and watch over their now-dispersed offspring.

Time passed, and even those of near immortality faded and vanished.

The land about Nimue's cottage drained, and the region eventually became known as Somerset.

Generations came and went, but crafted of spelled gold, the headpiece endured and continued to hold and protect the timeless moonstone imbued with Nimue's and Merlin's spells...

Over time, a house, crafted of sound local stone and timbers from the surrounding Balesboro Wood, was built on the site of Nimue's cottage. The house became known as Nimway Hall. From the first, the house remained in the hands and in the care of a female descendant of Nimue, on whom devolved the responsibilities of guardian of Nimway Hall. As decades and then centuries passed, the tradition was established that, in each generation, the title of and responsibility for the house and associated estate passed to the eldest living and willing daughter of the previous female holder of the property, giving rise to the line of the Guardians of Nimway Hall.

THE GUARDIANS OF NIMWAY HALL

Nimue - Merlin

.

Through the mists of time

.

1720: Moira
(to come)

.

1750: Jacqueline
by Stephanie Laurens - this volume

.

1771: Olivia
(to come)

.

1794: Charlotte
by Karen Hawkins - available March 22, 2018

.

1818: Isabel
by Suzanne Enoch - available March 29, 2018

.

1839: Miranda
(to come)

.

1862: Georgia

(to come)

.

1888: Alexandra
(by Victoria Alexander - to come)

.

1912: Fredericka
(to come)

.

1926: Maddie Rose
(By Susan Andersen - to come)

.

1940: Jocelyn
by Linda Needham - available April 5, 2018

CHAPTER 1

"*M*iss! Miss! You got to come and see!"

Caught in the act of crossing the great hall, Jacqueline Tregarth swung to face the front door, propped wide to let the sunshine stream in, just as Billy Brakes, one of the gardener's boys, came pelting in. "What is it, Billy?" Eyes widening, she walked toward him. "Has something gone wrong?"

Billy halted, wheezed, and shook his head. After a second, he managed, "The digging's going fine, miss. But Crawley's working over where the dowser says the spring should be, and he—Crawley—says as you need to come and take a look."

She frowned. "A look at what?" The Hall's groundsmen were digging out the bed of an old lake that had been allowed to dry up thirty years ago, as well as striking down to open up the spring that used to fill the lake. Over the recent winter and spring, the stream that had provided water to the house and most of the estate for the past thirty years had steadily failed; it was now not much more than a trickle. In that region, water was known to change its course, sometimes with little warning, but with summer in full swing and the first crops ripening in the lower fields, the estate desperately needed a good, reliable source of water, especially to drive the estate's mill.

"I dunno, miss." Billy blinked guileless blue eyes at her. "I think they hit a lump of something. Crawley just said to come and get you so you could look and decide what you wanted to do."

A lump of something? Jacqueline glanced down the great hall, but none of the tasks awaiting her couldn't be put off. "Very well. I'll come." She waved Billy ahead of her, picked up her skirts, and followed him out of the front door, down the steps, and onto the gravel path that led around the eastern side of the house.

Neat, well-tended lawns rolled away to the line of trees marking the edge of the wood that protected the Hall in an arc from the southwest through the east to the north. Bees buzzed in the lavender bushes bordering the path, and the sun, still high in a cloudless blue sky, shone down with welcome warmth.

As she followed Billy past the corner of the house and onto the wide north lawn, Jacqueline reflected that she really should have stopped to find a hat—freckles were thoroughly unfashionable. The thought made her grin. Being fashionable didn't feature on her list of aspirations. Leading her people and taking care of the Hall and the estate were all that really mattered to her.

The lake lay a hundred or so yards behind the house, in the north-eastern quadrant of the area the household deemed "the grounds." A narrow path of beaten earth followed the low berm that circled the wide, shallow lake.

At various points on the lake bed, in groups of two and three, men were working with shovels and wheelbarrows, removing the soft earth that had once been underwater. Jacqueline paused to survey the results of their efforts; they'd done a good job of deepening the lake in preparation for releasing the blocked spring. The men saw her and paused, raising their heads and looking expectantly her way; she smiled and nodded in approval and encouragement, then continued walking. The Hall's gardener, Crawley, was waiting at the far end of the lake with Mr. Mainard, the dowser she'd called in.

As Jacqueline neared, she saw that Crawley was standing over a deeper hole into which both he and the dowser kept glancing. She halted on the path nearby and arched her brows at Crawley; Billy had rejoined the nearest group of men. "Billy said you found something."

"Yes, indeed, miss." Crawley lumbered over to offer her his hand and steady her down the slope of the bank to the lake bed. "Seemed a bit odd, so before we went further, I wanted you to look and tell us what you think."

Gripping Crawley's gnarled hand, Jacqueline raised her skirts and went down in a controlled rush. She was relieved to find the earth firm enough beneath her leather-soled slippers. She released Crawley's hand and her skirts and walked over to the deeper hole.

On the other side of the hole, Mainard frowned into its depths and shifted from boot to boot. He glanced at her, bobbed his head respectfully, then looked down again. "This is the right place. I'd take my oath the spring is down there."

She halted at the edge of the hole and looked in. At first, all she saw was a hole several feet deep and a yard or so square, its floor and sides composed of rich, friable earth. Then she caught a gleam of something beneath the dirt in the center of the hole. She crouched and stared. "What is that?"

"It's a stone of some sort." With a grunt, Crawley dropped back into the hole, his boots landing well clear of the object. "I just glanced it with my shovel, then I thought it best to wait and get your orders."

Country folk were superstitious, and the locals of this county, and especially those on the Nimway Hall estate, were wary of disturbing unexpected finds. Local legends too often carried warnings of dire consequences.

"What, exactly, is it?" She couldn't make out the object's size or even the material from which it was made. "Brush away the dirt, and let's see."

Crawley took a rag from his pocket and bent and cautiously wiped away the first layer of dirt, then the next, revealing the upper surface of what appeared to be a smooth, pale, milky stone.

Jacqueline caught the glint of metal—brass, copper, or gold—like fingertips holding the stone. "It looks like some sort of ornament." She studied it, then caught Crawley's eye. "Can you test around it to see how big it is or whether it's attached to something larger, then see if we can lever it up? Preferably without damaging it."

Crawley studied the lump, then grunted. He straightened, looked out over the lake, then bellowed to another of his lads, "Matthew! Fetch me a trowel."

Jacqueline rose from her crouch. Crawley bent again to the buried ornament and carefully felt in the dirt around it.

Mainard looked troubled. "I swear, Miss Tregarth, that the spring is down there." He pointed at the object Crawley was tending. "If I had to be precise, I'd say it's right below that spot. And before you ask, that ornament, whatever it is, couldn't have distracted my dowsing. I only react to water, nothing else."

"I'm sure we'll find the spring, Mr. Mainard—I don't doubt that." She gave him a reassuring smile; he was the best dowser in the area and came with an excellent reputation. "I have no idea why that ornament was buried there, but if we need to remove it to get to the spring, then that's what we'll do."

Mainard continued to frown. "I can't imagine why anyone would bury such a thing on top of a spring—on the spot a spring used to be."

Nor could she, but she wasn't about to allow any object, no matter how unexpected or strange, to keep her people from the water they needed.

By the time Matthew came running with a trowel, Crawley had cleared around the ornament—a smooth, roundish stone, about the size of a man's fist, trapped and held in claws of some burnished metal.

Crawley took the trowel, crouched beside the dirt-encrusted lump, and carefully inserted the trowel's blade at an angle such that it would strike well below the object.

They all watched with bated breath.

The trowel sank smoothly in to the hilt.

Crawley grunted. He tried again from a different angle with the same result. "Right, then." He glanced up at Jacqueline. "Looks like it's not stuck to anything—we should be able to free it."

She nodded at him to proceed.

Five minutes later, Crawley waggled the trowel one last time, and the dirty lump rolled free. Crawley rose, handed the trowel to the waiting Matthew, then, once again, drew the rag from his pocket. This time, he handed it to Jacqueline. "Here."

She took the rag, then Crawley bent and carefully lifted the ball of dirt enclosing the stone and the structure housing it. He held it up, then turned and offered it to her.

After spreading the rag over her hands, almost ceremoniously, she accepted the stone. The weight was similar to an ornament of that size fashioned from gold and crystal. Balancing the stone in its mounting on one palm, she used the edges of the rag to wipe more of the dirt away; it clung to the metal more tightly than it had to the smooth stone.

"I'll have to use water to clean the rest off." She peered at the stone. "But it does seem to be some sort of ornament."

Crawley grunted. "Strange place to bury an ornament."

The men returned their attention to the hole.

Intending to shake the loosened dirt from the rag, Jacqueline tipped the ornament, stone first, into her palm—

The stone softly glowed.

Quickly, she righted it, but even as she stared at it, the glow faded, and the stone returned to its previous, not-quite-translucent milky-white state.

She felt her heart thud.

"Well, I'll be damned!"

Startled, she looked at Crawley—it was he who had spoken. He was staring at his feet.

Following his gaze, she saw water bubbling up through the hole left by the ornament.

Cradling the stone closer, she beamed. "We have water!"

"Water!" The call was taken up and relayed to all the men.

Most came running to look.

As Crawley clambered out of the hole, Mainard shook his head and met Jacqueline's eyes. "That"—with a nod, he indicated the ornament—"was buried right on top of the spring. Like a plug."

Smiling, she held up the ornament, supporting it with both hands. "It seems it's something of a good luck charm, then." She glanced around at the men. "At least, for this household."

Everyone grinned and agreed.

Crawley called the men to order, pointing out that the deeper hole was filling fast and would soon overflow and start to fill the basin of the lake. He gave orders for the men to finish off preparing the lake bed.

Leaving Crawley and the men to that task, Jacqueline accepted Mainard's support to climb up the bank and onto the path. Carrying the ornament partially wrapped in the rag, she walked with the dowser back toward the house.

When they reached the path at the rear of the house, Mainard halted and bowed to her. "Thank you for sending for me, Miss Tregarth. It was an interesting exercise, opening up your old spring." He glanced back at the activity around the lake. "I confess I have never come across a... stopper like that plugging the neck of a spring."

She glanced at the ornament, now nestled in the crook of her arm. "Indeed. It does seem hard to believe that someone buried it in that very spot." She looked up and met Mainard's eyes. "But there are stranger tales about these parts, several of which involve Nimway Hall. This is simply another to add to our list."

"Indeed, miss." Mainard bowed. "My horse is in the stable. I will leave you here. Once again, thank you for your custom."

She inclined her head and watched the dowser walk off to the stable, then she looked again at the ornament. She raised it to the sunshine, watching the light slide over the surface of the now-dull stone. "I fancy you will clean up very nicely, and then I'll put you on show to be feted as the Hall's good luck charm."

Smiling, she lowered the ornament. Holding it between her hands, she walked toward the house.

"I have never been lost in my life!" Tired, dusty, and frustrated, Lord Richard Edward Montague Devries—deeply reluctant darling of London society—plunked himself down on a fallen log. Exasperated, he stared at the trees surrounding him, at the woodland stretching in every direction as far as his eyes could see. "Damn it, Malcolm! Where the devil are we?"

His horse, a hefty dappled-gray gelding who went by the name of Malcolm the Great, continued to forage through the leaf mold carpeting the ground and didn't deign to respond.

With his forearms on his knees and Malcolm's reins loosely looped in his long fingers, Richard hung his head and sighed.

He'd fled London two days before, leaving his lodgings in St. James as if merely going for a morning ride in the park. At the corner of Jermyn Street, he'd been joined by one of his closest friends, Sir Toby Lackland, and they'd ridden into the park. Then through the park and on. They'd kept riding, ultimately out along the highway and on via Andover and Salisbury. The ruse had been necessary; after the events of the night before, he'd needed to avoid alerting anyone to his departure and, even more, his destination.

He'd been glad of Toby's company—to ensure he escaped London without hindrance.

That was what his undeniable good fortune had reduced him to—fleeing the capital, with his friends watching his back.

Richard picked up a twig and poked at the dead leaves between the toes of his riding boots. As the second son of the wealthy and powerful

Marquess of Harwich, ever since Richard had gone on the town at twenty, he'd featured on the matchmakers' lists. His mother being a Montague only increased his eligibility, his desirability as a husband for the swarms of young ladies who every year descended on the capital to hunt through the ballrooms for a suitable match.

He'd nearly been caught—trapped—long ago, but he'd learned his lesson well. Subsequently, when one of his father's distant cousins had died and left Richard a manor house in Wiltshire along with substantial accumulated wealth, he'd foreseen the inevitable reaction and had remained alert and very much on guard. He'd successfully avoided the ballrooms for more than a year and thereafter neatly sidestepped the multitude of snares the matchmakers had laid before his feet. He'd been twenty-five at the time; as the years had rolled on and he'd continued to decline to succumb, the matchmakers had grumbled and largely given up, viewing him as a lost cause.

As a gentleman unlikely to stumble and fall into their grasping arms.

All had been well for several years, his life relatively peaceful, then earlier that year, his paternal great-aunt, Lady Dulcimea Caverthorne, had informed the family at large that she was naming him her heir. Dulcimea was nowhere near her deathbed, but she was an exceedingly wealthy, childless widow, and other family members had been prodding and pricking her to declare the disposition of her estate. So she had. Apparently, said other family members had forgotten that Richard was Lady Dulcimea's favorite and had been for decades; pushed too far, she'd declared enough was enough and had stated her final wishes, which she'd signed and sealed in her will.

Being her heir, combined with the land and wealth he already commanded, rendered him almost as potentially wealthy as his older brother, Gideon, who would inherit their father's title and entailed estate. Given that the prospect of Dulcimea's wealth would immediately catapult Richard to the giddy pinnacle of the matchmakers' lists, he'd been relieved that only the family had been privy to Dulcimea's declaration.

A week ago, someone had blabbed and let the until-then familial secret out, and the news had flashed through the ton like wildfire.

Within a day, Richard had been drowning in invitations to balls, soirées, entertainments of all kinds, and house parties galore. Bad enough, but as soon as he'd shown his face in public, he'd been accosted by older gentlemen clearly hounded by their wives to secure his presence at their dinner tables—on two occasions, he'd been buttonholed in the street, followed by three separate incidents in his clubs. In his clubs, for God's sake!

For several days, the situation had been an open joke among his closest friends.

Their laughter had come to an abrupt end three nights ago.

After spending a convivial evening with Toby and a group of like-minded others, Richard, Toby, and another of their close circle, Lord Charles Herries, had ambled out of the door of what was presently the most fashionable hell in town and had turned their footsteps toward their beds. It had been late, somewhere in the small hours, and with the street flares burning low and its streets and lanes cloaked in shadows, London had slumbered around them. On reaching Piccadilly, the three of them had gone their separate ways; Richard had headed south via a lane to St. James, his usual route into that precinct of well-heeled bachelors, while the other two went north into Mayfair, toward their parents' houses.

Luckily for Richard, Toby and Charles had halted in Piccadilly to argue some point. They'd been within earshot of Richard's battle cry when, in the dark confines of the alley, he'd been set upon by four ruffi-ans. Two, Richard could have managed on his own; he'd been carrying his swordstick and was an expert with a blade. But four...

Toby and Charles had come running, naked steel gleaming in their hands, and the ruffians, already nursing several wounds, had sworn and run off, dragging with them the one of their number Richard had already incapacitated.

After catching his breath, with his friends at his back, Richard had given chase.

He, Toby, and Charles had burst out of the alley to see the ruffians piling into a coach. One man hung on the back, and at the sight of them, he'd called to the driver, who had whipped up the horses. The coach door had swung, then been hauled shut, and the coach had clattered off along the empty street.

That the four ruffians had had a coach waiting...understanding had sent a chill through the three of them and through Richard in particular.

The men had come to seize him—to kidnap him.

Ascertaining their motive required little thought.

Someone had paid the blackguards to kidnap him in order to stage some compromising situation, which would force him to offer for some young lady's hand; although he'd spent the rest of the night discussing possibilities with Toby and Charles over several large brandies, they'd all felt certain of that.

They'd also agreed that he needed to treat the incident seriously and take himself off, out of harm's way, given that none of them could immediately discern a way to nullify the root cause of his problem.

Charles had dropped a heavy hand on Richard's shoulder. "We'll find some way, but for now, you need to play least in sight."

Toby had grunted. "Better still, disappear altogether. And not just out of London. Nowhere in society is safe for you now."

Grim, Richard had nodded. "And I won't be safe until we find some way to make me less eligible."

Toby had soberly appended, "Without doing something of which your mother wouldn't approve."

They'd all agreed on that as well; all three had a healthy respect for the Marchioness of Harwich.

Richard heaved another part-irritated, part-exasperated, part-resigned sigh. He'd spent the last twelve years gracing the circles of society's upper echelons. Leaving London as he had—being driven from it—had felt like a form of rejection. A repudiation of his birthright.

In truth, while riding west with nothing to do but think, he'd reached the point of deciding against marriage altogether. After his one and only brush with love had ended so disastrously—with him learning from the young lady's own lips that her liking for him arose from considerations of his wealth and station and had nothing to do with affection or even respect for him, the man—his view of matrimony had cooled. Given what he'd since been privileged to see of his brother's marriage—a union based on dynastic considerations and mutual respect that had deteriorated into a hellish relationship that had deeply scarred Gideon and left his wife, Melissa, a temperamental shrew—Richard's aversion to marriage had only grown.

The latest attempts to force marriage on him had deepened his distrust of matrimony, the state, to the point of outright rejection. His brother had already fathered two sons; there was no pressing need for Richard to marry.

Taking refuge with his maternal uncle, the Bishop of Bath and Wells, a devout bachelor, had seemed the obvious answer to his immediate need. He could sit in His Grace's palace and lick his unexpected but nevertheless stinging wounds while taking sage counsel.

That had been his plan as he'd ridden out of London on the morning following the attack.

After a thankfully uneventful journey, he and Toby had parted ways the previous afternoon in Yeovil. While Toby had continued on to visit his ancestral acres near Sidmouth, Richard had struck north. He'd spent last night in a small inn just north of Yeovil, and this morning, he'd set off on what should have been a relatively easy last stage of about twenty miles, riding across country to Wells.

His gaze on his boots, he shook his head. By now, he should have been relaxing in the comfort of his uncle's library, regaling the bishop with the details of his close escape. Instead, he—who had hunted since he could walk and had never been lost in any woods or forests before—was sitting in this accursed wood with no idea which way to go.

He dropped the twig, raised his head, and looked around again. There were no real paths, not even bridle paths, to follow through the trees, just spaces and clearings through which to navigate, all covered with a carpet of long-fallen leaves.

Malcolm the Great stood nearby, cropping a patch of thin grass. Other than the chirping of birds in the canopies high above and the occasional rustle of a squirrel or rabbit, the wood remained quiet.

Given the sunshine slanting through the shifting leaves to dapple the forest floor, it was difficult to imagine the somnolent quiet as menacing, yet Richard nevertheless felt trapped and, worse, as if something—the very air—watched and waited.

For what, he didn't know.

He'd noticed a sign just before he'd ridden into the trees, naming this Balesboro Wood.

A bale was an evil force; he should, quite clearly, have taken due note and stuck to the lanes. But the lanes would have led him far afield, the route much longer, and he knew that all he had to do was head directly north and he would eventually reach Wells.

"Yet here I sit..." Stifling another sigh, he rose and stretched, then walked to Malcolm the Great.

The huge gelding was favoring his off-front leg—another unexpected problem. Richard lifted the hoof and inspected it again, but the thick sliver of wood was still there, wedged between the iron shoe and the pad of the hoof. If he tried to tease the sliver out with his knife, he could well send a splinter deeper into the softer part of the hoof and do significantly greater damage. He needed to find a farrier who would have the right tools to safely remove the sliver.

Lips setting, he released the hoof, straightened to his full height, and set his fists on his hips. Enough of bemoaning his state. The angle of the sunbeams and the cooling temperature told him the sun was setting, the day slowly dying. He had next to nothing with him beyond a few changes of clothes thrust into his saddlebags. He hadn't been able to bring anything that looked like luggage with him, much less his valet and groom. It might be summer, but spending the night sleeping rough in this wood didn't appeal; quite aside from appeasing his rumbling stomach, he needed to find shelter, and that, relatively soon.

From the slanting light, he could deduce which way was north, but to that point, the knowledge hadn't helped him. "Which way?" he murmured.

Almost as if in answer, he heard the distant rumble of voices. Male voices.

Perhaps woodsmen who could direct him to the nearest village. With a tug on the reins and a click of his tongue, he got Malcolm the Great's attention, and leading the huge horse, Richard started walking toward the voices.

The men weren't moving, either toward him or away; the sound of their voices grew louder the farther Richard walked.

Innate caution stopped him from calling out; there were at least two men, and he was, after all, a lone traveler lost in these woods, and his horse was worth a pretty penny, not to mention the ring on his hand and the sword at his hip.

Eventually, he reached a glade that ended in a shallow rise beyond which, if all he could see and hear spoke true, lay a dip of some sort. The men were in the dip and still speaking. They weren't talking loudly but seemed to be standing and discussing something.

Richard halted a few yards from the upward slope of the rise. Ears flicking, Malcolm the Great halted silently beside him.

From beyond the rise, in a plainly educated voice, came the words, "Very nice work, Morgan. I knew I could rely on you. Your contrivance has achieved exactly what I needed. Well done!"

Something in the gentleman's tone—a tinge of unholy excitement—fed Richard's caution. The question of what "contrivance" a gentleman might be examining deep in a wood gave him further reason to exercise discretion.

"Thank ye, sir," came a reply in a deeper, rougher, countryman's voice—presumably the lauded Morgan. "Do you want it left as it is? Or should we look to gradually dismantle it, like? When you give the word, o'course."

After a second's debate, Richard looped Malcolm the Great's reins around a branch, then silently crept up the rise. He was an expert huntsman; he knew how to move through woodland without alerting his prey.

"No, don't repair it—at least, not yet." The gentleman went on, "I want the farmers as well as the miller in dire straits before I make a move." After a moment's cogitation, the gentleman decided, "It will serve me best to leave this construction of yours in place until I'm certain of gaining all I want from it."

Richard was curious to discover what "the construction" was. He dropped to all fours as he neared the crest of the rise. He thought the men were facing his way, and he now had no wish to be spotted eavesdropping.

As he eased toward the top of the rise and, very gradually, raised his head, he heard Morgan reply, "Aye, sir. As they haven't found it yet, there's no reason they will. I'd say it's safe to leave well enough alone—no need to keep checking on it."

"No, indeed," the gentleman concurred. The scuffing of feet on leaves suggested the pair were now moving away, heading to Richard's right. "The less chance of any of us being spotted near here, the better. Come on. We'd better get going."

Sure, now, that something underhanded was afoot, Richard raised his head enough to peer over the rise. He found himself looking down into a narrow valley. A decent-sized stream burbled over a rocky bed that wended its way along the valley bottom.

The men—judging by their clothes, a gentleman and a rough laborer —were walking along the stream's opposite bank. They were already well to Richard's right and making for two horses—one a reasonable-looking hack, the other a cob—tied in the trees at the mouth of the small valley. Richard raised his head further and looked along the rise, but the rise continued, curving away from the end of the valley, which opened into a clearing. If the men rode out through the clearing, they wouldn't see Malcolm the Great.

Satisfied on that score, with the men no longer speaking, Richard turned his attention to whatever construction the pair had been examining. He studied the stream; the men had been standing on the far bank, more or less opposite Richard's present position, looking at something while facing him...

The men mounted and turned their horses. Richard flicked a glance their way, but didn't catch any clear view of either man. He hadn't seen their faces, only very oblique profiles and their backs as they'd walked away.

He grimaced. He waited, unmoving, until the men's horses' hoofbeats faded, then he rose, dusted the woodland detritus from his clothes, and walked back to Malcolm the Great. Richard untied the reins and led the great horse up and very carefully down the other side of the rise and into the valley.

Determined to discover what was going on, Richard secured Malcolm the Great beside a small copse of trees opposite where the men had tied their horses. Then he leapt over the stream and walked back along the other bank. Once at the spot where the men had stood—easy enough to define via the footprints in the softer earth—he looked around, trying to see what the pair had been discussing, what the "construction" was.

It took him several minutes to grasp the implications of what he was seeing—that the stream burbling down from the head of the valley, now to his right, lost volume as it passed along that stretch until, to his left, it was reduced to a trickle.

The construction wasn't easy to stumble upon; if he hadn't known something had to be there and actively searched, he would never have found it.

It was also ingenious.

He spent long minutes working out what had been done. The bed of the stream was over two feet deep. Tunnels had been carefully bored into the stream bed below the level of the rippling water. None of the tunnels were big enough to show suction or appear as a gaping maw, but all working together, the series of tunnels was enough to drain the stream of much of its flow.

Richard turned and looked away from the stream. At that point, on that side, the valley didn't slope upward but ran roughly level to a rocky line beyond which the ground fell away. Richard strode to the line of rocks and discovered that they marked the edge of a short drop, the first of a series of what might, centuries ago, have been landslips along the edge of an escarpment.

Standing on the lip of that escarpment, he looked out and found himself surveying the wide swath of land known as the Somerset Levels.

On the northwestern horizon, he saw a peak bathed in the rosy glow of the westering sun. The peak looked vaguely familiar...then he realized he was looking at Glastonbury Tor.

Instantly, he could place where he must be. The Tor lay southwest of Wells, which meant there was no chance at all that he would reach the comfort of his uncle's hearth that night.

With a disgusted grunt, he turned back to the stream and his examination of what was, in essence, a cannily concealed diversion. The tunnels channeled the water away under the bank and continued underground, but only for so many yards. Thereafter, the water had been allowed to ooze out and spread over the surface, but by that point, the ground sloped gently toward the escarpment, so the water continued in that direction, camouflaged by rocks and leaf litter, until it spilled over the edge.

Crouching and peering over the edge, he visually traced several rivulets snaking down the escarpment's rough and tumbled face. Immediately below, at the foot of the first drop, the grass grew in a particularly verdant shade of green, more like a boggy water meadow than a normal tract of cliffside grass.

He rose and walked back to the stream. "So the gentleman and his man diverted the waters of the stream, but to no discernible purpose."

Of course, the gentleman *had* a purpose; Richard simply didn't know what it was.

The air was starting to lose its warmth as the sun dipped toward the horizon. Richard leapt over the stream and strode along the bank to where he'd tethered Malcolm the Great.

Untying the reins, he stroked the horse's long nose. "Come on. I might be lost, but there's one woodsman's trick that's guaranteed to work even in this accursed wood. If you want to find habitation, just follow water downhill."

He set off with Malcolm the Great clomping behind.

As he walked beside the dwindling stream, Richard wondered just what the gentleman had meant by his "getting all I want" from the diversion he'd arranged.

CHAPTER 2

*S*everal hours later, with the long summer twilight deepening to dusk, Richard finally—*finally!*—stepped out of Balesboro Wood onto a neat gravel drive that curved through a wide clearing in which stood a large manor house. The drive swept in a gentle arc to the forecourt before the house's front door.

Richard glanced at the eager, smiling faces of his companions—a woodcutter and his wife. Their footsteps crunched on the gravel, a counterpoint to his own and the clop of Malcolm the Great's heavy hooves.

His idea of following the stream had been a good one; it had led him to the woodcutter's cottage and not a moment too soon. The couple had been about to leave, having been summoned to the local manor house for a celebration.

As their cottage—a single-roomed hut—was far too small to accommodate the likes of him and they had no stable, the pair had suggested he walk with them to the manor. They'd assured him that the Tregarths, the owners of Nimway Hall and the woodcutter's employers, were very nice gentlefolk and would be happy to offer him shelter.

Naturally, both woodcutter and wife had taken in the quality of his clothes, his sword, and Malcolm the Great and correctly identified him as a gentleman. Accepting their cheery and plainly confident assurances of welcome, Richard had joined them on the short trek to what he understood was an impromptu celebration occasioned by an old spring running again.

Given they were in Somerset, he'd refrained from leaping to conclusions. If there was a connection to the gentleman's diversion of the stream, he would find out soon enough.

As they walked up the drive, Nimway Hall rose before them. Built of the local pale-gray stone with impressive corner towers three stories high, the central block comprised two neat stories with dormer windows above and the hint of a basement level below. Ivy, the creeper's leaves a bright summer green, covered sections of the wall, but the clinging tendrils had been neatly trimmed away from around the numerous multi-paned windows. The lawns surrounding the house stretched wide, smooth and scythed. Although there was no fountain or sculpture to break up the rolling sward, the enfolding arms of the wood and the majesty of the house rendered such ornamentation superfluous.

That evening, every window on the lower level shone with the welcoming glow of candlelight.

The woodcutter and his wife increased their pace. "Looks like most of us are already here." The woodcutter's wife's face was alight with joyful anticipation.

Richard noted a narrower extension of the drive curving around the house to the left, presumably leading to the stable. Several gigs and traps and at least one coach were lined up along its verge. No saddle horses were visible, but others must have ridden to the house. As, beside the woodcutter, he approached the front porch, Richard wondered what to do with Malcolm the Great. The horse needed care; Richard didn't like leaving him hitched to a bush and unattended. Aside from any other consideration, if Malcolm got loose, given the door was open, he might follow Richard inside.

But then a tow-headed lad, no doubt alerted by the crunching gravel, peered out of the open door. On seeing Richard—or, more correctly, Malcolm the Great—the lad's eyes grew wide, and he hurried to step out, onto the porch, where he paused uncertainly.

"There you are, Young Willie," the woodcutter boomed. He was a large robust man with a large robust voice. "This gentleman got lost in our wood, and we've brought him here to beg shelter. And his great horse has fallen lame, too—best you take the beast around to the stable while we take the gentleman indoors to speak with the Tregarths. No doubt Hopkins will be interested and will come to see to the beast."

Radiating suppressed eagerness, the lad descended the three steps and readily approached. "I can take him to the stable for you, sir."

Richard smiled and held out the reins. "Despite his size"—the horse more than lived up to his name—"he's very even tempered."

The lad stroked the long velvety nose, and the horse—who was also intelligent enough to know who to butter up—chuffed encouragingly. "What's his name?"

"Malcolm the Great."

The lad grinned, as did the woodcutter. "I'll take good care of him, sir," the lad vowed. He nodded to the horse's lame foreleg. "And if you speak with Hopkins—he's the stableman—I'm sure he'll come out and do what he can to make the beast more comfortable."

Richard nodded and, as the boy led the big gray away, followed the woodcutter and his wife up the steps and inside. He stepped over the threshold and paused.

He stood in what he recognized as the antechamber to a medieval great hall. The large rectangular space that opened up two paces on had unquestionably been a great hall in its time; the large, solid, polished-oak beams that ribbed the walls and arched across the ceiling testified to its past. At several points in more recent centuries, it had been built onto, with wings to either side and stories above, until the house had attained its present form. Richard judged that the great hall now operated as the central hub of the manor house. And, as at that moment, the space provided the perfect venue for communal celebrations.

A mass of people—all solid country folk as far as Richard could see —thronged the room, yet it wasn't overcrowded. This wasn't a ton "crush" but a pleasant gathering of people comfortable in each other's company; the hum of conversations interspersed with easy laughter bore witness to that fact.

"Evening, Mr. Cruickshank."

Richard turned as the woodcutter bobbed his head to a man—tall, thin, and garbed in the long-tailed black coat favored by butlers every-where—who had materialized out of the shifting crowd.

"This here gentleman"—the woodcutter gestured to Richard—"got lost in our wood. He found his way to us, and we thought to bring him to the manor for shelter. Him and his lame horse."

The butler—Cruickshank—assessed Richard's station, or as much of that as Richard allowed to show, in one swift glance, then bowed appro-priately. "Sir." He straightened. "Mr. Tregarth and Miss Swinford are by the fireplace. If you will follow me, I will make you known to them."

Richard inclined his head. "Thank you." He turned to take his leave of the woodcutter and his wife, but both had already been claimed by friends.

Richard caught the man's eyes and inclined his head gratefully, then with his customary easy smile curving his lips, he turned and followed the butler. The man led him down one side of the room, skirting the knots of guests filling the space.

Several people glanced his way, but that was hardly surprising; he was taller than most, and even in his traveling clothes, deliberately chosen to be unremarkable, he cut a sufficiently striking figure to draw eyes—he always had. Unperturbed, he idly surveyed the crowd. He recognized their type—good, honest gentlefolk, squires, small landholders, tenant farmers, and those who served the manor, their lives spent, busy and content, managing their acres or fulfilling their duties unconcerned with and largely oblivious to the exercise of wider power. These were the people his mother referred to as the backbone of England, and she wasn't wrong. Without them and their labors, his class—the ruling class—would have little to rule.

Halfway down the long hall, a lady, part of a large group in the center of the room, swung around and blatantly studied him. She was, he judged, somewhere in her twenties, yet there was no challenge in her gaze, only frank and straightforward assessment. Her gaze steady and assured, she surveyed him for several seconds, then briefly, she met his eyes.

Openly noting him—taking note of him—yet with no judgment or, indeed, any reaction that Richard could see.

That last piqued his interest, far more so than had she smiled invitingly.

Smoothly, the lady returned her attention to her companions, none of whom had noticed her momentary distraction, while Richard continued on.

Without conscious direction, his mind had cataloged the lady's appearance—glossy fair hair in a warm shade of honey blond piled artlessly atop her head, a wide forehead and finely arched eyebrows above eyes whose color he hadn't been able to discern. A straight nose and delicately curved lips, beautifully sculpted, with cheeks plump and just touched with a healthy rose...and a firm and determined chin. It was, he realized, that chin that had made the biggest impression on him, that had drawn his interest enough for him to have noted all the rest.

Her gown ranked as among the more expensive in the room, fashioned of teal silk in the current style, with a front panel of fine ivory lace.

Idly—he reminded himself that any interest on his part could be nothing more than idle—he wondered who she was.

Just because he'd set his mind against marriage didn't mean he'd set his mind against female companionship altogether. The sight of the lady —who might well be married—had evoked a familiar pressure in his loins, reminding him that it had been weeks since he'd last indulged. Unfortunately, given his partners in pleasure were, by his invariable rule, of his own class and also well and truly wed, then unless he was exceedingly lucky and found a willing and suitably qualified lady, he might be facing a prolonged period of abstinence.

The butler—Cruickshank—reached the far end of the hall and led Richard to a settle flanking a massive stone-manteled fireplace. An older, rather faded, but sweet-faced lady sat on the settle, her hands clasped in her lap, and alongside her, ensconced in a Bath chair with a rug spread over his knees, from under bushy eyebrows, an older gentleman surveyed the throng.

Cruickshank bowed to the pair. "Mr. Tregarth. Miss Swinford. This gentleman found himself lost in our wood and has come asking for shelter."

"Heh?" The older gentleman—Mr. Tregarth—squinted at Richard, his gaze as openly assessing as the unknown lady's had been.

Richard smiled, stepped forward, and bowed with his customary grace. "Mr. Tregarth." Straightening, he inclined his head to the older lady. "Miss Swinford. My name is Richard Montague." He often used his last given name, also his mother's family name, whenever claiming that of his exceedingly powerful and well-known father might not be in his best interests. With a self-deprecating smile, speaking to both his hosts impartially, he continued, "This morning, I set off from Yeovil for Wells, on my way to visit a relative in the bishop's household, but to my abiding astonishment, I became quite turned around in the nearby wood. I fear I am, indeed, reduced to throwing myself on your mercy and asking for shelter for myself and my horse."

Miss Swinford's hands fluttered, and she beamed up at him. "Well, of course, dear. We'll be only too happy to put you up. Won't we, Hugh?" She glanced at the gentleman.

Hugh Tregarth was scrutinizing Richard. "Got lost, did you? In our wood, you say?"

"Balesboro Wood," Richard replied. "I believe it forms part of this estate."

Slowly, Hugh nodded. "Indeed, it does." Hugh eyed Richard for a moment longer, then Hugh's wrinkled face creased in a genial smile. "And Elinor's quite right—you are, indeed, very welcome."

Richard half bowed to them both. "Thank you."

"You mentioned your horse?" Hugh inquired.

"Yes, and sadly, he's gone lame. A sliver of wood wedged into his off-front shoe."

"Nasty. We can't have that. Good beast, is he?" Hugh asked.

"A Trojan," Richard averred.

Hugh shifted in his chair, scanning those around, then he raised an arm and waved. "Hopkins! Over here, man."

Richard watched as a man as old as Tregarth, heavy chested with the bow-legged stance of one who had ridden on most days of his life, drained the tankard he held, set it down on a nearby dresser, then weaved through the crowd to present himself with a crisp nod. "Aye, sir?"

"This gentleman"—Hugh indicated Richard with a flick of his hand —"Mr. Montague, got lost in our wood and will be staying for the nonce. His horse picked up a sliver and is lame. Thought you might see to him."

The stableman's interest was immediate. "Aye, sir—that I will." The man raised his gaze to Richard's face.

"I left the beast with your stable lad—Young Willie," Richard said, answering Hopkins's unvoiced question. "I believe he took the horse to the stable."

"Aye, he would've done. Not wanting for sense, Young Willie." Hopkins nodded to Hugh Tregarth. "I'll get along there and see what's what."

"If you don't mind," Richard said, "I'll come with you." He met Hopkins's faintly surprised gaze. "I'm rather fond of Malcolm the Great."

Hopkins blinked. "That's the beast's name?"

"I bought him at a horse fair in Scotland. The name seemed appropriate. You'll understand when you see him."

Hopkins's eyes widened. "In that case, sir, if you'll come this way?" Hopkins waved to an archway giving onto a corridor that led away from the great hall in the direction of the stable.

Richard bowed to Tregarth and Miss Swinford. "If you'll excuse me, ma'am, sir. I'll return once I've seen the beast settled."

"Of course." Tregarth waved him away. "Commendable thing, to take care of one's cattle."

Richard hid a smile and followed Hopkins from the hall.

As he'd assumed, the corridor led directly to a side door that opened to a short stretch of lawn on the other side of which the stable squatted, long and low in the fading light. The glow from a lamp inside the stable spilled out of the open door; inside, they found Young Willie leaning on the front of a stall and crooning to Malcolm the Great.

Young Willie had brushed the horse down and fed and watered him, for which Richard thanked him and surreptitiously slipped him a penny. Hopkins had already opened the stall door and, after offering the horse his hand and stroking the long nose, then the arching neck, had gone into the stall.

Having surveyed the dappled gray's size, Hopkins grunted. "See what you mean about his name. Fits him, right enough. Now." Hopkins bent and lifted the off foreleg, angling the hoof to the light. After a moment of studying the damage, he grunted again. "Young Willie—go fetch Ned Ostley." The boy instantly raced off. Hopkins glanced up at Richard. "Ostley's our farrier. He's the best one to see to this."

Richard blew out a breath. "I thought it would take a farrier—I'm just glad you have one."

"Oh aye—we have most of the trades here." Hopkins gently set down the damaged hoof, leaned against the side of the stall, and folded his arms, clearly prepared to talk while they waited for the farrier to arrive. "An old estate, you see, and we're a mite isolated, what with the wood all around and the escarpment to the west."

Richard propped a shoulder against the front of the stall, more than willing to exploit the situation. "I was on my way to Wells when I got lost. I found your woodcutter, and he and his wife brought me here." He tipped his head toward the house. "They said the celebration was something to do with an old spring running again." The woodcutters hadn't seemed to know more, and not wanting to advertise his interest, he hadn't pried.

Hopkins nodded. "Aye. See, our stream's been running low. Very low. We didn't get the flush we usually do after the winter thaw. Our farmers were getting into a pother—not enough water would make for a hard year. And the mill can't run, not with the stream so low, so that's another worry —even if they get the crops in, they'll have to pay for someone else to mill the grain. But the mistress, Miss Jacqueline, remembered about the old lake." Hopkins tipped his head beyond the rear of the house. "Used to be at the far end of the grounds, but it's been dry for years. Seems the spring that fed it got plugged up somehow, but Miss Jacqueline had the dowser in, and this afternoon, they had the spring gushing again. So now the lake's filling, and once it's full, the estate will have water aplenty. We'll still have to figure out how to supply the mill, mind, but if any of our farms need water, we'll have it to give them. So that's what the celebration's about." Hopkins eyed Richard—measuringly, much as Tregarth had done. "Might not seem such a big thing to you, but to us in the country, fixing a situation like that…it's a victory of sorts. Worthy of celebration."

Richard allowed an entirely genuine grin to split his face. "I might live in London for some of the year, but I was born and brought up in the country. So I fully appreciate the triumph of…Miss Jacqueline." He arched his brows. "I presume she's Mr. Tregarth's daughter?"

"Nah—she's his great-niece." Hopkins straightened as the sound of heavy footsteps neared. "He's her guardian, so to speak, ever since her parents died. It's Miss Jacqueline who owns Nimway Hall."

Richard blinked, but then a heavyset man arrived and introduced himself as Ned Ostley, the farrier. After taking a quick look at Malcolm's damaged hoof, Ostley fetched his tools, and in short order, the offending sliver—a surprisingly thick and sharp-edged shaft of hardwood—was removed.

Both Ostley and Hopkins—along with Richard—studied Malcolm the Great's subsequent reaction. The big horse still found the foot too sore to use. Hopkins grunted. "It'll take a while to settle, no doubt. His weight… you wouldn't want to rush him back into using it before he's ready."

"No, indeed." Somewhat grim, Richard said, "We'll see how he is tomorrow."

The others grunted agreement, and leaving Young Willie to settle Malcolm, the three men returned to the great hall and the celebration that was still in full swing.

Richard estimated he'd been absent from the hall for about thirty minutes. He parted from Ostley and Hopkins with sincere thanks, then found himself offered a mug of ale and a pasty, both of which he gratefully accepted. The pasty, simple and hearty country fare, went some way to filling his empty stomach. Two more pasties and another mug of ale did the trick. Sufficiently fortified, he wondered which of the younger ladies he'd spotted in the crowd—all three of whom he was making a point of ignoring—was Miss Jacqueline Tregarth. Further wondering if he should find the housekeeper and retire rather than linger when he knew so few, he made his way back to the fireplace where Tregarth and Miss Swinford continued to hold court.

He'd only just rejoined them when, with a rustle of silks, the lady he'd noticed earlier—she of the assessing gaze and determined chin—stepped out of the crowd and halted beside Hugh Tregarth.

Richard realized he was about to meet the owner of Nimway Hall.

In confirmation, Miss Swinford fluttered and beamed at the lady. "There you are, Jacqueline. You must meet Mr. Montague—Richard Montague. Mr. Montague, please allow me to present my charge, Mr. Tregarth's great-niece, Miss Jacqueline Tregarth."

As Richard bowed and Miss Tregarth dipped into a regulation curtsy, Miss Swinford rattled on, "Mr. Montague was riding to Wells to visit a relative in the bishop's household, but he got lost in our wood and his horse went lame, and so here he is, come to beg shelter."

Miss Swinford lowered her restless hands to her lap, her face alight with satisfaction, apparently over having delivered such news. She looked from the lady to Richard, transparently pleased.

Richard felt Miss Swinford's approving gaze, but didn't meet it. His eyes were trapped, stare for stare, by the most striking blue-green gaze he'd ever seen. Miss Jacqueline Tregarth had eyes of mingled cerulean blue and spring green, both shades bright; she also possessed a gaze of such directness, of such unstated confidence and unshakeable inner strength, that the combination literally stole his breath.

It had been a long time—a *very* long time—since anything about a lady had rendered Richard Edward Montague Devries speechless.

Jacqueline studied Richard Montague with her customary outward calm, yet inside, to her surprise, she felt her senses fluttering, her nerves leaping, and a very real curiosity stirring. In other ladies—more susceptible ladies—she imagined he stirred another sort of interest entirely, but she knew herself to be fully armored against that particular weakness.

Regardless, it was, apparently, impossible not to react to his presence. He was of above-average height, with broad shoulders, a narrow waist, and long rider's legs, and he moved in a way that marked him as quite different from the country gentlemen to whom she was accustomed. Richard Montague was a...the label her mind supplied was "warrior." He wore a sword at his hip, and his fluid prowling gait was that of an experienced hunter.

Did he hunt through woods or ballrooms?

She suspected the answer was both.

The line of his lips was frankly sensual, the thickness of his dark hair a blatant invitation to feminine fingers to stroke, thread through, and grip. He wore the walnut-brown locks drawn back into a queue at the nape of his neck, exposing the chiseled planes of his face. His nose was a patrician blade, his chin rugged and uncompromisingly square, and his deeply set hazel eyes looked out on the world with—if she had to guess—a cynicism to match her own.

Certainly, the gaze she held was as unrevealing and as unapologetically assessing as hers.

She raised her chin a fraction and continued to meet his eyes. "Welcome, Mr. Montague. As I'm sure my uncle and my chaperon have assured you, you are welcome beneath this roof."

His lips quirked fractionally, then relaxed into an easy—practiced—smile, and he bowed again, remarkably elegantly. "Thank you, Miss Tregarth."

She glanced at the door through which he'd returned to the hall. "Your horse, sir? Has it been stabled?"

"Thank you, yes. Your stableman and farrier have seen to him. They removed a splinter from his hoof, and we've agreed to see how he is come morning."

The emotion that fleetingly shadowed his face suggested he was truly concerned for his steed. Her curiosity deepened. "Have you ridden far?"

His gaze returned to her face. He hesitated for a second, then replied, "I left London several days ago. I rode with a friend to Yeovil, and we parted there, and this morning, I turned north. I expected to reach Wells by this afternoon, but sadly, your wood defeated me."

She widened her eyes. "I admit I'm surprised you didn't keep to the lanes." Most travelers did.

His lips thinned slightly as if in remembered irritation. "I might have had I known of the confounding nature of Balesboro Wood. However, as I've hunted since boyhood and in forests far larger and have never before encountered any difficulty in finding my way, striking north across country seemed the obvious and fastest route."

She noticed Hugh snap to attention, his gaze focusing a great deal more sharply on their unexpected visitor. Before Hugh could commence an interrogation, she smoothly stated, "The folklore of these parts includes several tales of travelers getting lost in the woods." *Specifically, in Balesboro Wood.* "The stories often involve some magical being that haunts the woodland and ensnares certain mortals." She smiled reassuringly. "Of course, such tales are generally considered myths."

A faint frown tangling his dark brows, he replied, "In light of my experience in your wood, I can understand how such tales come about."

She'd expected him to laugh and dismiss all ideas of magical beings with a contemptuous wave.

She wasn't at all sure what to make of Richard Montague. What was he doing there? Could she take his story at face value? Up to now, the gentlemen who had sought to woo her had openly ridden up to the house, more or less declaring their purpose, but if Richard Montague had heard of her and decided to make a bid for her hand, then she had to admit that gaining entry to the household by claiming shelter with a story of getting lost in her wood was a novel and effective way of getting past her first line of defense.

He was inside her walls and assured of a bed, at least overnight.

That in the process, his horse, who he plainly cared about, had picked up a splinter and gone lame might simply have been an unintended consequence of his plan.

"Will the bishop's household be expecting you, Mr. Montague?" She had to wonder if that part of his tale was true.

"If they are," Elinor hurried to say, "I'm sure we can send a messenger…" Her face clouded. "But it's already late, so perhaps not until morning, and by then, you might be ready to journey on."

Richard Montague smiled gently at the older woman. "I'm a frequent visitor to the palace at Wells, but this visit was a spur-of-the-moment decision, so they won't be expecting me. And, as you say, if my horse recovers the use of his hoof quickly, I'll be in Wells tomorrow."

Elinor relaxed under the reassuring warmth of Montague's smile. Jacqueline gave the man credit for being kind enough to calm her chaperon, who was a dear but prone to plunging into distracted and distracting flusters.

Based on that calming kindness and that Montague had, to that point, shown no signs of setting himself to charm her, she decided that, at least for the moment, she would proceed as if he was nothing more than he claimed—a traveler intent on reaching Wells who had been temporarily waylaid.

By Balesboro Wood.

Of course, it was early days yet.

She glanced around, her duty as lady of the manor tugging at her, yet she was reluctant to leave Montague to his own devices. "Perhaps, Mr. Montague"—she returned her gaze to his handsome face and coolly arched a brow—"you might accompany me on my rounds, and I can introduce you to some of our neighbors."

He half bowed. "I am yours to command, Miss Tregarth."

She seriously doubted that, but, when he gallantly offered his arm, consented to lay her fingertips on his sleeve. As he turned her toward the groups of people dotting the great hall, she tried to ignore the clamoring of her senses occasioned, evidently, by the feel of steely muscles beneath the cool fabric of his coat sleeve and the sheer impact of his powerful body in such close proximity to hers. Surreptitiously, she swallowed, then she tilted her chin upward and gestured to one of the nearer circles. "I should speak with Mr. Harris. He's the local alderman."

With a brief, acknowledging dip of his head, Montague led her to join the group.

Unsurprisingly, they were welcomed with undisguised interest and the avid curiosity of country folk on finding a stranger—an exceedingly handsome one who, despite his neat and conventional appearance, carried the dangerous edge of an experienced commander—suddenly in their midst.

Determinedly suppressing the effect he had on her, Jacqueline introduced him to Mr. and Mrs. Harris and the two other couples—the owners of neighboring smallholdings—then asked Mr. Harris about the upcoming wool fair.

"Indeed, Miss Tregarth." The alderman puffed out his chest. "There was something of a battle between East Pennard and West Pennard, but in the end, it was decided to hold the fair in our usual field, to the west of West Pennard."

"I have to admit," Jacqueline said, "that that suits us rather better—driving our flocks across to East Pennard would have meant an extra day."

"Aye—a lost day." One of the other gentlemen nodded in agreement.

Mrs. Harris smiled at Montague. "You're from London, sir? I daresay you find such pastimes as wool fairs and the like supremely boring."

Montague returned her smile, his own one of easy, confident grace. "Although I spend much of my time in the capital, I'm not one to turn my back on country pleasures." He glanced at the men. "And these days, the wool clip and similar harvests from the country form the backbone of our nation's wealth—none of us should forget that."

The comment had Jacqueline's brows faintly rising and, of course, made Montague an instant ally of the men—farmers all. Montague's attire, subdued and self-effacing though it was, his dark-brown coat relatively plain with simple gold buttons but devoid of braid or other showy embellishments, nevertheless marked him as hailing from London; given their quality, his garments couldn't have originated from anywhere else.

Subdued his clothing might be, yet everything about him screamed of wealth.

The gold signet ring on his right hand and the jewel-encrusted hilt of the sword she'd seen peeking out from beneath his coat confirmed that assessment.

Whoever he was and whatever his reasons for being there, Richard Montague came from a wealthy family.

Given he was a Montague, there was little surprise in that.

They remained chatting with that group for several minutes, then Jacqueline touched Montague's arm, and they made their excuses and moved on to the next knot of locals.

Once again, Montague proved to be a dab hand at reassuring others uncertain of how to deal with him. After making a joking comment about his woeful experience in her wood, he engaged the men in what evolved into a lively discussion of hunting in the neighborhood. Montague's recollections of the sport to be had around Wells, and his ready exchanges with Mr. Willis and his son, Thomas, both of whom hunted in that area, left Jacqueline reasonably certain that Montague's claim to be a frequent visitor at Wells was true.

As they moved from group to group, under cover of the chatter, she watched him closely, but somewhat to her surprise, he appeared to… subtly retreat from the ladies' advances. Certainly, he deployed what she sensed was a shield of smiling yet steely reserve between him and those ladies who, with their smiles and gushing comments, sought to draw him to them.

He resisted most definitely and remained by her side.

Yet he made no move to engage her, stoking her curiosity even more. Indeed, to a point where her escalating inquisitiveness made it easy to ignore her nonsensical, still-overactive senses.

Perhaps Richard Montague was exactly who and what he claimed to be and nothing more.

Regardless, he gained her very definite approval when, as they were passing through the crowd, he dipped his head to hers and murmured, "One moment, if you please."

Then he diverted to where Hammond, one of the Hall's woodcutters, was standing with his wife and several others, all workers on the estate.

All turned in some surprise, but bobbed bows and curtsies to her and to Montague.

Montague smiled upon them all, then settled his gaze on Hammond. "I wanted to thank you and your wife"—he dipped his head to Mrs. Hammond—"for taking pity on a stranger and bringing me here. Not everyone would have been so helpful."

Hammond flushed and insisted that they'd done no more than what anyone would have, but Montague only smiled and inclined his head. "Nevertheless, I'm grateful to you both for your kindness and hope prosperity shines upon your labors."

With that and a general, easy nod to the others, he steered Jacqueline on to the next group of guests.

After making the introductions, in response to several questions, she described calling in the dowser and finding the old spring, yet Montague making the effort to thank the Hammonds remained high in her mind. It had, quite simply, been a nice thing to do. And not something to which gentlemen of Montague's ilk tended to stoop.

The longer she spent in his company, the higher Richard Montague rose in her estimation.

Apparently, without intending to.

Richard saw no reason not to stick by Miss Tregarth's side—a decision that, once he realized he'd made it, struck him as distinctly odd; normally, he avoided the company of marriageable ladies like the plague. But Miss Tregarth had displayed not the faintest interest in claiming his attention for herself. Indeed, if asked to define how she viewed him, he would say "suspiciously."

Regarding him as a highly desirable, eminently eligible parti—which he unquestionably was—apparently did not feature in her, from all he could judge, otherwise clear-eyed view of her world.

If one part of him saw her obliviousness as a challenge, that part and any impulses to which it might have given rise were smothered beneath a tide of relief. Although he was escorting a striking young lady about a social gathering, for once, he felt safe.

He'd thought that he would have to reach Wells and the august presence of his uncle before he would be able to relax. But while he still had to keep a wary eye out for the other young ladies—and several not so young—who saw him as a marriageable entity and couldn't believe their luck, while he stuck by Miss Tregarth's side...he was safe.

That gave him time and the mental space to observe more broadly and consider other things.

Of course, many of the older gentlemen, those of the type to take a paternalistically protective view of Miss Tregarth, were eyeing him askance, some with expressions bordering on incipient animosity. He could have soothed them by informing them that he had sworn off marriageable females, possibly for all time, but their wish to scare him off was proving useful.

From the instant he'd been informed that Miss Tregarth owned the estate, he'd been curious as to how she managed it. Being the owner of an estate himself, he knew what the management of such properties entailed. It was pure curiosity on his part, wondering how a pretty, still-youthful lady would handle the demands of the position.

During their various discussions, several gentlemen—Alderman Harris among them—had dropped comments to the effect that Miss Tregarth managed the reins entirely on her own. Richard suspected that the alderman and others who had made similar remarks thought that by painting a picture of a lady of managing disposition, they would frighten him off. Instead, their revelations only further fueled his curiosity.

As he and she progressed up the great hall, stopping at each circle of guests to chat and converse, he overheard a not quite low-voiced-enough exchange between three disapproving older ladies and learned that Miss Tregarth had dismissed a string of suitors. The older ladies deplored her unwed state, declaring that, at twenty-four years of age, she should be married with a brood of children rather than discussing the price of wool with two of the estate's farmers, as she presently was.

Richard enjoyed the puzzle of understanding people, of figuring out what drove them. It was an interest his parents had encouraged as useful in one of his station, and over the years, defining people had become an ingrained habit. He could comprehend and catalog most people without any real effort. Jacqueline Tregarth, however, was proving to be a challenge.

That she was, apparently, uninterested in marriage—which went some way toward explaining her lack of matrimonial interest in him—and, instead, was focused on managing her estate was precisely what made her so interesting to him.

So different, ergo fascinating, entertaining, and intriguing.

She was presently discussing the estate's expected wool clip and the price she and her farmers might get for it. Having not that long ago been privy to a similar exchange between his father and his brother, Richard judged her to be well informed.

Given she was competent, intelligent, and strikingly attractive—albeit romantically reserved—and endowed with what, from all he'd gleaned, was a sizeable house and estate, he had to wonder just why Miss Tregarth had turned away what sounded to be legions of suitors.

They were in between groups when the strains of a viol drifted down from above. Glancing up, Richard saw movement in the gallery above the end of the hall as the musicians who had taken up position there put bows to strings and struck up a jaunty country dance.

Those milling in the center of the hall shuffled toward the sides, creating an impromptu dance floor. Richard looked at Jacqueline. She was smiling encouragingly at other couples, then she laughed and made a shooing motion, directing those others to the floor.

One glance around the room was enough to confirm that he was the ranking male of appropriate age and station to lead Miss Tregarth out, at least to begin with. Electing to grasp the opportunity Fate was dangling, he caught Jacqueline's eye, swept her a flourishing bow, and with a laughing smile, asked, "Might I beg the honor of this dance, Miss Tregarth?"

For one instant, she looked taken aback, as if participating in the dance hadn't crossed her mind. But then she smiled, sank into a curtsy, and rising, gave him her hand. "Thank you, Mr. Montague. I would enjoy that."

He set his mind and his considerable expertise to ensuring she did.

It was a simple country dance, one he could perform in his sleep, but with her as his partner, he remained alert and focused.

As she dipped under his arm in a slow, graceful twirl, from beneath her lashes, she met his eyes. "Do they dance such dances in town?"

Ruefully, he shook his head. "The hostesses prefer the more complicated contredanses, yet everyone needs to concentrate so ferociously on the steps, such dances feature more as torture than enjoyment."

She laughed—as he'd intended.

They parted, then came together again, and he seized the moment to ask, "I've heard, of course, of the cause of this celebration—that an old spring is running again and a previously dry lake is refilling. But what prompted you to search for the spring?"

The stableman had explained, but Richard wanted to hear her reasons. In her various exchanges on the topic, she hadn't touched on those.

She bobbed, then drew closer and turned, giving him her hands. "Our stream's been drying up—the flow never picked up after winter. So we— the estate—needed water. Quite desperately. We still have to find a way to supply the millstream, but one hurdle at a time—at least we now have water enough for the Hall's and our farmers' needs."

"I see." After another circle and changing of hands, he asked, "The stream that's failing—is it the one that runs past your woodcutter's cottage?"

"Yes. You must have noticed how poor the flow was."

He nodded as they swayed, but continued to hold his tongue regarding the gentleman and his diversion of the stream. Clearly, they were talking of the same stream, yet his father had drilled it into him never to jump in and volunteer information in situations he didn't fully comprehend, and he had no way of telling if Miss Tregarth and the gentleman were acting together for some reason he couldn't yet discern.

The dance separated them for several minutes.

By the time they came together again, he'd decided that, if he hadn't learned more one way or the other before he was ready to ride on, he would mention the gentleman and the diversion in the wood before he left.

The dance came to an end, and he bowed, and she curtsied. He gave her his hand and drew her to her feet, returning her smile—one more genuinely relaxed than he'd yet seen from her.

Others gathered around, and they continued chatting while the musicians decided on their next measure. When they once more started playing, Richard—too well brought up not to know his role—solicited Miss Swinford's hand.

Although she blushed and disclaimed, when he inquired, Miss Swinford admitted she loved to dance. Thereafter, he ignored her fluster and inexorably drew her into the nearest set.

If her wide smile when the dance ended was any indication, Miss Swinford had thoroughly enjoyed the exercise.

While dancing with a succession of her neighbors, Jacqueline watched with approval as Richard Montague dutifully progressed through the ladies, most of whom were somewhat older than he, but who nevertheless clearly enjoyed his company.

His attentions, she noticed, he kept to himself. Given the dearth of younger ladies, that might have been expected, but more than one lively matron attempted to catch his eye in a more meaningful fashion, yet although his smiling courtesy never wavered, he studiously maintained a respectful distance.

He was, she realized, accustomed to this—to country entertainments and country ways. She suspected that meant he was a landowner himself or, at the very least, the son of one. That, indeed, fitted with some of his earlier comments to her farmers and neighbors.

After a time, she excused herself from the dancing and returned to the hearth to check on Hugh and Elinor, who had returned to her seat beside Hugh. Hugh's legs had weakened, and he was confined to his Bath chair, propelled around the house and grounds by his devoted valet, Freddie. Freddie had retreated to stand by the wall, so when Jacqueline paused by Hugh's chair and exchanged a smile with her erstwhile guardian, she felt no hesitation in declaring, "I find myself quite content to have had Mr. Montague join us." She turned to watch the dancers and picked him out amid the lines—simple enough given he was taller than most and easily the most striking man in the room.

Hugh humphed, the sound one of approval. "He's certainly joined in —no standing on ceremony."

Jacqueline nodded. She had a strong suspicion Richard Montague was at home in significantly more elevated circles, yet at no time had he shown the slightest sign of being high in the instep.

Elinor sighed. "Such an easy and undemanding guest. He's the sort of guest it's a pleasure to have."

"Indeed." Jacqueline felt reassured at having her reading of Montague confirmed. Hugh and Elinor might live as sheltered a life as she did, but each had years of experience at their back, and she'd long ago learned they were rarely taken in by pretty faces and polished manners. As for charm…like her, they instinctively distrusted it, especially in gentlemen.

Despite his easygoing handsomeness, Richard Montague hadn't tried to charm anyone.

With a nod, she moved on. She accepted an offer from a blushing

Thomas Willis for the last dance and found herself in the same set as Montague. Thomas was younger than she by three years and was clearly in awe of Montague's polish, but with a smile and a nod, Montague set the boy at ease, and the dance passed off splendidly, leaving the four in their set laughing and smiling and in excellent accord.

Most of the estate's workers had already left, slipping away with nods and bows. The rest of the guests, mostly neighbors, took the end of the music as signaling the end of the event and started gathering their parties to depart. Coaches were called for and farewells tendered. Jacqueline stood to one side of the open front door and waved her guests off, into the softness of the summer night.

Finally, all were gone. She turned inside to find Cruickshank waiting to close and bar the door.

While he did, she walked slowly back into the great hall. Elinor had already gone up, and Hugh and Freddie had retreated to Hugh's rooms at the rear of the house. Somewhat to Jacqueline's surprise, Richard Montague was helping the footmen muscle back into place the heavy round table that normally stood in the center of the great hall.

Once it was settled, she approached. With a nod and a smile, she dismissed the footmen, then met Montague's hazel eyes. "You didn't have to do that."

He smiled and lightly shrugged. "I was here, and it seemed the least I could do to repay you and your household for your collective willingness to put me up for the night." He tipped his head. "And for allowing me to join your celebration—you didn't have to do that."

She laughed. "Very well. Let's call ourselves quits."

From the corner of her eye, she caught a glint of candlelight on gold and looked toward the hearth. Now freed of all dirt and polished until the gold mounting gleamed and the surface of the stone, a moonstone, shone, the orb—Hugh, Elinor, and she had agreed that was the only word for it —stood on the mantelpiece, in the middle, in pride of place.

Smiling, she turned and crossed to the fireplace. "If you'll wait just a minute, I'll show you to your room. I should put this away."

He trailed after her and watched as she reached up and lifted the orb down.

As it had several times before, when her fingers brushed the moonstone, the stone appeared to softly glow. Just for an instant.

Frowning, he peered at the orb. "What is that?"

She wasn't sure if he was asking about the orb or the curious glow. "We found it lodged on top of the spring—like a plug." Cradling the orb in her hands, she started toward the drawing room on the other side of the hall. "Now, of course, it's become the Hall's good luck charm—we're calling it 'the orb.' The way the estate's workers are talking of it, it'll feature in the tales they tell their children for years to come."

"I see." He strolled beside her, but his gaze remained on the orb, his expression one of puzzled curiosity.

They walked into the drawing room; the room had been left open for guests to sit and rest, and several candelabra still shed a warm glow throughout the chamber.

She crossed the room and halted before the dresser set against the far wall directly opposite the door.

His gaze still on the orb, he halted beside her, then glanced up and saw her studying him. The lines at the corners of his eyes crinkled, and his lips quirked. "It's a curious thing—I was thinking it looks a bit like the top of a scepter."

She nodded. "The more fanciful suggestion is that it's the head of a magical staff, but regardless, it's now the Hall's charm." She looked up at the top shelf of the dresser; she couldn't reach it, not without dragging over a chair.

"Top shelf?" he asked.

"Please." She held out the orb.

He lifted it from her hands. His hands were so much larger, the orb was all but engulfed by his palms and fingers.

And it glowed. Briefly.

Just as it did whenever she touched it.

They both frowned as the glow quickly faded, leaving the moonstone once more just a large, smooth, pale, milky, semi-translucent stone.

"Perhaps it's something to do with the warmth of our hands," he muttered.

Except it hadn't reacted that way when either Hugh or Elinor had held it. "I thought it might be due to some hidden facet or fracture catching the light just so," she offered.

He made an uncertain sound, then looked up at the empty top shelf of the dresser. "In the middle?"

"If you would."

He placed it carefully, turning it on the base of old gold, an engraved working that reminded her of the ruff above an eagle's claw. The mounting holding the moonstone in place almost certainly represented claws.

He stepped back to view his handiwork. "Is that how you wanted it?"

She couldn't have done better. "Yes, thank you."

She turned and deviated to pick up one of the candelabra as she crossed to the door. He stood back to let her precede him into the great hall, then followed at her shoulder as she led the way to and up the stairs.

His manners, his courtesies, weren't actions he consciously thought about; his attentiveness to others was ingrained. As he followed her down one of the corridors leading from the gallery, she was quite sure of that.

She halted before the door of the room the Hall's housekeeper had earlier informed her had been prepared for him. She lifted the latch, set the door swinging wide, then stepped back and waved him inside. "I hope you'll be comfortable." With a gracious nod, he stepped past her, and she added, "If there's anything you find you need, please ring no matter the hour. Cruickshank and Mrs. Patrick—the housekeeper—will be distressed if you don't. To their minds, they have their own standards to uphold, and we don't get many unexpected visitors, so you've put them on their mettle—please don't be shy."

Richard cast a comprehensive glance around the room, taking in the comfortable four-poster bed, his saddlebags set on the top of a large tall-boy, and the ewer, basin, and folded towel on a washstand in one corner. The wide window was uncurtained and stood open to the soft, scented night air.

He turned to his hostess and smiled. "I can't see any reason to disturb your staff."

He reached out and lifted the candlestick left waiting on a side table by the door. He tilted the tip of the candle to one of those in the cande-labra she held. Once the wick was alight, he straightened the candlestick and raised his gaze to her face—to her lovely blue-green eyes. "You and your staff have my heartfelt thanks for taking pity on a benighted traveler —and his even more benighted horse."

She laughed as he'd hoped she would; the silvery sound fell like music on his ears.

He saluted her with the candlestick and reached for the door.

She dipped her head to him, her golden curls burnished by the candle-light. "Goodnight, Mr. Montague."

He executed a courtly half bow. "Goodnight, Miss Tregarth."

Still smiling, she set off along the corridor, heading back to the gallery.

Richard turned into his room and shut the door.

It had been a long day. He was tired, but…despite the frustrations of the day, he'd landed on his feet, and unexpectedly, they'd led him to a welcoming, comfortable, and altogether intriguing place.

CHAPTER 3

The following day was Sunday. As usual, the old minister, Reverend Henry, came walking up the drive, followed by the estate workers, and they joined with the household for the customary service in the chapel above the great hall.

Sunday service in the chapel had been a Hall tradition from time immemorial.

Afterward, Jacqueline met with Mrs. Patrick to review the stores after the depredations of the unexpected celebration. They'd agreed on the items for an order to be placed with the merchant in West Pennard, the nearest village of any size, when one of the young footmen, Harold, arrived to inform her that Sir Peregrine Wallace had called and that Cruickshank had Sir Peregrine waiting in the great hall.

Jacqueline muttered an imprecation; she did not like Sir Peregrine. "Thank you, Harold. No need to go back to Cruickshank—I'll go straightaway."

She might not like Wallace, but the sooner she saw him, the sooner they could all be rid of him. Admittedly, Sir Peregrine hadn't yet crossed her personal line—meaning he had yet to tout himself as an acceptable suitor and urge her to yield him her hand—but if she was any judge at all of men, it was only a matter of time.

She quit the morning room, but halted in the corridor before the door giving onto the great hall. She shook her skirts straight, checked her fichu was in place, then drew in a breath and pushed through the swinging door.

She turned toward the front door and had to fight to keep her lips straight. Cruickshank, bless him, had kept Wallace kicking his heels in the antechamber just inside the door. He hadn't shown Sir Peregrine to the more comfortable chairs before the fireplace, much less into the drawing room. Instead, Wallace was perched on an uncomfortable bench set against the wall a yard inside the door.

Jacqueline clasped her hands at her waist and, head high, glided forward. "Sir Peregrine. How nice to see you."

Wallace came to his feet and stalked to meet her, reaching her as she drew level with the central table.

She halted as he did, with less than a yard between them. Perforce, she had to offer him her hand.

He took it and bowed over it. "Miss Tregarth. I hope I see you well."

"Indeed." She retrieved her hand, reclasped it with the other at her waist, fixed a politely inquiring gaze on Sir Peregrine's once-handsome but now-dissolute face, and waited for him to state his business.

He glanced frowningly at Cruickshank, but unperturbed, the butler remained standing by the front door, his gaze trained above Jacqueline's head as if awaiting orders. Apparently accepting that he would not be left alone with her, Wallace returned his distinctly bloodshot gaze to her face.

Bloodshot, and it wasn't even noon.

She was not going to invite him into the drawing room or even to sit. As far as she was concerned, the sooner Wallace left, the better.

Then he looked past her, and she heard the faint squeak of the door to the servants' hall and the soft steps of a woman's slippers. Reinforcements; she hid another smile. Mrs. Patrick had come in as if needing to speak with her or Cruickshank and, from the direction of Wallace's narrow-eyed gaze, had taken up position at the rear of the hall.

A dark expression in his blue eyes, Wallace finally looked back at her and smiled.

The transformation was startling—as a young boy, he must have looked like a cherub with his perfect features, cerulean-blue eyes, and cap of golden curls—but Jacqueline had already glimpsed what lay beneath the faded beauty and had a shrewd suspicion of what, in the intervening years, Wallace had become. More, she was immune to charm, no matter how pretty.

"I have come, my dear Miss Tregarth, because I learned via the grapevine of the dreadful news that your stream is failing. As I heard it, your mill can no longer function and even your farms on the levels will soon face difficulties, what with the worst of summer still ahead of us. I imagine the loss of crops will be substantial. You and Mr. Tregarth must be quite beside yourselves as to how to come about."

She kept her expression as uninformative as she could and wondered where Wallace was attempting to lead her.

He made to reach for her arm, but as she'd tucked her elbows into her sides—she'd adopted that pose for a reason—there was no opening for him to take her elbow without having to grab and pull. His arm lowered to his side. Fleetingly, his lips thinned, but then his smile returned. "Of course, the instant I heard of your difficulties, I came riding over to offer what assistance I can. As you know, I recently acquired Windmill Farm, beyond your north boundary, and the farm boasts a spring-fed stream that's running strongly, and the lake there is full. If it would ease the Hall's plight, I would be happy to arrange for my tenant there—Wilson—to cart water to your farmers and even to the millstream."

Jacqueline stared at Wallace's eager, smiling face and wondered what Farmer Wilson—who had only the previous evening been dancing in this very room—would say to such a proposal. As if he would have time to cart water to the Hall! Luckily…

Smiling entirely sincerely, she calmly said, "That's a very kind offer, Sir Peregrine, although I do think Wilson would be hard pressed to comply. Fortunately, we won't have to put him to the trouble. I'm happy to be able to inform you"—no lie, that—"that we've been successful in locating and reopening our own spring, the one that feeds the lake behind the house. The lake is, even now, steadily filling, and we'll shortly be able to commence carting water to the farms and elsewhere as needed."

Sir Peregrine's expression fell. "Another spring? A *lake*?" He stared at her.

Jacqueline looked into a dissipated countenance that displayed weakness and willfulness in equal measure. This, she suspected, was much closer to Sir Peregrine's true face, stripped of the mask of assumed politeness.

In his eyes, she detected frustration and something darker, more harsh. Emotions evoked by some train of thought she didn't understand.

"Yes." She felt obliged to respond even though she assumed his questions were rhetorical; hearing her own voice grounded her. "The old lake has been dry for years, but Hugh recalled that it was spring fed, so I called in the dowser..."

Upstairs, Richard stepped into the gallery. He'd broken his fast with Hugh and Miss Tregarth, then attended morning service with the rest of the household. After that, he'd gone out to the stable to check on Malcolm the Great, only to be informed by both Hopkins and Ostley that the big gelding wouldn't be able to put weight on the affected hoof, at least not that day.

Not entirely surprised, he'd accepted their advice and returned to the house and spoken with Hugh and Miss Swinford, who he'd found in a rear parlor, Hugh reading, Miss Swinford—Elinor, as she'd suggested he call her—embroidering. Miss Tregarth had been meeting with the house-keeper, but both Hugh and Elinor had assured Richard that he was welcome to remain until Malcolm the Great recovered the use of his hoof. Both had been amused by the horse's name, but then neither had yet seen him.

Richard had returned to his chamber via the rear stairs to put Malcolm the Great's favorite curry comb, which he'd taken to the stable, back into his saddlebag. Deciding that, regardless of the assurances of Hugh and Elinor, he should seek Miss Tregarth's permission to remain, he'd left his room with the intention of finding her.

He heard her voice floating up from the great hall below, smiled, and strode on. Then her words registered, and he slowed. Plainly, she was speaking to someone who had not known about her rediscovered spring and the refilling lake. Richard paused in the shadows of the gallery and looked over the balustrade.

The gentleman to whom his hostess was speaking looked vaguely familiar. Then Richard noticed that Cruickshank's gaze was trained on the newcomer and realized that, if the man was a visitor, then it was odd he hadn't been shown into the drawing room. Richard's sharp ears registered a creak from below the gallery. Careful not to get too close to the balustrade and draw the stranger's eyes, Richard shifted until he could look down... He could just see the edge of a woman's reddish curls and the front of her plain gown. The housekeeper, Mrs. Patrick, was also present—standing guard.

His eyes narrowing, Richard returned his gaze to the man. Who was he? And why did Miss Tregarth's experienced staff consider him a threat? A threat to her?

Then Miss Tregarth reached the end of her explanation, and the stranger shifted, straightening, and spoke.

"I see. Well, that's…wonderful. Of course." The stranger nodded; from where Richard stood, he couldn't see the gentleman's face. The man continued, "It's good to know that your farms won't run dry and will continue to prosper through the summer."

The man's tone suggested he was, at least metaphorically, speaking through clenched teeth.

Regardless, Richard recognized the voice of the gentleman he'd last seen deep in the wood, walking away from the diversion of the stream.

So this is what the diversion is about.

This, Richard realized, was the man's purpose—the impact of the diversion on Nimway Hall and the estate's farms. And thus, on Jacqueline Tregarth.

Clearly, Cruickshank's and Mrs. Patrick's instincts were sound. The effect on the estate hadn't been any unintended consequence.

His gaze locked on the unknown gentleman, Richard studied the man —what little he could make out from his elevated angle—while Jacqueline thanked the gentleman, Sir Peregrine, for his kind offer of assistance, plainly building toward a dismissal.

Even from where he stood, Richard could read Sir Peregrine's frustration—his fists had clenched, and the tension in his frame suggested he was on the brink of some violent eruption—yet from Jacqueline's calm if controlled expression, it seemed Sir Peregrine was endeavoring to hide his reaction behind a passably polite mask.

Richard hailed from a family steeped in social and political power; his instincts regarding people had been honed from the cradle. He did not doubt that Jacqueline Tregarth herself was Sir Peregrine's immediate target, yet nothing in what Richard saw or sensed in the tableau before him suggested any degree of amorous or romantic inclination on the gentleman's part.

Hmm.

Jacqueline reached the end of her expressions of gratitude, inclined her head, and gracefully stepped toward the front door—forcing Sir Peregrine to accept her implied dismissal and swing around to keep pace with her.

Richard eyed Sir Peregrine's back. He wasn't wearing a hat or greatcoat as he had been in the wood. While on sight alone, Richard had to admit he could not have sworn it was the same man, there was also nothing to make him revise his conviction, based on Sir Peregrine's voice and his interest in the estate's water supply, that this was the man responsible for the stream's diversion.

Cloaked in the gallery's shadows, Richard watched with approval as Jacqueline, head high, glided toward the front door, all but towing Sir Peregrine in her wake. Cruickshank stepped up in support to stand beside the already-open door.

Then Sir Peregrine—glancing almost scowlingly sidelong at Jacqueline—halted. He raised his head and stared over Jacqueline's—through the open doorway and into the drawing room. "I say! What's that?"

Two steps farther on, Jacqueline stopped and turned back.

Before she could prevent him, Sir Peregrine strode across the hall and into the drawing room.

In a flurry of skirts, Jacqueline rushed after him.

Richard tensed—to go down or not? But Cruickshank was already striding for the drawing room. The butler halted in the doorway, then stepped back as Jacqueline reappeared, literally dragging Sir Peregrine away…

From the orb?

That had to be what Sir Peregrine had seen—the orb sitting on the top shelf of the dresser directly opposite the drawing room door.

As Jacqueline, both hands gripping one of Sir Peregrine's arms, drew him back into the great hall, even as his feet reluctantly complied, Sir Peregrine's head remained turned, his gaze locked on what had seized his attention. "You found it buried above the spring, you say?"

"Yes." Jacqueline's tone suggested she'd reached the end of her patience.

Sir Peregrine lost sight of the orb and refocused on her. "Actually, I'm something of an authority on arcane objects. Would you like me to—"

"No." Jacqueline's jaw was set, her tone definite. "It's just an old thing from the house, but given where we found it, the household and the estate workers now view it as our good luck charm. But it's nothing more than an old ornament."

Sir Peregrine was in no way convinced of that; Richard read as much in the man's shifting gaze and his calculating expression as he glanced over his shoulder, back toward the drawing room. But then Sir Peregrine, who Jacqueline had continued to urge toward the front door, dropped his resistance, turned, and went willingly.

He patted Jacqueline's hand, wrapped about his arm—as if about to grasp her hand.

Abruptly, Jacqueline released him and drew back her hands. She hauled in a breath, recomposed her expression, and briskly led her unwelcome visitor to the front door.

Surprisingly meekly, Sir Peregrine kept pace.

Cruickshank had gone ahead and now waited to one side of the open doorway. She halted on the other side and turned to Sir Peregrine.

He met her gaze, then glanced toward the drawing room. "If you're sure...?"

"Quite." Tipping up her chin, she held out her hand. "Thank you for calling, Sir Peregrine." When he didn't immediately respond, she added, "I really must get on, sir."

Sir Peregrine's gaze returned to her face, a frown fleetingly visible in the blue of his eyes. For a moment, he regarded her with that harsh, hard stare that she couldn't interpret, then finally, he grasped her fingers and, rather perfunctorily, bowed over them. Straightening, he inclined his head. "Until next we meet, Miss Tregarth."

With that, he walked out, across the porch, and down the steps to where Billy Brakes held the reins of a showy hack. Jacqueline noted that Hopkins and Ned Ostley had also come to the forecourt and were loitering within easy reach of the front door.

With Cruickshank at her elbow, she stood on the threshold of the Hall and watched Sir Peregrine mount, viciously wrench his horse's head around, and ride away down the drive.

The instant the trees hid Sir Peregrine from sight, Jacqueline felt a weight lift from her shoulders—and indeed, she sensed the same nebulous pressure lifting from the staff around her and from the Hall itself. Apparently, she wasn't the only one to take against Sir Peregrine; just having to grip his arm had made her skin crawl.

She took a moment to consider what her instincts were telling her. Outwardly, Sir Peregrine was personable enough, but there was something nasty lurking behind his glamor. She'd also got the impression he was intent on something—that he knew some secret and was keen to seize some advantage.

She suspected he was or could become a threat, but she wasn't as yet sure in what way.

Regardless, he was definitely a person to guard against.

With a nod to Hopkins, Ned, and Billy, she turned back into the hall.

As was customary on such glorious summer days, they left the front door propped wide. Cruickshank followed her into the body of the great hall.

She'd reached the central table when footsteps on the stairs drew her attention.

She halted and watched as Richard Montague descended the stairs, step by step. Unhurriedly yet purposefully. A faint frown tangled his dark brows, and his gaze was fixed unwaveringly on her.

It was impossible to stop her senses from leaping, her lungs from seizing, then constricting. She might consider such reactions to the mere sight of a man ludicrous, the hallmark of a silly girl rather than the lady she was, yet when it came to Richard Montague, she was helpless to prevent them; he triggered her senses.

It was also impossible to prevent her conscious mind from making the comparison between him and Sir Peregrine, from cataloguing the differences. While they were of similar height and not much different in build, Montague was the heavier, the more physically powerful. Also, beneath his undeniable social polish, which held a significantly higher gloss than Sir Peregrine had ever displayed, Montague possessed a hard-edged intelligence combined with eyes that saw and a mind that assessed with experience and knowledge, all tempered by an innate understanding of how their world worked.

While her inner sight had already labeled him a warrior, it now also saw him as embodying justice. As standing for justice. She had a fleeting vision of him wielding a sword in Justice's name.

He stepped onto the hall tiles and walked to meet her.

As Montague halted a yard before her, Cruickshank stepped past. With nothing more than a deferential nod to Montague, Cruickshank continued down the hall, following Mrs. Patrick, who, after one glance at Montague, had already turned and walked back through the door to the servant's hall.

Her staff's assessment of Richard Montague could not have been clearer. Hiding a smile—no matter how serious he appeared, she, too, did not see Montague as any sort of threat—Jacqueline met his hazel gaze and arched her brows in question; he was plainly dwelling on something.

He held her gaze, his own direct and open, for several seconds, then said, "I was in the gallery, coming to see you—my horse's hoof is not yet healed, and I wanted to request your permission to remain for at least another day."

"Yes, of course. You're welcome to stay until your horse is fit to ride again."

He inclined his head, then his gaze moved past her to the open front door. "I couldn't help overhearing the latter part of your conversation with your recent visitor."

"Sir Peregrine Wallace. He's…a neighbor of sorts. He hails from Lydford, to the southeast, but he recently took possession of the farm that adjoins our northern boundary."

"Indeed?" Richard paused, trying to place Wallace in London society and failing; presumably, he and Wallace moved in different circles. He refocused on Jacqueline Tregarth's delicate features and, feeling his way, ventured, "I didn't hear all of your conversation with Wallace, but if I understood correctly, he came with an offer of help to ease the water shortage caused by your stream drying up."

She nodded. "The lake on the farm to the north fills from a different, spring-fed stream. He offered us water from that, although how poor Farmer Wilson would cope with having to cart water over to our farms, I do not know. Luckily, now we have our spring running again, we won't need to bother him."

Richard's jaw tightened, his expression hardening. He held Jacqueline's questioning, now-curious gaze. "Yesterday, when I was lost in your wood, I heard two men talking. I was unsure what manner of men they were and what they were up to, so despite wanting help finding my way, I approached cautiously, and neither saw me. I found them in a narrow valley—one man was clearly a gentleman while the other was a much rougher sort, a laborer, perhaps. The pair were discussing a series of tunnels the laborer had constructed that cunningly siphoned water from the stream running along the bottom of the valley."

Jacqueline Tregarth wasn't lacking in wits. Her face, her whole bearing, stiffened.

Still holding her gaze, Richard continued, "By the time I saw them, the men were already moving away—I saw only their backs. I can't be certain of identifying either by sight. But their voices had reached me clearly, and I'm perfectly certain that the gentleman I heard in the wood discussing the diversion of that stream was the gentleman who recently stood in this hall, speaking with you. Sir Peregrine Wallace."

Jacqueline blinked, then her gaze grew distant.

"I didn't speak last night," Richard said, wanting to clear up that point, "because at that time, I wasn't sure what was going on and who was connected to whom. I didn't know Sir Peregrine's purpose. Now, I do."

Jacqueline refocused on his face; her blue-green eyes were flinty, and her chin had firmed. "These tunnels that divert the waters of the stream—they're still there?"

"Yes. I heard Wallace tell his man—the laborer—to leave all in place. They knew no one had discovered the diversion, and it wasn't easy to find. I stood over it, searching the ground for several minutes, before I realized what had been done."

She tipped up her chin. Her eyes flashed. "Are you willing to lead me and my men to this diversion?"

Holding her challenging stare, he raised his brows. "Yes, of course." He paused, then added, "Assuming your wood cooperates."

Immediately after luncheon, they rode into the wood.

Half an hour later, Jacqueline sat atop her mare and watched Crawley and his lads, assisted by Fred Penn, the Hall's old groundsman, work to collapse the tunnels that had been bleeding the lifeblood from the Hall's stream.

Without the slightest tension, the estate's men had accepted Richard Montague's direction. He now stood alongside them, hands on his narrow hips, his head bent as he assessed their endeavors. Occasionally, he pointed to this or that and made a suggestion, with which her men instantly moved to comply.

Jacqueline might have lived a relatively sheltered life, but she recognized leadership when she saw it, and Richard Montague was born to the role. Not once had he had to push to get his way; he guided and led by example and with sound common sense, and the men followed.

She also recognized the vengeful animosity with which her men attacked the tunnels, their spades and picks striking with force. They were furious. She was more so.

How dare Wallace try such a trick?

This was her wood—Nimway Hall's wood—and as with the Hall itself, the wood was hers to protect.

Sensing her flaring anger, her mare shifted beneath her.

Reining in her ire, Jacqueline patted the silky neck and crooned soothingly. She and the horse were on the opposite bank of the stream, a few yards from the area in which the men were working, yet close enough to hear all that passed between them. The other horses were tethered some way to her right, in the clearing beyond the entrance to the narrow valley.

If Richard Montague hadn't stumbled upon Sir Peregrine's scheme and thought to investigate, she was convinced they would never have found the diversion; it was too well concealed.

Once the mare had settled again, Jacqueline determinedly turned her thoughts to practical matters—to whether they would be able to patch the holes in the stream bed well enough to completely halt the trickle of water over the escarpment, and if they managed to do so, how long it might take for the stream to resume its customary flow. They would need the mill in action within a month or so to grind the early grain.

She mentally listed her questions, but her eyes remained trained on the men—more specifically, on Richard Montague.

He was fast becoming a lodestone for her senses.

Unbidden, her gaze drew in, focusing solely on him, as the old tales of those who got lost in Balesboro Wood floated through her mind. His story of getting inexplicably lost—completely lost when normally he was assured of finding his way through forests far more extensive—resonated with one set of the long-told tales. The ones of people snared by the wood for a purpose, that purpose being to aid the Hall and, most especially, the Hall's guardian.

If one believed in the old tales...it was easy to cast Montague's entrapment as being necessary to protect the Hall. He—specifically he, with his particular character and traits—had had to be there, to surreptitiously overhear Sir Peregrine discussing his diversion, to be curious enough to investigate further and find the tunnels, then to carry the tale of the diversion to the Hall, to Jacqueline, the present guardian, and subsequently, to lead her and her men to the valley in which they now worked, so they could put right a man-wrought wrong.

Sir Peregrine Wallace's diversion had been a calculated crime against her and her people, one she would neither forgive nor forget.

Richard worked with the men, directing them in shifting stone, rocks, and clay to block the holes in the stream bed, then collapse the tunnels that had drained the water away.

Finally, he deemed the work around the stream done. As a trial of the effectiveness of their repairs, he had the young lads drag a pick through the rubble just before the edge of the escarpment, parallel to the drop. Along with the men, he stood and watched as the long slash in the earth at first filled and overflowed...but then the water in the groove stood, then slowly sank into the earth, and the incoming flow eased, then ceased altogether.

The ancient groundsman grunted. "Good enough. With the amount of clay in the soils here and with the spring flush over and done, the bank will have time to dry and bind and seal up our work. It'll hold."

Along with the other men, Richard was happy to accept that assurance.

They hoisted their tools and trudged back to the horses. As they walked along the now merrily gurgling stream, they were all pleased to see that the level of water was already rising along that stretch, returning to its correct level.

Richard walked to the horse he'd been given to ride—an aging but still powerful chestnut gelding that had been Jacqueline's late father's horse. She came trotting up on her mare as he swung up and settled in the saddle.

"All done?" she asked, holding the spirited mare in.

He nodded. "As your old groundsman says, it should hold, and I'm sure he'll be back to check in a week."

She smiled faintly, the gesture lightening her until-then-serious expression. "Indeed. We can rely on Fred Penn to keep an eye on it."

With a dip of her head, she led the way forward, on and across the clearing. Richard tapped his heels to the chestnut's sides, then reined in its resulting surge and brought it to pace alongside the mare.

As they left the clearing, he glanced back. The men had come on a range of beasts, some two to a back. They were sorting themselves out and preparing to follow. Richard faced forward. As he settled into the saddle, he gave voice to a puzzle. "Yesterday, I couldn't find my way through this wood, not even to the Hall. Yet this afternoon, I led you and the others directly to this valley. I didn't have to think. I knew which way I needed to go to return here, just as I normally would when in any other forest." He glanced at Jacqueline.

Briefly, she met his gaze, then shrugged. "I can't explain that any more than you can."

He humphed, but let the confounding matter rest.

As they ambled beneath the trees, the air warmed by the slanting sunbeams, he debated, then deciding that his assistance with the stream gave him a certain license, he surrendered to what he recognized as a protective impulse and inquired, "Do you have any insights into Wallace's motives in diverting the stream?"

She let the question lie between them for a full minute before replying, "I've been wondering about that."

After several seconds, to Richard's satisfaction, she went on, "From his visit this morning, it seems clear that he'd hoped to bring about a situation whereby I would accept his help, thereby placing me and the estate in his debt. Not monetarily but morally. Although he has yet to allude to the prospect, I strongly suspect that he—as with so many others—has it in mind to offer for my hand. I assume he believed that by assisting the estate in such a way—indeed, in stepping in as a savior of sorts—he would ingratiate himself with me and make me subsequently more amenable to entertaining his suit."

Judging by her flat tone, Wallace had severely miscalculated, a realization that warmed Richard's heart. But in delivering her answer, his pretty hostess had made no effort to conceal her antipathy toward gentlemen who wished to marry her. Such cynicism in a gently bred lady, especially an attractive one in her mid-twenties, seemed strange. Recalling all he'd overheard the night before, although he sensed he was straying onto thin ice, he couldn't resist prompting, "I heard that you've turned away a good few suitors."

She snorted. "Indeed." She shot him a sidelong glance, a rather sharp one he made a point of not meeting. "I daresay," she said, looking forward, "you heard that from the older ladies. There are several in the neighborhood who view my position as an unmarried lady in possession of considerable lands and an established manor house as a situation to be deplored. More, as one in urgent need of rectification."

"Clearly, you don't agree with that assessment."

Her laugh was harsh. "If you knew of my suitors—those who have presented themselves to date—you wouldn't, either. Every one has come to me with only one thought in his head—to gain control of the Hall's farms, along with the right to supply wood to the bishopric of Bath and Wells, which right is attached to the Hall's title. Both farms and right are valuable in that they generate significant income. At present, however, most of that income is plowed back into the farms and the Hall, spent in supporting the fabric of the estate and the people who work on it and care for it."

The glance she threw him then—one he felt forced to meet—was steady and held palpable feminine power. "Nimway Hall does not exist for the benefit of any man. It's here to support those who labor in its fields, all those who care for its wood and who maintain the Hall itself. Those who are its keepers."

She paused, then looked ahead. "The tradition of the Hall is one that reaches back through the mists of time. Unlike the case with most other estates, the Hall and its lands pass in the female line, usually from eldest daughter to eldest daughter. Each daughter who becomes the lady of the Hall accepts the role of guardian. Consequently, any man who aspires to be her husband must understand and accept that the reins of the estate remain in the lady's hands, and that the preservation of the Hall, of this wood, and the lower fields is the guardian's duty—a duty that takes precedence over any other she might undertake."

Richard couldn't hold back a wry smile. "I can see how that might not align with the views of gentlemen looking for a bride."

"Indeed," she scoffed. "To date, deciding how to respond to my would-be suitors has required little thought." She paused, then in a more even tone amended, "I should make clear that my disgust is not leveled at the institution of marriage, but at the gentlemen wishing to secure my lands via securing my hand."

He dipped his head in acknowledgment, struck by the thought that her situation was, in many ways, the female version of his. More, that her distinction between marriage and suitors was a valid one, one he hadn't considered overmuch with regard to his own situation.

That was something to ponder, perhaps when he finally reached the safety of his uncle's hearth.

For now, however, in the matter of Sir Peregrine Wallace and his interest in the lady of Nimway Hall, Jacqueline Tregarth had her feet firmly on the ground and appeared well armored against any attack, especially from any man aspiring to her hand.

She tapped her heels to her mare's sides, and Richard urged his gelding to keep pace alongside. He glanced at her, took in the fetching sight she made in her green velvet riding habit, and facing forward, smiled to himself. Pretty she might be, of the caliber to draw eyes and focus predatory senses, but one look into those wide, blue-green eyes and one glance at her determined chin ought to be enough to warn any man against taking the lady for granted.

Given how attractive he found her, it was lucky he wasn't on the lookout for a wife. Conversely, he knew very well that she was attracted in much the same way to him, which made her disinterest in suitors something of a relief.

They were mirror images, it seemed. Just as he was being hunted for his wealth and his name, she, too, was being courted for her possessions rather than the person she was.

As Nimway Hall appeared before them and, side by side, they cantered up the drive, he acknowledged there was a certain comfort in knowing that the lady in whose company he was shared his aversion to being pursued.

~

They returned to the Hall in time for afternoon tea. After partaking of scones and cakes as well as a dish of the fragrant brew, with the shadows lengthening, Richard walked out to the stable to check on Malcolm the Great.

Having contributed to the well-being of the estate by assisting with the repair of their stream, Richard felt more comfortable over making use of the house's amenities. Consequently, when he inquired of Hopkins as to the state of Malcolm's hoof and Hopkins shook his head direfully and informed him it would be days yet before the horse was fit to ride, he didn't feel compelled to search for alternatives to continuing at the Hall.

"Come." Hopkins beckoned. "Ned has the beast with him. Let's see what he thinks."

Richard followed the bow-legged man with his rolling gait through the stable and into the farrier's domain at the rear of the building.

When appealed to for his opinion on Malcolm the Great, who was hitched to a railing nearby, Ostley, too, shook his head. "I'd thought he'd be right as rain by now but...here." He crossed to the big gelding and picked up the hoof in question. Angling it so Richard could see, Ostley pointed to a pinkish section on the pad, next to the spot where the large sliver of wood had been wedged. "There's no cut and it's not infected, but I've seen that sort of thing before. He's not taken to the wood—the type of wood, see?—at all. If you try to ride him, especially given his weight"—Ostley set down the hoof and glanced at Richard—"aye, and yours, too, then odds are that'll open up, and then it will get infected."

Richard pulled a face, but nodded in acceptance. "He's too valuable to risk. It seems I'll have to wait for a few days yet."

Ostley nodded. "That'd be my recommendation. The times I've seen this before, it's been maybe five more days before the swelling's gone down."

"Five days?" That was longer than Richard had imagined. He looked inward, expecting to find impatience if not frustration, only to discover that, instead, the prospect of having the time to further investigate the curious behavior of Sir Peregrine Wallace and, if possible, thrust a more definite and permanent spoke in the man's wheel vis-à-vis Jacqueline Tregarth was distinctly appealing.

He wasn't, indeed, averse to spending more time at Nimway Hall. It was a pleasant and peaceful place, with pleasant, accommodating, and undemanding people—a place in which he didn't need to fear being set upon and trapped into matrimony. Quite the opposite. And with Wallace to deal with, he wouldn't be bored.

He was on the verge of inwardly smiling and accepting Fate's decree when Hopkins, regarding him earnestly, said, "If you was in a hurry to get on to your business in Wells, we could loan you that gelding you rode today. He'd carry you there, easy enough, then I could send one of the lads with your beast once he's recovered."

Richard paused and thought again, but… Slowly, he shook his head. "I don't have business, as such, to attend to in Wells—my visit was purely social and unplanned at that. No one there is expecting me, so no one will be concerned that I haven't yet arrived." And now that he was here, in the relative safety of Nimway Hall, there was no urgent need for him to race for the protection of his uncle's bachelor household; those who wished to pursue him could have no notion of where he'd found refuge.

He met Hopkins's gaze and smiled. "Thank you for the offer, but I would simply be sitting idle in the bishop's household, and truth to tell, I would rather be here, where I can at least ride and enjoy the countryside. After months in London, that's a welcome relief."

If he continued to Wells, he would have to remain indoors; venturing forth, even there, would be too dangerous. It was too soon after his near escape in town, and his connection to His Grace of Bath and Wells was no secret, after all.

He would also rather not leave Malcolm the Great wholly in others' hands; he was the only person the huge gelding allowed on his back. That thought settled the matter. With a brisk nod, Richard glanced from Hopkins to Ostley. "I'll stay."

They both smiled, clearly of the opinion that he'd made the right decision.

"Presuming," he added, "that my remaining won't inconvenience the household in any way."

Both Hopkins and Ostley exchanged a meaning-laden look, then both waved aside Richard's concern with the dismissiveness they plainly felt it deserved.

"Can't see why anyone would mind you hanging about," Hopkins stated.

"Aye—and it's the right decision an' all." Ned Ostley nodded to where Malcolm the Great had shifted to rest his huge head on Richard's shoulder. "Attached as the great beast is to you."

Richard chuckled and stroked Malcolm's long nose, then stepped away. With a wave to Ostley, Richard headed back to the stable with Hopkins.

Leaving the stableman issuing orders to his lads, Richard strode on, back toward the house.

Far from feeling obstructed by not being able to continue his journey, he felt…lighthearted. Strangely free.

Looking ahead, he studied the house, its gray stone burnished by the sun's waning light. He had to admit it was a welcoming sight. He mentally looked ahead to the coming days…and that welling sense of freedom nearly made him giddy. How long had it been since he'd felt so unencumbered—so free of social expectations and constraints?

Obviously, it had been too long if the mere prospect of freedom for a few days could affect him like this.

Recalling the meaningful look Hopkins and Ostley had shared, Richard wondered what had been behind the exchange. Perhaps it was simply that, with gentlemen like Wallace sniffing about their lady's skirts, the men—devoted to a fault, Richard had no doubt—considered that having a gentleman like him, younger and more able than Hugh Tregarth, on hand about the place wasn't a bad thing.

Richard reached the side door, opened it, stepped inside, and inwardly admitted that, in that regard, he, too, thought him remaining at Nimway Hall for a few more days was an excellent—nay, inspired—idea.

CHAPTER 4

*W*hen Richard entered the breakfast parlor the following morning, there was no one else there. However, seconds later, Cruickshank whisked in with a large teapot and the information that the platters were on their way. The footmen duly ferried the covered dishes to the table, and Richard settled to assuage his appetite.

He always slept well in the country, and last night had been no exception. Nimway Hall was old and its timbers creaked and even groaned, but he'd grown up in houses nearly as old, and to him, those sounds were the equivalent of a lullaby.

Ostley's and Hopkins's predictions of his continuing welcome had proved accurate. On returning to the house after speaking with them, Richard had gone to the family parlor; once again, he'd found Hugh and Elinor there. As before, both had happily extended the household's welcome for however long he required, and later, when he'd joined the family in the drawing room before dinner, Jacqueline had added her voice to the chorus. Graciously, she'd declared that, in light of the service he'd rendered to the Hall over the stream, he was welcome to remain for as long as he wished.

Over dinner, he and Jacqueline had described to Hugh and Elinor the structure that had diverted the stream's waters. After considerable discussion, it had been agreed that, as they had only Richard's memory of a voice on which to base an accusation, better they kept their counsel and did not warn Sir Peregrine that they were aware of his perfidy, but rather, being forewarned, kept a close eye on his activities henceforth. Given that, courtesy of his acquisition of the farm to the north, Wallace was now a neighbor of sorts only strengthened that argument; having a feud with a neighbor was not a situation Jacqueline wished to court.

Richard wasn't certain he agreed with what he saw as Jacqueline's leniency toward Wallace, but as a guest in her house, he'd held his tongue and, outwardly at least, deferred to her decision.

Later, Hugh had mentioned to Richard that Wallace had come by the deed to Windmill Farm via a wager and a game of cards that others present had thought strangely one-sided. But again, there was no evidence sufficient to accuse Wallace—just a suspicion that he had cheated. Richard had little doubt that Wallace had; it seemed the man was a cad through and through.

Warmed by the bright morning light streaming through the breakfast parlor windows, Richard was considering ways and means of dealing appropriately with Wallace when Jacqueline walked into the room. She was garbed in her riding habit, which, from Richard's perspective, boded well.

She smiled at him and went to the chair opposite, which Cruickshank hurried to hold for her.

Once she'd sat and poured herself tea, then helped herself sparingly from the various platters, Richard ventured, "I confess I find myself somewhat at a loose end."

Her gaze flicked up to his face, then her lips curved, and she said, "I intend to ride down to our farms—they lie to the west below the escarpment—to see how well the stream is recovering. I would like to get some idea of how quickly we might expect the flow to return to normal, especially with respect to the millstream. If it's going to take some time, we might need to think of carting water down from the lake."

He nodded and skewered his last slice of ham. "How is the lake? Is it full yet?"

"I checked it this morning. It still has some way to go, but within a day or two, it should reach capacity."

He frowned, chewed, and swallowed. "Will the spring continue to fill it, so that it overflows?"

She widened her eyes. "It hasn't in the past, so I presume it reaches some sort of balance."

He nodded; he'd seen similar systems elsewhere.

She caught his gaze and continued, "Would you like to accompany me on my ride? And later, perhaps we can take a look at the lake." She frowned abstractedly. "I was wondering if it might be possible to construct a tunnel, similar to the diversion tunnels, and use that as a channel to lead water to the stream, to supplement the flow if and when required."

He grinned. "Taking something positive from Wallace's attack?"

Her lips firmed. Her eyes refocused on his, and she nodded. "Just so."

He set down his cutlery and inclined his head. "I'm entirely at your disposal, Miss Tregarth. Whenever you're ready, lead on."

After making a quick breakfast, she did. They stopped in the kitchen to pack a light luncheon into their saddlebags, then, side by side, walked to the stable. She'd sent word requesting that the horses they'd ridden the previous day be saddled. When they reached the stable yard, Hopkins had both horses waiting. After securing the saddlebags, they mounted and rode out.

On the back of the chestnut gelding, almost as powerful as Malcolm the Great, Richard felt his heart lift as he followed Jacqueline and her mare at a quick jog-trot down a bridle path that led west from the stable. Minutes later, the trees ended and Jacqueline drew rein on a clear area of rocky ground at the edge of the escarpment. The trail led on, snaking downward over what was, at that point, a gentle enough descent. But Jacqueline's gaze had gone outward, scanning a view that was simply breathtaking.

How far they could see, Richard couldn't even guess, but between them and the hazy horizon to the west stretched a patchwork of fields in myriad shades of green, some tinged with the golden hue of ripening grain. Low hills lay to the south and the north, natural boundaries to the vast plain of the low-lying Somerset Levels. In the far distant past, history said the area had been mostly underwater and riddled with springs and bogs. Like the fens not far from his boyhood home, over the centuries, the land had been drained, but in wet seasons, areas could still become waterlogged.

Jacqueline pointed to the northwest. "That's the Tor. And if your eyesight is acute enough, you should be able to glimpse the ruins of the old abbey."

Richard recognized the unmistakable outline of Glastonbury Tor. Nearby, the crumbling arch of the abbey glowed as the sun, now well risen, danced over the ancient stones. "Yes—I see it."

After a moment, he glanced at Jacqueline and found her watching him, patently waiting to gauge his reaction. He smiled. "This is a stunning vista." He directed his gaze toward the nearer fields, intending to ask which were attached to the Hall, but trees growing up just below the lookout obscured the closer view.

"Come on." She shook her reins and sent the mare over the lip of the escarpment and on down the descending trail.

Lighthearted and eager, he followed.

The trail tacked back and forth as it wended its way down the escarpment. Several times, the path drew near the rocky stream, now gurgling and gushing—a cheery sound as the waters splashed over rocks in a rush to reach the lower ground.

At the base of the slope, the trail skirted a spot where the reinvigorated stream flowed into a small pool before burbling on. While the stream was clearly running freely, the pool was only half full.

Slowing her mare to an amble, Jacqueline studied the pool and the stream leading from it. "It's already much better than it was, but it looks as if it'll take several days to build up to its usual state."

She tapped her heels to the mare's sides and led the way on, and Richard followed.

The trail became a well-beaten path that, not long after, joined a cart track that led between fields, green and lush and burgeoning with grain. To any countryman, the view was an exceedingly pleasant one, and for Richard's money, it was made even better by the vision of Jacqueline Tregarth, neatly garbed in green velvet with a jaunty cap perched atop her golden curls, seen against the landscape of wide fields and arching skies. After several moments of covertly drinking in the sight, he turned his head and scanned the fields about them. "Are these the Hall's farms?"

"Yes." Jacqueline threw him a glance. "My ultimate goal for this visit is the mill, but I usually call in at the farms on the way."

He waved her on. "By all means."

Her gaze lingered on his face, then she faced forward and nudged the mare into a canter. After a moment, she called, "Are you interested in farming?"

He drew in the gelding alongside the mare. "My father's lands lie in Essex, so although this isn't exactly the same sort of country, the fields are low-lying and fertile...there are similarities." He paused, then added with a smile, "I'm sure there will be enough of interest to keep me amused throughout our ride."

Jacqueline tipped her head in acknowledgment and rode on. So his family hailed from Essex and actively farmed; she tucked the tidbit of information away.

Minutes later, she slowed and turned down the path to the first farm. After halting her mare in the yard before the farmhouse, she slipped her boots free of her side-saddle's stirrups and slid to the ground—before Richard could dismount and lift her down. She caught the faint frown on his face, but ignored it—she was no helpless ton lady—and walked forward to greet the woman who had come to the farmhouse door.

Jacqueline wasn't surprised to learn that the farmer and his sons were out in the fields, but the farmwife was delighted to welcome them. On its route to the mill, the stream ran through the farm at the rear of the farmhouse; the farmwife took them to view it, pointing out that the level of the stream was steadily rising. "Way it's going, it'll be back to normal in a day or two, we think."

Jacqueline agreed. After parting from the farmwife, she walked directly to the mounting block in the yard and used it to clamber into her saddle. Again, she felt Richard's gaze on her, but when she didn't glance his way, he snorted softly and went to catch the gelding's reins.

Once they were mounted and settled, she led the way back to the cart track and continued cantering west. The mill sat to the south of the track, some way farther on. The millstream was a branch off the main stream; it steadily narrowed, increasing the pressure of the water pouring through, until the tumult reached the mill race and forced the heavy water wheel around. Immediately beyond the mill lay the millpond, a deep pool with an outlet through which the waters rejoined the main stream.

The track they were following would lead them on a circuit past farms and mill; she'd never been one to miss an opportunity to let her people tell her if anything was awry.

She and Richard were still some way from the track to the next farm when a high-pitched wailing had them reining in. The big gelding danced, and the mare tossed her head as Richard and she circled, looking and listening, trying to pinpoint the direction of the forlorn sound. Then it came again, drawing their gazes to the right of the track.

Lips setting, she urged the mare on. "There's a path to a cottage just ahead."

She found the path between two fields and rode quickly down. The wailing came again, growing louder and more insistent the closer they got to the worker's cottage set between the fields.

A large old oak tree grew before and to one side of the small white-washed cottage. As Jacqueline slowed the mare and trotted into the yard, she saw an aproned woman crouched beside a young girl of about six or seven years, trying to console the wailing child.

The harassed-looking mother glanced up as Richard followed Jacqueline into the yard; the woman's eyes went wide, and she shot to her feet. "Now see who you've brought with your wailing, Ginny." As Jacqueline slid to the ground, the woman smoothed down her skirts and bobbed a curtsy. "Miss Tregarth. I'm so sorry, miss, but it's nothing, really."

Jacqueline smiled reassuringly, but her gaze followed Richard as, after fluidly dismounting, he followed the little girl's fixed gaze into and up the oak tree, then he walked to stand beneath the wide branches and stared upward. The girl, freed from her mother's enveloping arms, darted after him; she skidded to a halt by his side and gazed upward, too.

Richard glanced down at the girl's dark head. "Your kitten?"

The girl turned her head and looked up at him—all the way up to meet his eyes. Hers were huge and swimming in tears. "Timmy," she whispered. Her lower lip trembled. "He's gone up, and he can't get down."

Richard was fairly certain the kitten—a small, furry, orange-and-white lump sitting wedged into a fork high on the trunk—would eventually find its way down. But that might not happen until nighttime or even the next day, and until the child held the kitten in her arms again, she would fret; that much was clear.

The mother and Jacqueline joined them. The woman put her hands on the child's shoulders. "Ginny—I told you. Timmy will come down when he gets hungry."

The little girl's eyes remained trained on Richard's face. "But what if he doesn't come down soon? What if the owls in the wood get him?"

Unanswerable questions, and from the mother's silence, also valid ones. Richard looked up at the bundle of fur and spotted two small greeny eyes staring down at him. The kitten was quivering, plainly wanting to come down. As he watched, it tentatively put out a paw, but even as it tried to shift its weight, its back legs slid, and it immediately scrambled back to huddle once more against the trunk.

Richard looked at the tree's lower branches; even the lowest was above his head, but the large branch to his left looked to be within reach. He glanced at the girl, then at Jacqueline and the woman. "Stand back."

The woman drew the little girl with her as she and Jacqueline stepped away.

Richard fixed his gaze on the branch, then leapt, locked his hands over the smooth wood and swung, then he managed to pull himself up until he was sitting astride. It had, he reflected, been quite some years since he'd last climbed a tree. After a second to reassure himself of his balance, he pushed to his feet, into a crouch. He shuffled closer to the thick trunk, then bracing his hands on it, he carefully rose to his full height.

The kitten was still several yards out of reach. He grimaced and set himself to climb.

The beast tracked his approach with wide eyes.

When he paused to settle his weight on a branch, still lower than the animal's refuge and farther around the trunk, the kitten blinked at him, then mewed pitifully.

"Hopefully, now, you know better." Moving slowly so as not to frighten the tiny creature, he reached up.

At the last moment, the kitten panicked, but Richard pounced and gripped its head, then gently shifting his gloved fingertips around, he grasped the kitten by the scruff and eased it out of the cleft into which it had wedged itself.

Slowly, he lowered the dangling beast toward his chest, grateful for his gloves as the animal wildly batted and scrabbled with its paws, claws extended.

But when he gathered the furry lump against his coat, the kitten quieted.

A second later, it started to purr.

He snorted softly. He had to let go of the trunk and lean one shoulder against the bole to free his other hand so he could open his coat pocket and deposit the purring lump of fur inside.

That done, with the weight of the lowered flap of the pocket just sufficient to keep the kitten inside, he started making his way back to the ground.

Minutes later, he sat on the lowest branch, then dropped to the ground, landing in a crouch.

Before he'd even straightened, the girl had pulled free of her mother's hold. She came racing up, her eyes alight. "Timmy!"

Richard grinned. Rather than extract the animal himself, he opened his pocket and bent his knee and, with a nod, encouraged the girl to reach inside and retrieve her kitten.

Her face a wonder of relief and resurging happiness, she lifted out the ball of fur, cradled between her small hands. "Timmy—you bad cat!" Then she hugged the kitten to her cheek and looked up at Richard as he straightened and resettled his coat. "Thank you, mister."

Richard let his grin widen into a smile. "That's quite all right. I think you'd better have a few firm words with Timmy about the dangers of getting too far from your side, at least until he's bigger."

"Yes." The girl held the cat out so she could look into its eyes. "I will have to do that."

The girl carried off her pet, already talking to it in serious tones.

Unable to keep a highly amused and appreciative smile from her face, Jacqueline approached with the girl's mother.

The woman bobbed a curtsy to Richard. "Thank you, sir. That was kind of you."

Richard's smile remained. "It seemed the easiest way to stop her wailing."

The woman, transparently relieved, offered them both a smile and a mug of her scrumpy. With a look at Jacqueline, Richard accepted; pleased he had, she accepted the offer, too.

The scrumpy, made from last year's apples from the cottage's small orchard, was sweet and delicious and distinctly heady. Beside Richard, Jacqueline sat on a bench by the cottage's door and slowly drank. She asked the woman what her husband thought of his upcoming crop; all those who worked on the Hall's farms were used to her inquiries, and the woman answered without hesitation. It seemed that now the issue of an adequate water supply had been resolved, all were looking forward to a bumper crop.

The girl, Ginny, returned with her kitten. Ginny crouched on the grass beyond the end of the bench, and Timmy, in the way of young felines having already forgotten his ordeal, darted in and out, tempting Ginny to play with him. Richard, sitting on that end of the bench, laughed, then when Timmy—hearing the sound—promptly rolled over, exposing his stomach and waving his paws in the air, Richard reached down and obliged both kitten and girl by scratching the kitten's belly.

Jacqueline smiled, sipped her scrumpy, and watched the large man, small girl, and tiny kitten play.

Finally, Jacqueline stood and, with thanks, handed her empty mug to the woman. After draining his larger mug, Richard added his thanks to hers, then followed her as she crossed to where they'd left the horses hitched to a post.

She gathered the mare's reins, intending to lead it over to the bench so she could scramble up to her saddle, but when she turned, she found Richard before her, an easy smile on his face.

"Allow me."

Without waiting for any answer—apparently assuming she would agree—he reached for her waist, gripped, and lifted her effortlessly up to her saddle.

She bit back an unladylike squeal. About her waist, his palms and fingers seemed to somehow sear her, yet as he eased his grip, and his fingers and palms slid away, a strange feeling of loss speared through her.

Senses careening, wits in sudden and shocking disarray, she managed to summon enough dignity to incline her head and murmur a rather breathless "Thank you."

He merely smiled back—as if there'd been nothing whatever in the moment to give him the slightest pause—then he turned and walked to where the gelding waited.

Jacqueline raised her head and forced a huge breath deep into her lungs. She wasn't accustomed to having gentlemen at the Hall, much less to having one perform that simple courtesy. Inwardly frowning, she settled her boots in the stirrups, arranged her velvet skirt, and picked up the reins—and told herself her reaction had simply been occasioned by surprise.

She led the way back to the cart track and continued on.

They reached the next farm and found the farmer in his yard, herding a group of pigs. Leaving his lads to continue corralling the animals, the farmer leaned on his fence and readily answered her questions. As she'd hoped, now the stream was running again, the farmer's outlook was rosy.

Somewhat to her surprise, Richard—who had been studying the sows from the back of his gelding—asked what breed they were, and a swift exchange about the various benefits accruing to this breed or that ensued. By the time they farewelled the farmer and rode on, she had added several observations to her mental picture of Richard Montague.

At the next farm, after the farmer came to meet them in the yard and confirmed all was well in his world, he asked her for advice on his brother's behalf. Apparently, his brother was negotiating to purchase a piece of farmland not far away. Jacqueline had to confess the matter lay beyond her ken. She glanced questioningly at Richard Montague—and wasn't all that surprised when he responded with several points, valid points, that he suggested the farmer's brother should pursue prior to finalizing the sale.

As, with the farmer's thanks ringing in their ears, they rode on, she adjusted her mental vision of Richard Montague yet again.

He knew about farming, about crops and yields. He knew something of livestock. He understood the legalities of land and farms—his recent comments had been predicated on a sound knowledge of the mutual obligations involved in tenant farming. And most telling, at least to her mind, he had an easy, confidently assured way about him when dealing with her people—her farmers and their families.

She hadn't asked about his background—it hadn't been relevant to the question of whether to grant him shelter—but she would now take an oath he was, in fact, an active landowner himself. When she'd first set eyes on him...his subdued but expensive clothing might have belonged to a wealthy merchant, but his behavior and his knowledge had, from the first, marked him as being of different and distinctly higher station.

She glanced sidelong at him as they rode along. He sat his saddle with the easy grace of a man who had ridden since he could walk. Or possibly before that.

The ring on his finger, the sword at his hip. The quality of his horse. All underscored the accuracy of her deduction.

She looked ahead and told herself it didn't matter what his background was. He was merely a guest for the next few days, a stranger who had walked out of her wood and who had, thus far, brought nothing but blessings.

Who Richard Montague was in the wider world didn't matter.

They'd turned in to the narrow lane that led to the mill when, on rounding a bend, they came upon three boys wrestling and attempting to rain blows on each other.

Jacqueline reined in her mare. Richard was out of his saddle before the gelding properly pulled up. She watched as he waded into the fray. He caught two boys by the collar, one in each hand, and by main force, wrenched the trio apart. The third boy staggered back, blinking in astonishment.

Richard released the other two and looked from one to the other. "What's this about?" The command in his tone cracked like a whip and had the boys straightening.

Jacqueline nudged the mare closer to the gelding and leaned across to seize the gelding's reins.

After several seconds passed with Richard, his hands now on his hips, frowning at the boys while they exchanged wary glances, the third boy sniffed and, with his gaze on Richard's boots, mumbled, "We're off to fish in the millpond. Now the stream's running again, the fish'll be biting." The lad glanced swiftly at the other two, as if saying he'd done his part.

Jacqueline had placed the three as the sons of three of her farmers whose farms lay farther afield; she'd thought the trio were good friends.

When the boy who'd spoken volunteered nothing more, and neither of his peers showed any sign of speaking, Richard said, "That doesn't tell me why you were fighting."

His unmoving presence communicated without words that he wasn't going to let them go until he'd heard the whole tale.

One of the boys he'd manhandled shifted. His eyes on the ground, the boy said, "We all want to fish, but we've only two withies."

"And"—the boy yet to speak ran his sleeve beneath his nose—"we don't have a knife to cut another. Our das say we're not old enough to have hunting knives."

Jacqueline watched as Richard surveyed the fishing baskets and lines, along with the two withies at the center of the dispute, all discarded haphazardly in the grass bordering the lane. He glanced briefly at Jacqueline, then returned his gaze to the boys—who were still studying the beaten earth rather than looking at him. "You're heading for the millpond. I'm going to the mill with Miss Tregarth. If you behave yourselves and wait patiently at the fishing spot, once Miss Tregarth has finished her business with the miller, I'll come and find you and cut enough withies to last you for some time."

All three boys looked up, hope in their faces. Then the expression of the boy facing Richard clouded. "Gentl'man like you—why'd you want to bother with the likes of us?"

Richard glanced over his shoulder at Jacqueline. "Because Miss Tregarth would much rather see you fishing than scrapping, especially over something as senseless as a withy."

The boys sent Jacqueline careful glances, which she met with a stony stare, then Richard asked, "So what's it to be?"

The boys exchanged glances again, then the boy facing Richard— Jacqueline thought he was the oldest—nodded. "All right. We'll wait at the fishing spot—it's past the mill and along the bank, nearly opposite from here."

Richard nodded in acceptance, turned, and walked back to his horse.

Jacqueline handed him the reins, and with a swift smile for her, he mounted, then looked at the boys; they were busy collecting their equipment, such as it was. "While you wait, you might look around for trees with suitable withies."

The boys straightened, nodded, and raised their hands to their foreheads in salute to Jacqueline as, with a regal nod and "Boys," she led Richard on.

She slowed as he drew alongside, and when he glanced at her, she caught his gaze and arched her brows.

He grinned and looked ahead. "I know what it's like to be the boy without the withy."

"Really?" She tried to hide her smile.

He nodded. "Younger son. Trust me, with an older brother and his friends forever about, you learn to stand up for yourself."

She considered, then added, "And fend for yourself, no doubt."

He inclined his head. "I certainly learned how to cut withies."

She grinned, then laughed. His smile deepened, and they rode on.

They found John Miller at the mill, standing beside the millstream where it fed into the mill race; as John was also a farmer, Jacqueline hadn't been sure she wouldn't have to send for him. At that moment, the great wheel was locked and raised out of the race; as they clattered into the yard, John was staring down at the roiling water rushing through the stone-walled channel.

A heavyset man, ready to be pleased with life and slow to anger, John looked up with a welcoming smile. "There you be, Miss Tregarth. I thought you'd be around." He waved at the water. "It does my heart good to see it running again."

"Mine as well." Jacqueline slid down from the mare's back and crossed to stand beside John. The flow looked strong—much stronger than the trickle they'd stared at the previous week.

As Richard joined them, John looked at him, then bobbed his head. "Heard tell you were the one stumbled on our problem."

Richard smiled easily. "That's an apt way of putting it—courtesy of the wood, I was lost at the time."

"Aye, well." John tugged at his earlobe. "Seems like it was meant to be, then." He glanced at Jacqueline. "But now we've the stream running again, I reckon we'll be ready right in time for the early grain."

"Excellent." Jacqueline felt a weight she hadn't truly acknowledged lift from her shoulders. Without the mill, the farmers and the estate as a whole would have faced a very hard year. She exhaled as the tension left her. "That's a big relief."

"For all of us." John turned to the mill and caught her eye. "I was just about to take a look at the grinding stones and gears and all—if you'd like to check things over with me?"

She accepted, but Richard stepped back. When she looked his way, he tipped his head toward a path leading around the edge of the millpond. "I'll go on and speak with those lads."

She smiled encouragingly. "I'll come and find you once I'm finished here."

Richard tipped her a salute and set out along the path. He could see the boys at the edge of the pond, at a spot nearly halfway around, where a wooden platform had been built out over the water, allowing keen fishermen to cast their lures into the deeper waters of the pond.

As he strode along the path, he glanced at the sun. It was nearing midday, not, in general, a propitious time to go fishing. But with the waters of the stream running fresh into the pond, the fish might have been stirred enough to rise. The boys might not be wrong in thinking it worth a try.

They saw him coming. Even at a distance, he saw their faces light; they hadn't been sure he would keep his word. They scrambled to their feet as he neared, forming up at the edge of the wooden platform.

On reaching them, he halted and asked, "Have you found any useful willows?"

"There's a good clump this way." Eagerly, one boy pointed into the surrounding wood.

"And if that won't do, there's more over there." The oldest boy waved along the path.

"Right, then." Richard drew out the penknife he always carried and opened the blade. "Let's see what we have."

The three trotted at his heels as he walked into the wood. Four yards off the path, three willows stood clustered in a group. They'd been coppiced at some time in the not overly distant past, and all three offered numerous withies of the thickness, strength, and bendability that was perfect for fishing rods.

Assisted by the boys, whose opinions he solicited, Richard selected and cut three long, pliable rods. He handed one to each boy, then turned back to the pond. "We may as well take a look at the other clump."

That, too, was a ready source of rods; Richard cut four and handed them over. "With the two you already have, that makes nine in total—three each. Even if you lose one, you'll still have enough to put two lines in at any one time."

The boys beamed at him. "Thank you, mister," they chorused.

Richard hid a grin and waved them to the fishing platform. "Come—I'll trim the withies for you, and then we can get you set up."

He spent a pleasant fifteen minutes remembering how best to string rods and teaching the boys all he could remember of that and how to best set their bait—worms—on the hooks and how to sling their lines well out, into the deepest part of the pond where the larger fish would be lurking.

He'd just settled the third and youngest boy, Rob, and all three were concentrating, apparently willing fish to their hooks, when Richard heard footsteps on the path. He straightened and turned to see Jacqueline making her way toward them.

He smiled.

Jacqueline met his gaze, saw that smile, and thought that inside every man lurked a boy—just under the surface, ready to emerge and join in such pastimes with simple, sincere enjoyment; that was what she saw in Richard Montague's face.

She returned his smile and looked at the boys. Each glanced briefly her way, dipped his head in polite acknowledgment, but immediately returned to silent contemplation of the pond.

She noted the careful arrangement of their tackle boxes, each set neatly beside each boy, and that the three were sitting sufficiently well spaced so that they wouldn't interfere with each other's rods or tangle their lines. She was perfectly certain they hadn't thought of such things on their own.

Glancing at Richard, she arched a brow and quietly asked, "Ready?"

He nodded and softly called, "Good luck, boys!"

All three turned and, as one, called softly back, "Thank you, sir!"

Then they returned to their fishing.

Grinning, Jacqueline shook her head and turned to walk with Richard back around the pond. Once they were out of hearing of the boys, she murmured, "Their mothers would find that scene hard to believe. Those three are never quiet."

Richard slid his hands into his breeches pockets and paced easily beside her. "I explained to them how fish don't like noise." As they rounded the pond, he glanced at the three. "I also warned them they might have to wait until the sun started setting before they got a bite. For their sake, I hope the fish will prove me wrong."

They walked on in companionable silence. Jacqueline realized she was still smiling—still amused by his deft handling of the boys and by his ready connection with them. Indeed, now she thought of it, she'd been smiling a lot today, and for most of the time, it hadn't been due to relief. And the waves of calm contentment that were washing through her— those occasioned by her laughter as well as her relief—could all be laid at Richard Montague's door.

As they reached the mill yard, she shot him a measuring and appreciative look.

He caught her eyes, read them, then arched his black brows. "What is it?"

She held his gaze for a moment, then boldly replied, "I was just thinking that I owe the pleasures of this day to you. If you hadn't got lost in our wood and discovered the diversion of the stream, all this"—she spread her arms and twirled, then continued toward her mare—"would have been very different." She halted by the mare's side and looked over her shoulder to find him following in her wake. She met his eyes. "Even the boys wouldn't have come to fish—the pond would have been unstirred."

He halted behind her and looked into her eyes. "Careful," he murmured, his voice low. "You'll give me a swelled head."

She laughed.

Then he reached for her, closed his hands about her waist, turned her, and hoisted her to her saddle.

Battling a blush, she murmured, "Thank you," and busied herself settling her boots and skirt and gathering her reins.

The instant he'd mounted, she rode out, clattering back along the lane. She turned to circle on, determined to focus on her duties and keep her mind from dwelling on the sensations his entirely innocent and unexceptionable touch had sent lancing through her.

When they halted at the next farm—one of the larger ones—it was half an hour past midday, and the farmer and his wife invited them to join the family about the table; for farmers, it was the main meal of the day. Jacqueline glanced at Richard; his expression stated he was happy to join the company. She accepted the invitation, and Richard went to fetch their saddlebags to add their provisions to the family's fare.

What followed was, to her mind, a pleasant interlude in a day of pleasant moments. While she chatted with the farmwife and the three other women of the large household, she kept an eye on her guest, yet as she'd more than half expected, without the slightest stiffness or any sign of awkwardness, Richard joined a discussion about the latest theories of crop rotation and the benefits of using barley as well as peas and beans to enrich the soil.

From there, the men's talk spread to wider fields of agriculture, including livestock, with Richard openly sharing his experience of farming on the plains of Essex.

Farmers were always keen to hear of other places with different ways, and Nimway Hall's farmers were no different. Yet the more Richard interacted with Briggs and his sons, the more certain Jacqueline grew that Richard Montague was accustomed to dealing with tenant farmers in a practiced and practical rather than theoretical way. More, his confidence in himself, in the reality of who and what he was, showed in his directness, in the way he utterly ignored the distinctions of class.

In her admittedly limited experience, only a gentleman assured of his own station was likely to treat that station and its customary social trappings in such a laissez-faire manner.

Richard Montague, she was increasingly sure, hailed from a very elevated stratum of society.

After the meal, she turned to Farmer Briggs and asked what he thought of the likely harvest now the stream had been restored.

Briggs leaned back and expansively confirmed what she'd heard elsewhere, that a bumper crop was quite possibly in their cards.

Making a mental note to look into the situation of their storehouses—whether they might need more space to accommodate a bumper harvest—she took her leave of the Briggses and their sons and their wives. Leaving Richard exchanging farewells with the group, she seized the mare's reins and quickly made use of the mounting block to scramble to her saddle.

When Richard followed and saw her already perched high, he met her eyes, then smiled that easy smile she was coming to recognize as quietly smug and overly understanding. Then he caught the gelding's reins and fluidly mounted.

Not waiting to see more, with a brisk salute to the Briggses, she led the way out.

Richard followed, content and curiously satisfied. He'd been more than entertained and amused by the events of Jacqueline's day.

To his surprise, her last stop, just short of them rejoining the trail up the escarpment, proved to be vegetable fields. Fields and fields of various types of vegetables. The plots were clustered around and spread out from the spot where the stream tumbled down the last stretch of the escarpment and onto the relative flat of the Levels.

Obviously, these fields more than any others would have been at great risk had the stream dried up.

Luckily, it was running again, bubbling and burbling along its bed, which, obviously by design, led through the middle of the vegetable fields.

In scope and in intent, he'd never seen the like, not on any of the numerous estates he'd visited up and down the country.

When he said as much, Jacqueline smiled. Eventually, she said, "We have the climate to grow virtually everything we need, so we do. Not just for the house but for the entire estate."

He considered that, then clarified, "Who farms these fields?"

"The estate as a whole, not any one farmer. We're all responsible, and the work is done by everyone, including those at the Hall." She walked her mare along the track that bordered the fields, raising her head to scan the crops. "We sell whatever excess we have, and that gives us the money for buying more of the few things we can't grow here." She glanced at him. "Like oranges."

He arched his brows. "You could grow oranges in an orangery." His mother did.

She thought, then dipped her head. "Perhaps we should consider that now we have the lake filling again. We could build an orangery behind the house."

Richard trailed her as she walked her horse up and down the aisles between the various plots of vegetables, stopping to chat to the few workers—all older women—who were working the plots that day. From the exchanges, he gathered everyone on the estate worked on some sort of rota; it was, he had to admit, quite ingenious, especially if one wanted to ensure the health of the estate's workers.

Finally, presumably having learned all she wished for the day, Jacqueline turned the mare's head for the trail and the escarpment.

He followed. As they climbed, the horses slow on the upward slog, he glanced back and out—over the acres of fields and farms they'd visited that day.

When he'd first laid eyes on Jacqueline Tregarth, he'd been surprised to learn that she ran the estate. She'd seemed too delicate; he hadn't seen how steel of sufficient caliber could possibly reside inside her. Yet through all she'd said and done that day—not just her words and actions but also her bearing and her attitude while interacting with her farmers and their families—he'd been impressed by her firm grip on the estate's reins and, even more, by her sure touch in dealing with her farmers, all established men who he wouldn't have expected to readily take to having a female at the estate's helm.

Now that he'd seen more of her, that those farmers, to a man, accepted her as their overlord no longer surprised him. Unlike many of his ilk, he knew very well that women—even ladies—were more than capable of managing land as productive acreage and handling all the challenges that entailed. For many years, his mother had been his father's right hand in managing the marquessate's lands. With his father so often absent on or engrossed with political affairs—called to court or dispatched on some political errand for the king—if it hadn't been for his mother's steel trap of a mind and rock-solid hand on the reins, the marquessate's estates would have declined rather than thrived as they had.

As his gaze traveled over the Nimway Hall farms, Richard acknowledged that the day had dramatically altered his view of Miss Jacqueline Tregarth.

They reached the lip of the escarpment and paused to allow the horses to regroup. His gaze again scanning her outer fields, he couldn't resist murmuring, "I can now understand why would-be suitors are tempted by your lands."

She snorted and tapped the mare's side and started the beast ambling back toward the stable. "Indeed, but they only want the farmlands and the social standing of holding the diocese's wood right. They aren't actually interested in the wood per se, much less in the Hall and the household. They don't view the estate as a functioning whole—all would happily carve out the wealth-producing farms and leave the rest to decay or, worse, sell off the Hall and the wood."

After a moment, he admitted, "I can understand the logic. Many of those who aren't born to it but who seek to acquire the financial security well-managed land affords would regard Nimway Hall itself and the wood, being so isolated, as encumbrances better sold off."

She nodded. "That's exactly what they think, but the reality is that the Hall is the heart of the estate, and the wood...I suppose you might say it's the lungs. Regardless, both are vital to the continued good health of the estate."

He arched his brows. "The stream comes through the wood, and from what I saw today, it's very much the lifeblood of the estate."

She tipped her head. "Just so."

The stable loomed before them, and they guided their mounts into the yard.

Hopkins came out, asking about their ride.

Richard swung down and waited to see if Jacqueline would hurry to slide from her saddle.

But whether she was distracted by Hopkins and then sunk in thought or had simply forgotten, she was still sitting atop the mare when he reached the horse's side.

She glanced at him, held his gaze for an instant, then she slid her boots from the stirrups. She held her breath when he reached up and fastened his hands about her waist, and she caught her lower lip between her teeth as he lifted her and swung her down.

As he set her on her feet before him, she looked up and met his gaze...then she drew in a shallow breath and stepped back, out of his hold.

Her eyes had widened, but she didn't look away. "I'm going to walk around the lake to see if there's any possibility of us setting up some sort of tunnel system to channel water from the lake directly into the stream." Her tone was low, the words almost breathless.

He nodded and, as she turned, stepped forward to walk by her side.

And forced his lungs to inflate as if he hadn't been struck by scintillating awareness any more than she had. He looked ahead, albeit unseeing. "Let's survey the ground—we should at least be able to determine if the notion is viable."

She inclined her head. "Indeed."

Side by side, they walked out of the stable yard and, clinging to façades of bland normality, turned their feet toward the lake.

CHAPTER 5

Over the dinner table that evening, the atmosphere was relaxed and comfortable. Just how comfortable, how accepted Richard now felt within the Nimway Hall fold, was another of the many elements that continued to amaze him; it was as if he'd known these people all his life. Although he had, indeed, known people like them, given all at Nimway Hall struck him as particularly individual, his ease in their company—the remarkable degree of that—continued to strike him as strange.

He'd met them only two days before, yet they seemed as close as family.

Seated between Jacqueline and Hugh and opposite Elinor, Richard ate and drank and listened to Jacqueline's recounting of their day.

When appealed to, he contributed his observations, which Hugh—who Richard understood had been confined to his Bath chair for the past five years—apparently found enlightening.

"Always good fishing in that millpond, no matter the hour. The boys were right about that." Hugh sat back, a reminiscing smile on his lips. "Another one of those curious things that happen here."

Richard glanced at Hugh. Given the comment and Hugh's tone, Richard felt able to venture, "I admit I find it curious that, if I understood correctly"—he swung his gaze briefly Jacqueline's way—"Nimway Hall passes in the female line." Returning his gaze to Hugh, he said, "Jacqueline mentioned it was a very old tradition."

"Oh, indeed." Hugh's eyes, his whole countenance, lit with a scholar's enthusiasm. "Over the years, I've made quite a study of the Hall's legends, all the old stories the locals tell of this place. Had to do something to fill my time, heh?" He fixed Richard with a level look. "Did you know the Hall is said to derive its name directly from the sorceress?"

Richard frowned. "Sorceress...? Oh. You mean Nimue—Merlin's...companion?"

Jacqueline laughed softly. "Merlin's lover, yes."

"The story goes," Hugh continued, "that the Hall was built over Nimue's cottage by her descendants, and naturally, being the sort of lady she was, Nimue laid down the tradition that ownership of the place—or as we speak of it, guardianship of the hall and its lands—passes through the female line." He humphed. "Given the time period, that's not as odd as it now appears. Boadicea and all that. Many of the old tribes used that system. Women were the center of the tribes—the holders of their future as well as their past—while the men were all warriors, so in many ways, entrusting the protection of hearth and home to the females made excellent sense."

Richard arched his brows. Entrusting females to defend and protect people still made excellent sense.

"They changed the spelling, of course." Across the table, Elinor caught Richard's eye. "N-i-m-w-a-y instead of N-i-m-u-e." She smiled in her soft, vague fashion. "But that's just our English way, isn't it? Like b-o-r-o-u-g-h instead of b-o-r-o."

Hugh snorted. "Old spellings give way to the new, but how you spell a name doesn't change anything, including our wood." He skewered Richard with his gaze. "The tales of people getting lost in Balesboro Wood are quite interesting."

Before Richard could ask for more on that point, Jacqueline said, "That's true, but you haven't finished telling Richard what you've learned about the Hall itself."

"Indeed, indeed." Hugh met Richard's eyes. "The locals say..."

Richard listened, fascinated by the wealth of tales, mostly from local folklore, that Hugh had collected. Taken together, the stories wove a tapestry of strange events that suggested the presence of inexplicable forces centered on the Hall and permeating Balesboro Wood. After his personal experience of the wood, he was disinclined to scoff or even smile dismissively.

All the signs said there was something there, even if, in their modern wisdom, they couldn't grasp or understand it.

The lore of Nimway Hall was patently a subject close to Hugh's heart; he held forth at length, his deep voice rumbling pleasantly around the room.

As the courses came and went, Richard noted that both Elinor and Jacqueline seemed entirely content to allow Hugh the floor. Of greater note, despite some of Hugh's seemingly outlandish statements, neither woman sought to correct or contradict him...presumably because, to them, Hugh's conclusions weren't all that outlandish.

"Why, there's even tales of the lake—I must look up my notes about those." Hugh looked at Jacqueline. "I should add the latest chapter of you finding that orb blocking the spring."

Richard glanced at Jacqueline. When she merely nodded and said nothing, Richard turned back to Hugh. "Are there any stories about the orb?"

Hugh frowned. "I'm sure there must be—well, look at the thing. Never seen an object more likely to be the stuff of legends, what? But I hadn't seen it before, so I never thought to ask, and I'm fairly sure I've nothing jotted down..." After a moment, still frowning, he nodded. "I'll have to ask around."

They'd finished the last course—a creamy gooseberry fool. Jacqueline grasped the moment and Hugh's pause to push back her chair. "Do you gentlemen intend to dally over the port or...?"

Richard looked to Hugh, but her great-uncle had never been one for the custom.

"No, no." Hugh set down his napkin. "We'll take refuge with you in the drawing room, m'dears."

They quit the table. Richard, she was pleased to note, waved away the footman, grasped the handles of Hugh's chair, and wheeled the older man in Jacqueline and Elinor's wake through the great hall and into the drawing room.

There, they settled, Jacqueline in her favorite chair angled to one side of the wide window where the slanting evening light afforded sufficient illumination for her to work on her stitchery. Elinor, meanwhile, sank onto the high-backed settle that was positioned perpendicular to the huge stone-manteled fireplace and picked up her embroidery hoop; Cruickshank, knowing Elinor would sit there, had already lit the candelabra that sat on the small side table at Elinor's elbow.

Under Hugh's direction, Richard halted Hugh's chair so that Jacqueline's erstwhile guardian faced the empty hearth across the expanse of the large Turkey carpet. That done, at Hugh's request, Richard went off to the back parlor and returned several moments later with the book Hugh was currently reading, along with a volume on local history Hugh had suggested Richard might appreciate.

From beneath her lashes, Jacqueline watched Richard sit on the nearer end of the settle and open the thick, leather-bound tome. He studied the early pages, then leafed further into the book before spreading his long fingers over a particular page and starting to read.

She looked down at the fine stitches she was setting in a new altar cloth for the chapel. The household and, indeed, all those on the estate had always worshipped religiously, although their loyalties did not, in truth, lie with any church. That lack of specific allegiance to either Rome or Canterbury had, through the Reformation and the upheavals that followed, kept estate and household safe.

Major battles had been fought not far away—indeed, within sight of the lookout on the escarpment—but no one had considered Nimway Hall and its lands important enough to bother with. To disturb.

Nimue had chosen well.

Jacqueline glanced at Richard. She'd been intrigued by his reaction to Hugh's tales. Most men she'd met would have sneered or, at the very least, scoffed dismissively—even while their nerves twitched.

No one could live at Nimway Hall or even spend time within its purlieu without feeling—sensing—the reality of what still lingered there.

Impossible to put it into words, of course; mere words could never do it justice.

But it was there. Still there. Hovering in the air, breathed in and thus a part of all who lived on the estate.

She'd observed Richard closely, not just over the past hours but throughout the time he'd been at the Hall. She'd seen no sign of dismissiveness in him—only a strongly curious nature and a wish to understand.

When she looked at him…her senses told her he wasn't an enemy but rather could be an ally. Someone who was at home in the wider world, yet who did not hold against—attempt to resist—Nimue's legacy.

Lips firming, she studiously kept her gaze on her cloth and set another stitch.

Having a man like Richard Montague trapped by the wood and sent to the Hall—to her…

Despite all the signs, despite his attractiveness, she wasn't yet sure what she should make of that. Or of him.

Richard read through one long-ago tale—that of a family of travelers lost in Balesboro Wood who had sought refuge at the Hall, only later to discover that, in doing so, they had slipped from the net of soldiers sent to arrest them. With the aid of the household and estate workers, the family had fled to Bristol and escaped to France.

He turned the page and paused, his gaze resting on the next page, unseeing, as he let his senses stretch...and peace sank in.

A flow of soothing serenity wrapped about him, warm, enfolding —including.

Claiming.

It was the most curious yet richly alluring sensation, as if the house as well as the household accepted and embraced him.

As if he belonged.

As ephemeral as a sigh, the ambiance sank through him to his bones.

He raised his head and looked—at Jacqueline, industriously stitching in her chair across the room, the evening light falling over her, burnishing her hair to a warm gold and etching her fine features with feminine mystery. He glanced to his left, where Elinor, too, was stitching, quiet and absorbed. Turning his head to the right, he saw Hugh engrossed in his book.

Comfort, peace, belonging—all were palpable entities in that place, as if the house embodied such sensations and gave them life.

In that moment, he could almost feel that curious peace reaching into him, nurturing and tethering, setting its roots in his soul.

Protectively, not restrictively.

Welcoming and claiming.

For long moments, he stared unseeing, then he lowered his gaze and refocused on the pages of the book he held.

Entertaining fanciful thoughts—such highly fanciful thoughts— wasn't like him. The sudden susceptibility must have been provoked by the tale he'd read...

Frowning slightly, he turned the page and started reading the next story, one of strange lights that, after dark, appeared to travelers lost and far from home and led them to safety through Balesboro Wood.

∾

Richard jerked awake—instantly alert, his eyes searching the shadows, seeking the threat.

Seeing and sensing nothing through the dimness, he sat up in the four-poster bed, the better to scan the chamber.

Barely discernible in the weak moonlight streaming through the window he'd left uncurtained, the furniture sat undisturbed.

But something—some sound—had woken him.

Accustomed as he was to old houses, it had to have been an unusual, unexpected noise. The sort of noise his brain interpreted as heralding a threat.

He reminded himself that this wasn't his house.

But he was one of the handful of vigorous and capable males residing under the roof, and the others—the footmen—slept in the attics.

Accepting that he wouldn't get more sleep until he'd checked, he thrust back the covers and rose.

He was tying the flap of his breeches when the scrape of wood on stone reached him, followed by a succession of bangs and the unmistakable clatter of wooden furniture falling on stone floors.

He thrust his arms through his shirtsleeves and hauled his shirt over his head, then seized his sword, drew it free of its scabbard, and reached for the latch on his door.

He was first into the gallery and all but leapt down the stairs. Heavy footfalls thundered behind him, other men of the household racing down; the noise of the falling furniture had been loud enough to rouse everyone.

Richard landed on the tiles of the great hall. From the corner of his eye, he saw the door beneath the stairs start to open and whirled to confront whoever was there.

Wavering candlelight lit the gaunt face of Freddie, Hugh's valet. Freddie peered into the hall, a poker gripped tightly in one hand.

Tight-lipped, Richard nodded at Freddie, then swung toward the front of the house. He would swear the noise had come from there.

Cruickshank and the footmen came clattering down the stairs.

Richard yielded to instinct and strode for the drawing room. The others followed.

Even before he reached the doorway, by the cool night air wafting past him, he knew he'd guessed aright.

He halted in the drawing room doorway and surveyed the darkened room.

No one was there. He lowered his sword.

Cruickshank barked orders, and lighted candles appeared; seconds later, the butler held up a candelabra so that its glow spread past Richard and into the room.

The flickering light revealed that the shutters over the wide window facing the front lawn had been broken open—that must have been the sound that had woken Richard.

The latch of the glass-paned inner frames had been twisted and forced and the windows pushed wide, allowing an intruder to climb in.

Thereafter, with the room shrouded in darkness and not even moonlight to help, the intruder had run into unforeseen obstacles.

He'd stumbled over the footstool before Jacqueline's chair, tried to catch his balance by grabbing the chair, but had taken the heavy chair over as well. He must have staggered, then tripped on the edge of the rug and been flung against the settle. The cushions from the settle had slid onto the floor, and it looked as if the intruder had attempted to stand again, only to trip over them and pitch into the fire screen, knocking the fire tools over for good measure.

Unsurprisingly, the intruder hadn't dallied. As the front door remained shut and bolted, he must have scrambled out through the window, leaving a scene of chaos behind.

"The damned blighter's got away," one of the footmen grumbled.

Cruickshank gave orders for the footmen—and the stable lads and gardener's boys who had joined the crowd in the great hall—to search around the house. "See if he's loitering or has left any sign by which we might track him."

Richard grunted in agreement. Stepping out of the drawing room, he saw Jacqueline and Elinor descending the stairs. He propped his sword against the doorframe and rapidly tied his shirt points.

Their hair tucked into nightcaps, with voluminous robes swathing their figures and wrappers about their shoulders, the ladies joined him. Both were pale but unwaveringly composed. Their wide eyes sought his, their gazes questioning.

He stepped back and waved them into the drawing room, now lit by two candelabras. "Some man broke in here, but the furniture defeated him. Or so we think." He glanced around the room. "Did he manage to steal anything before he fled? Is anything missing?"

Mrs. Patrick, puffing slightly and bundled up in a heavy coat, came clattering down in her mistress's wake. She waved to get everyone's attention, then huffed, "Saw him."

Everyone stopped and waited for the matronly housekeeper to catch her breath. As soon as she could speak, she said, "Before I left my room, I looked out of the window." She waved to the east. "Out that way. And I saw a man in a great long coat running off into the wood like the hounds of hell were after him."

"Ah—that'd be our man." Hopkins had arrived. "I'll go tell the lads, and we'll search out that way."

At a nod from Jacqueline, Hopkins departed. Jacqueline thanked Mrs. Patrick and suggested the housekeeper sit for a minute on one of the chairs in the great hall.

After assisting Mrs. Patrick to a comfortable chair, Jacqueline returned to the drawing room. She halted by the window. With her hands on her hips, she surveyed the room. "I'm not at all sure what he might have been after."

Hugh, resplendent in a richly colored silk robe, arrived in his chair in time to hear her comment. From under his bushy brows, he scanned the chamber. His old eyes traced the path the intruder had taken. "He tripped and went the other way, but most likely he was making for the dresser." Hugh humphed. "Hardly surprising. That's where the silver is."

The large dresser dominated the wall opposite the door.

Richard considered it. "It doesn't look like he made it that far."

"No, indeed, Hugh, dear." Elinor straightened from placing the fallen cushions back onto the settle. "For see—all the plates are still there."

The row of silver plates lined up along the main shelves of the dresser looked the same as when Richard had last noticed them.

Hugh grunted. "Doesn't mean he didn't take a handful of the good cutlery. Need to check. Freddie? Cruickshank?"

"Indeed, sir." Cruickshank, along with Freddie, moved past Hugh and Richard and went over to open the dresser drawers.

Several maids had followed Jacqueline into the room and, together with their mistress, were setting the place to rights.

Jacqueline, her face a mask of reined anger, waited while the maids righted her heavy chair, then laid its cushions on the seat. "At least he missed my embroidery basket."

"Indeed." Elinor spread a hand over her breast. "Mine, too, thank heaven."

Cruickshank and Freddie shut the dresser drawers. Cruickshank turned to Jacqueline. "Nothing appears to be missing, miss."

"Thank you, Cruickshank. Freddie." Jacqueline nodded to the pair, then caught her wrapper and drew it more tightly about her.

"Oh no!" Elinor's exclamation drew all eyes. She'd looked at Cruickshank when he'd spoken, then her gaze had drifted upward over the dresser...

To the top shelf. The empty top shelf.

"Oh my heavens!" Elinor breathed. "He took the orb!" She pointed dramatically. "It's gone!"

For an instant, utter silence held sway.

Then Jacqueline said, "No, it isn't."

Confused—along with everyone else—Richard looked at her.

Lips firming, an expression on her face that he couldn't interpret, in answer to the question in everyone's eyes, she said, "When I woke just now, I saw the orb on my dressing table." The frown in her eyes materialized, tangling her fine brows. She glanced at the maids and at Mrs. Patrick, who had come to the doorway. "I can't remember taking it upstairs..." She paused, clearly waiting for one of the maids or Mrs. Patrick to admit to moving the orb. When the other women stared blankly back at her, Jacqueline swallowed and rather weakly concluded, "But I suppose I must have."

Relief showed in most faces.

His gaze returning to Jacqueline's face, Richard managed to catch her eyes. He held her gaze for a second—long enough to be perfectly sure she hadn't moved the orb—before she looked away.

For a moment, with the inevitable "Thank heavens" and "Thank Gods" flying around him, he stood silent and still and wondered.

The orb had been moved. Out of the drawing room, where it had been in danger of being stolen by some unknown intruder, to the safety of Jacqueline's bedchamber.

Neither the housekeeper nor any of the maids had moved it. Quite aside from the unlikelihood of any of the household touching the orb without consulting Jacqueline first, none of the women could have easily reached it.

Richard was the tallest man in the house, and he'd had to stretch to place the orb on the dresser's top shelf—actually the top of the dresser.

That the top shelf was otherwise empty testified to the fact that no one in the household could easily reach it; even Cruickshank would have to use a stool or a chair.

Yet the orb had been moved. Richard absolved Jacqueline of hallucinating, so...

Had *the orb* moved?

He blinked, then glanced around, once again tracking the intruder's unsteady progress across the room. Despite where the man had ended up, it was difficult to imagine he'd been heading anywhere but the dresser.

Elinor had picked her way through the smaller ornaments on the various side tables. "I can't see that anything's missing. Nothing at all."

Hugh harrumphed. "The daft beggar must have been after the silver, but never got that far."

Richard decided he wasn't going to argue with that assessment. Briefly, he met Jacqueline's gaze and knew she wasn't about to dispute Hugh's statement, either.

Even if she, as he, believed it was the orb their would-be thief had been after.

The orb that had somehow moved to Jacqueline's bedchamber. No, the silver being the man's target was a much better explanation.

The sound of hammering resonated through the room. Crawley, his expression grim, was securing the shutters in place. "I'll fix them tomorrow," he told Jacqueline before closing the second shutter.

Everyone lingering in the room turned and made their way out, into the great hall.

Richard brought up the rear. In the doorway, he paused and glanced back—at the dresser. He hadn't forgotten that Sir Peregrine Wallace had stood in much the same place, looking in the same direction, only two days before. When the orb had sat on the top of the dresser.

Inwardly shaking his head, Richard turned and walked into the great hall.

Cruickshank, having donned a coat over his nightshirt, came up to speak with Jacqueline. "Crawley and I will stand guard for the rest of the night, miss. Just in case the blackguard thinks to return. Crawley says the shutters won't be properly secured until tomorrow, so we think that best."

Jacqueline nodded. "My thanks to you both. That will ease everyone's mind, at least for the rest of the night."

"Just so, miss." Cruickshank glanced at Richard. "And I'll go around and check all the downstairs windows and doors, just to be sure."

"I'll come with you." With a half bow to Jacqueline, Richard followed Cruickshank.

With the pair of them going room to room, it didn't take long to ensure that all other doors and windows were locked tight.

Several hadn't been, prompting Cruickshank to catch Richard's eye. "Seems like whatever the blackguard wanted was in the drawing room." Cruickshank gestured at the scullery window, now closed but which had been half open. "He went directly there rather than looking around, as any real burglar would."

Curtly, Richard nodded and led the way back to the great hall.

Most of the household were trailing upstairs, returning to their beds. He glanced at the long-case clock; the hands were edging toward three o'clock. Seeing Mrs. Patrick making for the stairs, he moved to intercept her. She paused and looked at him inquiringly.

"The man you saw running away. Think back and picture the scene in your mind." He gave her a second to do so, then asked, "Was he tall or short?"

Her expression distant, Mrs. Patrick frowned. "Tallish, I would say—he wasn't a heavy man, more long and lean."

"You said he wore a coat. What sort of coat? Frieze? Or...?"

"No—it wasn't frieze. I couldn't tell the color in the poor light, but it was all one color—a palish color like dun or bone or pale tan."

"Did it have capes?"

Mrs. Patrick's face cleared. "Aye, now you mention it. Just the one, hitting mid back." The housekeeper's expression hardened, and she met Richard's eyes. "Like a gentleman's greatcoat, sir." Her chin firmed. "That's what I saw. Only caught a glimpse, but I'm sure of that—the blighter, God rot his soul, was wearing a gentleman's greatcoat."

Richard's smile was tight-lipped. He inclined his head. "Thank you, Mrs. Patrick. I won't keep you any longer."

After bestowing a bob and a "Sir," the housekeeper continued up the stairs.

Richard turned to survey the nearly empty hall and discovered Jacqueline at his elbow. He met her darkened gaze, then arched his brows.

Jacqueline nodded at Mrs. Patrick's retreating back. "I heard. Our burglar wore a gentleman's greatcoat."

"And he was tallish and lean rather than heavily built."

She met Richard's eyes. "Could it have been Wallace?"

He held her gaze and, after an instant, said, "I don't think there's any way we'll know for certain. All we can say is that it could have been him." He glanced around, then touched her elbow.

As, slowly, she started up the stairs, he fell in beside her and lowered his voice. "Other than those in the household, Wallace is one of the few who knew the orb was on the top of the dresser."

"And he was avidly interested in it."

"As an arcane object, a subject on which he claims to be an authority."

"Indeed." As they neared the top of the stairs, she murmured, "I wonder how Sir Peregrine spent his night."

"I suspect inquiring of his household would be wasted effort." They stepped into the gallery, and Richard added, "I think we can conclude that the would-be burglar was no tramp or itinerant, but sadly, we have no evidence that it was Wallace, and moreover, it would probably be wise not to leap to that conclusion."

She threw him a frustrated glance, but couldn't disagree.

Yet the thought of Wallace invading the Hall in pursuit of the orb—their orb—made her...

More worried and concerned than she cared to think about.

Never in her life had she felt physically threatened, certainly never in this house or on Nimway Hall lands.

In an instinctive attempt to shake off the unsettling feeling, she gave an almost-imperceptible shudder.

Immediately, she sensed Richard tense and knew, with an unquestioning certainty, that he wanted to protect her, that his first thought was to offer his support via a physical gesture—like putting his arm around her—but at the last second, he reined the impulse back.

Elinor was waiting a few paces along the gallery—an inhibiting presence preventing Jacqueline from doing anything to further explore Richard's impulses—to prod and provoke them—much as she wished to. Much as she realized she wanted to.

What dangerous idiocy had infected her?

She was about to thank him for his assistance and part from him—his room lay in one of the wings—when he shifted, clearly vacillating. She raised her gaze to his face. "What is it?"

His lips compressed, then eased, and he said, "I wonder if you would mind letting me see the orb. Just to reassure myself it truly is there."

Elinor cleared her throat. "I was waiting to ask the same thing, my dear. Not that we doubt you but...it would be *comforting* to see with our own eyes that the orb is still under the Hall's roof."

That, Jacqueline could understand. She waved them to her

bedchamber door farther along the gallery. "Truth to tell, I was so surprised to see it and then in such a hurry to get downstairs that I wouldn't mind seeing it myself, to make sure I didn't imagine it."

On the words, she opened the door, and it was instantly apparent that she hadn't been dreaming. The orb was on her dressing table. She walked through the door. Richard stood back to allow Elinor to precede him, then followed, but halted in the doorway.

Elinor stopped just over the threshold. "Oh my. Well, you couldn't possibly mistake that."

The object of their attention sat bathed in moonlight, the surface of the moonstone radiant and unearthly, the gold claws of the mounting like gilded fingers gripping and grounding the powerful creation. With respect to the orb, Jacqueline had a strong notion that the word "powerful" definitely applied.

Elinor sighed, then came forward to kiss Jacqueline's cheek. "I'm glad the strange thing's still with us, but it's time we all got some sleep."

After patting Jacqueline's arm, Elinor made for the door.

Over Elinor's head, Jacqueline met Richard's eyes as they rose from the orb. He held her gaze for an instant, then nodded. "Thank you for letting me see it. I doubt we'll be disturbed again tonight. I'll see you in the morning."

He stepped back, allowing Elinor to go out, then reached in and drew Jacqueline's door shut.

She eyed the panels, then sighed. She turned, and her gaze fell on the orb.

After a moment, she shook her head and walked to her bed.

Richard saw Elinor to her room, then walked down the corridor to the chamber he'd been given. He believed what he'd told the ladies; he seriously doubted their intruder would be back—whoever it was now knew the orb wasn't where it had been.

After closing the door, he halted in the middle of the room. Waiting for his eyes to adjust to the shadows, he stared unseeing at the open window.

He couldn't swear that the orb had been in the drawing room when he'd left it—when, at close to eleven o'clock, with Hugh, he'd finally quit the room and, in his case, had followed Jacqueline and Elinor, both of whom had retired a half hour before, up the stairs.

That said…he rather thought the orb had been there, caught from the corner of his eye as it sat, apparently innocently, on the dresser's top shelf.

Yet now it was in Jacqueline's room, wallowing in moonlight on her dressing table.

Even though no one remembered carrying it upstairs and placing it there.

For several fruitless seconds, he let thoughts whirl and clash in his mind, then he snorted, shook his head, and set about stripping off his clothes.

As he slid once more between the sheets, he recalled Mrs. Patrick's description of the man she'd seen fleeing into the wood.

The man might have been any tallish, lean-figured gentleman, yet the fact remained that it could have been Wallace.

And Wallace had wanted the orb.

The man's earlier attempt to lay his hands on the orb, blocked by Jacqueline, replayed in Richard's mind, including Wallace's words and, even more, his tone.

Richard closed his eyes. On one point he was entirely clear. Wallace possessed a covetous nature, especially when it came to anything arcane.

CHAPTER 6

*A*fter breakfast the next morning, Richard walked out to the stable to check on Malcolm the Great. The big gray greeted him with a toss of his head and greedily lipped the apples Richard offered on his palm.

Hopkins came ambling up. "So let's take a look at that hoof, then."

Ned Ostley arrived as Richard led Malcolm out of the stall. He patted the huge horse's side. "You're a right big fellow, but you have a nice nature. Better'n a lot of the nags I tend."

Richard grinned, then held Malcolm steady while the two older, more experienced men examined the affected hoof.

Ostley nodded and set the hoof down. "It's coming on nicely—the redness is fading and the swelling's going down—but it'll be a few days yet before it's safe to ride him."

Richard merely nodded and patted Malcolm's neck. "No thundering across the sward for you yet."

Hopkins snorted.

Richard smiled to himself. After the incident in the early hours, he was in no hurry to quit Nimway Hall, and he suspected that, in the matter of him staying, the other men were of like mind.

As if to underscore the likeness of their minds, Jacqueline breezed into the stable, garbed in her riding habit. She glanced down the aisle and saw them. Strolling closer, she asked, "How is he?"

Hopkins explained that it would be a few more days before Richard could chance riding on.

"I see." She smiled at Richard, then said to Hopkins, "I'll need the mare again."

"Yes, miss." Hopkins moved down the line of stalls. From behind Jacqueline, he directed a potent stare at Richard.

Beside him, Ned Ostley shifted, as if biting back unwise words.

Understanding full well what the men wanted, Richard leaned on Malcolm's stall door and returned Jacqueline's smile. "Wither away today?"

Her eyes twinkled as if she was fully aware of the protectiveness in the air. "Today, I'm off on a fact-finding mission. First through the wood to the woodcutters' cottages, then down and out to the outlying farms— the ones I didn't get to yesterday."

He widened his eyes, genuinely surprised. "You have more farms?"

She laughed. "Yes. Several more. And as the market is tomorrow and the wool fair the following day, I need to check with the spinners and the weavers, and the woodworkers, and the farmers and their wives over what items they'll be offering, especially at the fair. That only comes around twice a year, so I like to make sure that our people can make the most of it." She hesitated, then asked, "Would you like to accompany me? I fear it won't be all that different from yesterday."

He straightened and grinned. "Except there'll be no cat stuck up an oak tree, waiting to be rescued."

She laughed again; he decided he truly enjoyed hearing the sound. "True enough."

"So yes," he concluded. "If you'll allow me to trail at your heels, I'll gladly accompany you." He glanced out at the summer-blue sky. "I enjoy riding in the country—it's far better than riding in town."

Jacqueline confessed that she couldn't imagine how one rode in town, prompting Richard to describe Hyde Park and how restrictive the area was compared to riding over fields and through woodland.

By then, Hopkins had the mare and her late father's gelding saddled, and she and Richard mounted, then, as she had the previous day, she led the way out of the stable yard.

This time, she rode around to the front of the house, down the drive, then turned onto a bridle path that led deeper into Balesboro Wood.

Their first stop was the Hammonds, the woodcutter and his wife who had brought Richard to the Hall. Both were glad to see him again, and he chatted easily with Mrs. Hammond while Hammond showed Jacqueline the carved wooden toys he hoped to sell at the market and also at the fair. "I figure if the locals don't need them all, someone at the fair might be interested in having something to take home to their children."

Jacqueline nodded. "That's a sound idea. I'll have a word with the organizers of the fair when I see them at the market tomorrow about where it would be best to set up your table."

"Thank ye, miss." Hammond bobbed his great head. "Most helpful that would be."

From the Hammonds, Jacqueline led Richard on through the wood to the Tricketts' cottage. Another woodcutting family, the Tricketts specialized in crafting handles for all manner of tools. They, too, would have a stall at the local market as well as at the fair. After inspecting their merchandise and discussing prices, with Richard interestedly listening in, Jacqueline led the way on.

To reach her next destination, they had to swing to the northeast of the Hall, into a part of the wood where the trees grew thickly. She slowed, not wanting to risk the horses' legs in the more difficult terrain.

Richard urged the chestnut closer. "Who lives out here?"

"Our oldest woodcutter, Symonds. He's a grouchy old curmudgeon— a longtime bachelor—but he knows more about trees and logging than anyone else around."

As they plodded on, she felt Richard's gaze on her face. After a moment, she met it and arched her brows in question.

"You spoke with Hammond about his goods for sale, and with Trickett, you discussed the prices he might charge. With the tenant farmers I know, anything they make by selling crafted goods their manor takes no part of."

She smiled. "The Hall takes nothing of our tenants' extra income, either. But from experience, we've learned that, if I know what they wish to sell, I can do my best to arrange the most useful places for them at the market and, even more importantly, at the fair." She met his eyes. "It's part of our tradition that the guardian of the Hall helps the Hall's tenants to prosper." She looked ahead. "The more they make from their crafted goods, the more financially secure they are and the less likely the farms will suffer should we have a bad harvest or some other disaster strikes and reduces our customary income."

From the corner of her eye, she saw him slowly nod.

"That's an exemplary—and highly practical—stance."

She laughed. "Indeed. You've put your finger on one of the guardian's guiding principles. We live by the maxim that our people's prosperity is ours—indeed, underpins ours."

He nodded again, his expression stating he both understood and approved.

Symonds was as grumpy as ever, but highly curious about Richard Montague—a curiosity that was returned in full measure when Symonds started talking of the charcoal makers due to visit later in the year. The entire concept clearly fascinated Richard; as he explained when they rode on, they didn't have such a practice in Essex, at least not on his father's land.

She was tempted to ask about his father, but reminded herself that Richard was merely a guest and would soon be passing on. An inquisition wasn't appropriate.

They struck west and circled to another lookout, one farther north than the one at which they'd stopped the previous day. Today, beyond shooting glances over the landscape, they didn't pause but continued along the track that led down the escarpment, arriving at the bottom in a rush.

As they let the horses stretch their legs on the even surface of a track that led through wide and open fields, Richard remarked, "Oddly enough, I didn't feel lost once while riding through the wood."

The glance Jacqueline threw him suggested that, after hearing Hugh's tall tales, he really should understand.

He wasn't sure he did but wasn't inclined to ask outright for an explanation—one he wasn't sure he was prepared to hear. The thought reminded him of other tales Hugh had told... "Tell me about your parents." When she glanced his way, he elaborated, "How they met. Where your mother was born. Who your father was. Did they live all their lives at Nimway Hall or...?"

She smiled, a hint of fond reminiscence in her expression. "Mama wasn't born here—her father had estates in Ireland—but she and her brothers spent their summers here and some of their Christmases, too. But the Hall passed from Mama's mother to her, and when Mama was grown, she came to live permanently at the Hall, much as I do now."

"And your father?"

"He was one of the Tregarths of Truro, but he was the youngest of five sons, so had no estate. When he and Mama married, he was happy to stay here at her side."

"So they oversaw the Hall together."

She neither agreed nor disagreed, saying instead, "Papa was Mama's right hand, her staunchest supporter." Her voice lowered, more fragile as she said, "They died within hours of each other in the contagion of '45." Her tone had grown bleak, then she shook her head as if shaking off the memory. "We—those at the Hall—have, over the centuries, always steered clear of politics, and so we played no part in the rebellion and paid no price on that score. However, that year was one in which we lost...far more than we'd expected."

He considered uttering the customary trite words, but instead, said, "And you took over."

She glanced at him, clear-eyed, in control. "I was their only surviving child. My two brothers died as infants, so there was only me."

He nodded. Keeping his tone even and matter-of-fact, he stated, "And from all I've seen, you've done and continue to do an excellent job of managing the estate."

Her lips quirked, and she inclined her head. "Thank you kindly, sir."

Her prim tone made him laugh.

"Come on." She tapped her heels to the mare's side. "We can go faster along here."

They galloped for a while, both patently enjoying the wind in their faces, then she slowed and turned down a track leading to a farmhouse.

As he brought the gelding alongside her mare, he asked, "The orb. Did your parents ever mention it? Or was it buried above the spring from before their time?"

She blinked. Her brows slowly rose as she thought, then she shook her head. "I don't know. I can't recall them ever mentioning it, yet I do know the lake was full—the spring flowing—during their lifetime."

"So the orb must have been buried at some point during their lives."

Jacqueline frowned. "So it would seem."

They reached the farmyard to discover a harassed-looking Farmer Higgs and his two sons battling to separate three ewes from their yearling lambs.

Jacqueline swallowed her amazement when, after halting the gelding alongside her mare at the mouth of the track, effectively blocking that route of escape, Richard tossed her his reins with a "Here—hold these," fluidly dismounted, and waded directly into the melee.

Within seconds, she realized he'd done this before, that whatever else his father's lands held, they definitely carried sheep. Richard confidently directed Higgs and his boys, then together, Richard and Higgs held back one ewe, and after the boys corralled her lambs, Richard and Higgs released the bleating mother, moved on to the next ewe, and repeated the process.

In ten minutes, the deed was done and the ewes had been returned to the flock, somewhat forlornly bleating, while the boys guided the curious lambs around the side of the farmhouse and into a holding pen.

"You've done that before," Jacqueline observed when Richard came to take his reins. She'd already slid down from her saddle; she didn't need her wits and senses cast into a fluster, not when she had Higgs and Mrs. Higgs to deal with.

Richard grinned, triumph in his face. "It's been quite a while, but yes —I've done that many times before."

"Well, I thank ye for your help, sir." Higgs was still trying to catch his breath. He nodded respectfully to Jacqueline. "The missus was thinking you might call around—come in and take a look at what she's put by for the fair."

Mrs. Higgs was a weaver of very fine wool cloth. Although produced only in small quantities on the loom that stood in one corner of the farmhouse's main room, the cloth was of such exquisite quality that the household of the Bishop of Bath and Wells frequently sent to Mrs. Higgs for material for their clergy's undershirts.

Jacqueline ran her fingertips across the smooth surface of one of the swaths Mrs. Higgs had laid out on a bench, then smiled at the older woman. "As always, you'll get a pretty penny for these. Will you be sharing a stall with Martha as usual?" Martha Mullins, an experienced spinner, was Mrs. Higgs's sister and lived on a neighboring smallholding. Higgs produced the fleece, Martha spun it into yarn, and Mrs. Higgs wove the yarn into fine cloth.

"Aye—Martha has a good-sized basket of yarn to sell." Mrs. Higgs clasped her hands before her and somewhat hesitantly said, "We was wondering, miss, me and Martha, whether you might have a word with the fair's organizers to make sure we have our usual stall. Helps if we're closer to the gate and easier for fairgoers to find."

"I'm sure there'll be no trouble there—yours and Martha's work is always so popular. I expect to see the alderman at the market tomorrow— I'll speak with him then."

"Thank you, miss." Mrs. Higgs's lined face lit with a smile.

Jacqueline exchanged several more comments with Mrs. Higgs, then questioned Higgs as to his opinion of how his herd was faring and his expectations for the coming year. After taking her leave—and after Higgs again thanked Richard for his help—Jacqueline led the way back to the horses.

There was no help for it but to allow Richard to lift her to her saddle. She steeled herself—trying to lock her nerves against reacting to the feel of his hands gripping her waist, trying to stop her wits from noticing the flex of his powerful arms as he lifted her smoothly up. Or the gentleness with which he set her down and the way his fingers lingered at her waist before he drew his hands away.

Her only saving grace, or so she fervently hoped, was that she managed to keep her expression impassive and at least appear unaffected, despite her breathless state.

They rode on, and along the wider lane, he kept the chestnut level with the mare. After a moment, he remarked, "These farms—am I right in thinking they form an outer ring about the farms we visited yesterday?"

"An outer rim," she said. "The farms we saw yesterday were those closer to the escarpment and the stream and its ponds. Their fields are mostly given over to crops of one sort or another. These fields"—she gestured to the fields between which they were riding—"are primarily used for grazing."

"Mostly sheep, I take it."

"Yes. Some cows, of course—we do have a small dairy herd and a dairy."

It occurred to her that he'd learned a great deal about her and Nimway Hall over the past days. In contrast, she'd learned little about him. Yesterday, she'd told herself that who he was didn't matter. Today…regardless of logic, she no longer felt that way.

He was a younger son of a landowning family, and his father's farms lay in Essex; that much, she'd gleaned.

He dealt confidently with both household and estate workers, with the air of one accustomed to doing so. And he possessed a certain level of confidence—impossible to mistake and equally impossible to fake—that shone in his easy interactions with everyone and anyone, from Hugh and Elinor to the farmers' children. He was the opposite of pompous, the opposite of a man who felt compelled to shore up his station.

What else did she know of him?

That he was one of those rare gentlemen who was able to accompany a lady on business without needing to take over. Without arrogantly attempting to dominate. At no point over the past days had he questioned or judged her, much less spoken against her decisions. Throughout her dealings with her people, she'd sensed him at her shoulder, a steady, supportive presence, ready to help if required or requested, but otherwise content to follow her lead...

Vividly, she remembered her parents visiting the farms and her father hovering in just that way—supportive, protective, but never overbearing, never attempting to usurp her mother's place.

They reached the lane to the next farm, and she turned down it. "Do you spend most of your time in the country? Or in London?"

Richard glanced at her. He'd wondered when she would start asking more personal questions. "These days, I spend at least half the year in town. As for the rest, I visit friends all over the country—shooting, fishing, house parties in general." *The usual life of an idle gentleman.*

"So you spend more—most—of your time in society?"

Uselessly—to no good purpose. He inclined his head.

They reached the farmyard, and she turned her attention to the farmer who was approaching. Richard had noted that all of the farmers they'd visited that day had expected her to call, even though, as she'd explained, her intention was purely to learn how best she could assist them in making the most from the goods they would offer at the market and the fair. Obviously, the farmers regarded her help as something on which they could rely.

As he listened to the ensuing discussion—this time concerning the price of heifers—he could almost see the strengthening of the bond between tenant farmer and manor. He made a mental note to mention Jacqueline's habit to his mother. The marchioness could be counted on to be interested in anything that improved manor-tenant relations.

The next two farms appeared in rapid succession. As they'd done the day before, they took their midday meal at one of the farms, adding the contents of their saddlebags to the platters the farmwife, Mrs. Sturrock, set on the table.

One of the boys they'd met by the millpond the day before was the Sturrocks' son. He proudly pointed to the nice fat fish displayed on the platter in the center of the table. "I caught that—we each got three!"

Richard smiled. "Well done! Do you still have the withies?"

That started a conversation that commenced with the local fishing spots and, over the meal, extended to other forms of sport the locals indulged in. Jacqueline and Mrs. Sturrock smiled, then put their heads together to discuss feminine interests.

They left the Sturrocks' farm and continued in a sweeping curve, calling at three more farms before, with the sun sliding down the western sky, they turned their horses' heads once more up the track that wended its way up the escarpment.

It was then Jacqueline returned to her questioning. Over her shoulder, she threw him a glance. "You mentioned you were a younger son. Do you have many brothers and sisters?"

"One brother, three sisters." He debated how much to reveal, then added, "They're all married. My brother will inherit the family acres"—*and the titles and entailed wealth*—"and my sisters are settled with their husbands." *On their various estates.*

The trick—the challenge—was to answer honestly while not letting fall any clues as to his actual identity. That, she and the others there didn't need to know.

"If you spend most of your life in society, how do you fill your days?"

"The usual. Riding in the park"—*so tame compared to riding in the country*—"and attending the theater, balls, and parties." *All of which long ago lost their luster.* After a moment, he admitted, "I also attend lectures at the Royal Society on just about any scholarly endeavor." When, surprised, she looked his way, he flashed a self-deprecatory grin. "No, I'm not an aficionado of any particular science—I number among the purely curious. And I do enjoy reading."

"But you enjoy dealing with people." She waved toward the fields. "You liked chatting with the farmers, helping the boys fish, and even rescuing that kitten." She shot him a glance. "You enjoy using the knowledge you have and putting it to use helping others."

Her words gave him pause. After a second, he made himself shrug. "I suppose I've absorbed things over the years, and if I'm there and I can be useful…it's a way to pass the time."

Inwardly, he frowned as he guided the chestnut upward, close behind her mare.

After several minutes, she said, "Most people like using their talents, their skills—like all those we've been speaking with today. Everyone likes to have a purpose."

He humphed and made no answer, although his mind, entirely without his direction, drew the obvious conclusion: If one had a purpose, one had a reason for living.

So what was his?

They reached the top of the escarpment and continued along the bridle path that led to the Hall stable.

She turned her head and regarded him, her expression serious, her gaze level. After a moment, she asked, "Are you happy with your life?"

The question took him by surprise. He blinked, then slowly replied, "I'll have to take that under advisement." The honest—unsettling—truth was that he really didn't know. "I'm happy enough to be alive."

"But what about how you spend your life?"

She was cutting far too close to his bones. He assumed a lighthearted mien. "Can any man truly answer that he's content with all that is his lot?"

Her gaze held his, then she arched her brows. "Philosophy?"

Yes, and he was taking refuge in it. Reaching the stable yard spared him from having to formulate any further answer. Hopkins and Young Willie appeared, and the next moments went in dismounting and handing over the horses' reins.

For once, Richard made no move to assist Jacqueline from her saddle —not that she waited for him to lift her down—but up to then, he'd been intent on winning the entertaining tussle of wills they'd engaged in over that social point.

He knew her nerves leapt when he lifted her—as did his—and those possibly weren't reactions it was wise to unnecessarily prod, but assisting a lady to and from her saddle was a courtesy that was ingrained in him, and he felt curiously diminished and dismissed when she didn't allow him to pay it, to play what he saw as his appropriate role.

With multiple reasons contributing to his inner frown, he fell in by her side, and they paced toward the house.

To his relief, she didn't ask more questions; her inquisition to that point had unsettled him enough.

That morning, she'd referred to her day's purpose as a fact-finding mission. As matters had transpired, quite aside from learning what her farmers would be selling at the market and the fair, she'd gathered answers on subjects far removed from such matters.

They approached the side door, and he reached past her to open it, then waited for her to enter. Once she had, he drew in a deep breath and followed.

He hoped she was satisfied with the answers she'd wrung from him.

Unfortunately, those answers, as such answers were wont to do, had raised several even-more-unsettling questions—for him.

CHAPTER 7

*T*he market in nearby Balesborough was held in the village square.

At ten o'clock the following morning, Richard strolled with Jacqueline down one of the alleys formed by parallel lines of stalls. An explosion of color surrounded them—the bright hues of the bunting strung around many stalls, the myriad shades of the wares displayed, and the cheerful scarves many local women had tied about their hair clashed and contrasted with the more sober browns, tans, greens, blues, and blacks of the crowd's attire. As at any market, scents of all sorts assaulted their noses, and a cacophony of voices engulfed them—the calls of stallholders eager to attract passersby to their wares, and buyers commenting on said wares or haggling over prices. All in all, it was a good-natured roar.

Richard did his best to shield Jacqueline from the inevitable jostling of the largely happy throng. Many of those passing, certainly those better clad, recognized the mistress of Nimway Hall and smiled and nodded or bobbed in greeting. Time and again, Richard glanced back, keeping a protective eye on Elinor and Mrs. Patrick; with baskets on their arms, the older ladies were following in his and Jacqueline's wake, but were wont to become distracted by the offerings and stop to chat and buy.

Most of the household had traveled to the market; Richard spotted their now-familiar faces here and there, eagerly examining this or that. Even Cruickshank was there. As far as Richard knew, only Hugh and Freddie remained inside the house.

Richard was, therefore, pleased when, on scanning the crowd, he spotted Sir Peregrine Wallace standing in the shadow of one of the walls bordering the marketplace. If Wallace was there, he couldn't be at the Hall, searching for the orb and making trouble for Hugh and Freddie.

As far as Richard could discern, Jacqueline was there primarily in support of her farmers and their families. On first entering the market, she'd paused to have a word to the town clerk, who had been standing with a board and a list to one side. She'd smiled and thanked the man for ensuring the Hall's farmers had good positions that day. The man, small and unprepossessing, had bloomed in the light of her approbation.

Subsequently, with Richard keeping station by her side, she'd joined the throng examining the wares displayed. Although she occasionally paused at some stall not held by one of her people, to exchange greetings and comment encouragingly on the wares, her principal goal was clearly to halt at—and thus draw attention to—the Nimway Hall estate workers' stalls. They found both woodcutter families; the Hammonds were doing a brisk trade in their smaller carved toys, while there were several farmers waiting to purchase handles from the Tricketts' stall.

As they moved on down the avenue, the sights and sounds, the noise and the colors took Richard back to his childhood, to markets he'd attended with his parents at the villages attached to their various estates. He'd always liked markets.

Amid the bustle, several of the Nimway Hall estate people spotted him and smiled and nodded. One of the lads he'd helped with the withies grinned and waved. Richard smiled back and felt a pleasant warmth unfold inside him.

Jacqueline met and spoke earnestly with the alderman in charge of deciding the arrangement of stalls at the fair, impressing on that gentleman the importance of assigning various positions to her farmers. Richard helped by looming supportively, making the alderman just a touch uncertain; he caught the man's eye and, when the good fellow agreed to do as Jacqueline wished, smiled approvingly. No words had been needed; the man had understood.

Together with Jacqueline, Richard strolled on, heading down the next line of stalls, while that warmth inside him grew and spread.

Jacqueline paused to speak with Mrs. Higgs, who was standing behind her stall—a board on trestles, one half of which was covered with swaths of cloth, the other half with hanks of yarn.

Richard tucked his thumbs in his belt and waited, then the glint of silver at the next stall caught his eye. Buckles and horse brasses were displayed enticingly. After a glance at Jacqueline showed she was absorbed and would have to pass him in order to move on, he strolled over to examine the buckles.

He selected a pair of handsome shoe buckles in chased silver and had just handed over the coins to the metalworker when, from the corner of his eye, he saw Jacqueline abruptly turn and step back from the neighboring stall.

Her back was to him; he shifted and looked around her, surveying the gentleman she'd swung to face.

Corpulent, extravagantly overdressed, and overtly pompous, the gentleman stood before her, his coat of bright blue straining over his stomach; as Richard watched, the gentleman flourished a lacy white handkerchief and swept Jacqueline a leg—one better suited to the French court than a village marketplace in Somerset. "Miss Tregarth, your servant, my dear."

The man's voice was high pitched, almost childishly piping.

Richard bit his lip. Although he couldn't see Jacqueline's face, her reaction sang in the rigidity that had afflicted her.

Also in the frostiness of her tone as she said, "Sir Godfrey. I'm surprised to see you here, sir."

"Why," the gentleman replied, waving his handkerchief in an all-encompassing gesture, "the pleasures of the country called to me, my dear." The man's rather beady eyes, sunk between puffs of flesh, fastened avariciously on her. "As I believe you know, my dear Miss Tregarth, I count meeting your fair self as one of those pleasures."

"Indeed?" The ice in Jacqueline's tone would have quenched the pretensions of a satyr, but appeared to have little effect on Sir Godfrey.

Eyeing the other man, Richard felt it safe to assume that Sir Godfrey was one of Jacqueline's would-be suitors. Richard was about to step forward to Jacqueline's side, but then in the same frigid tone, she stated, "Be that as it may, sir, I fear I must deprive you of my company as I really have far too much to do." She gave a curt nod. "Good day, Sir Godfrey."

Sir Godfrey gaped like a landed trout.

Jacqueline spun about, saw Richard waiting, a pair of buckles in his hand, and immediately laid her hand on his arm. "Get me away from here," she muttered, "before I say something truly indefensible."

He smiled, all charm, but there was steel beneath. "With pleasure."

Without glancing at Sir Godfrey—now gobbling ineffectually behind her—Richard turned, and together, they continued down the line of stalls.

Once she felt certain Sir Godfrey wasn't following, she exhaled. "He's such a puffed-up popinjay, I took pity and smiled on him once—just once—but that was all it took to fix his attention, apparently unalterably, on me. And before you ask, I have refused him—several times!"

Richard chuckled. "In that coat, he truly is a popinjay. Does he always dress so brightly?"

"His coat today, for him, is reserved. But I don't want to talk about Sir Godfrey." He was one who tried her patience to its limit. "That said, he hates feathers—they make him sneeze." She pushed on Richard's arm, directing him to their right. "Let's go and view the animals."

His deep chuckle caressed her ears again—sending pleasant shivers down her spine—but he obliged and led her toward the area given over to the feathered and hairy.

Once there, she drew her hand from his arm—not because she wanted to but because she knew she ought to. In perfect harmony—and needing no conversation to maintain that state—they strolled the long line of animals. Most were of little interest to her, but toward the end of the line, she came upon a group of four black ewes. She dallied, studying the beasts, then when the owner looked at her inquiringly—hopefully—she stepped forward and asked from where he hailed and what the size of his flock was, while she bent and ran her fingers through the sheep's fleece. The wool was fine—as fine as any she'd come across.

Straightening, she looked at the four sheep. "There's someone I believe might be interested in these. I'll find him and send him over." She met the owner's eyes. "I suggest you might want to hold them until he sees them. If he wants to add them to his flock, he'll pay a good price."

The owner bobbed gratefully. "I'll wait for him if I can. Your name, mistress?"

"I'm Miss Tregarth of Nimway Hall, and the man I'll send over is Farmer Higgs."

"Thank you, miss." The owner beamed and bobbed again. "I'll wait right here."

Jacqueline turned to find Richard watching. He arched one black brow. "Higgs?"

She nodded as she joined him. "He's been looking for some blacks for a while, but most have too-coarse fleece for his—and Martha's and Mrs.

Higgs's—needs. Those"—she glanced back at the four sheep—"might be just what he's looking for."

Richard swung around to return to the Higgses' stall just as a gentleman came hurrying down the aisle, his protuberant gaze locked on Jacqueline.

She saw him. Her eyes widened, and she stepped closer to Richard—almost into him.

His protective instincts flared.

To all appearances oblivious of Richard's presence, the gentleman halted before Jacqueline and swept her an obsequious bow. He was more soberly dressed than Sir Godfrey, but his fixation on Jacqueline seemed every bit as acute. "My dear Miss Tregarth. Well met, my dear lady."

"Lord Wootton," Jacqueline acknowledged, her tone flat.

"My dear, my dear—I'm delighted to find you here!" A beaming smile wreathed his lordship's face. "I knew you would come, and so, of course, I came, too—it will be my greatest delight to escort you around the stalls—"

"Lord Wootton—"

"No, no—I insist! A pretty lady such as yourself needs must be escorted, and who better to do so than one who has her best interests at heart, and who, moreover, wishes—"

"My lord—"

"Indeed! Just so!" Wootton beamed fit to burst. "That's it, exactly, my dear. Why"—Wootton waved wildly—"the day is so fine and has only grown finer for me!" He prosed on, describing the wonders of his imagination.

Richard had to admit he'd never seen or heard the like. He now fully comprehended Jacqueline's aversion to would-be suitors.

One glance at her face showed her jaw clenched tight; he suspected she was grinding her teeth.

Then Wootton stated, "So you must allow me to know best and grant me the exquisite pleasure of escorting you through the marketplace."

"Lord Wootton!"

"And I have reserved a room at the inn for a private nuncheon." Undeterred, Wootton reached for Jacqueline's elbow.

She flinched back.

Simultaneously, his features hardening, Richard stepped forward, partially interposing himself between his over-eloquent lordship and the madman's object of affection.

Wootton's grasping hand landed on Richard's forearm.

Wootton jumped as if scalded. Then stared as if he truly hadn't noticed Richard—large and looming as he was—standing there.

Richard nearly rolled his eyes but suppressed the impulse in favor of capturing and holding Wootton's pale and now wide-eyed gaze. Letting menace seep into his voice, he stated, "I believe Miss Tregarth has been endeavoring to make clear to you that she has other calls on her time."

He glanced along his shoulder at Jacqueline, faintly arching his brows in question.

Lips tight, Jacqueline confirmed his words with an exceedingly curt nod. "Indeed, my lord. I fear we must leave you to your own devices —forthwith."

Boldly, she claimed Richard's arm, sternly quelling a frisson of reaction when he closed his hand, his palm warm and strong, over hers, anchoring her fingers on the fine fabric of his sleeve.

Grace and majesty combined, he nodded to Wootton. "If you'll excuse us, we must get on."

Richard swept her past Wootton and on; head high, she pretended not to notice his lordship's goggling as he watched them go.

Once they'd moved out of earshot, head still high, she explained, "I've never been able to get it through his head that I am simply not interested in being Lady Wootton."

"I now see what you meant about your decisions regarding such as he being easy—he's plainly uninterested in being the husband of the guardian of Nimway Hall."

She tipped her head in acknowledgment. "Indeed." She looked ahead. "And now we really must hurry and take word of those black sheep to Higgs."

Richard obligingly increased his pace.

They threaded through the crowd, with Richard shifting his broad shoulders this way and that, carving a way through the increasing press. They fought their way to the Higgses' stall. Higgs had been sitting on a stool behind his wife and his sister, minding their purse and supplies, but at the news that there were four fine-wool black sheep among the animals for sale, he quickly drew several coins from the purse and slipped them into the pouch at his waist, then with the two women shooing him on, he bobbed a bow to Jacqueline, tipped his hand in a salute to Richard, and hurried off toward the area where the animals were tethered.

Jacqueline agreed with Mrs. Higgs's fervent hope that her man would be in time to purchase the beasts. Turning away, Jacqueline shared a warm—faintly triumphant—smile with Richard, then she tipped her head along the aisle, and they resumed their wandering.

They'd lost Elinor and Mrs. Patrick long ago, but came upon the pair a few minutes later. The two older ladies had halted at one end of the market, in the shadow of a wall, to examine some lace Elinor had bought.

"See?" Smiling, Elinor held out the lace to Jacqueline. "It's just what I've been looking for to trim my blue silk."

While Jacqueline duly fingered the lace and exclaimed over its quality, Richard stood beside the three women and, raising his head, looked out over the marketplace and the still-surging crowd. There were three exits from the square, with two watchmen stationed at each, which probably explained the lack of cutpurses in the throng. Yet for ladies such as Jacqueline, the threats did not come from the beggars but from those far better dressed.

Richard was conscious that, while he'd been thoroughly amused by both Sir Godfrey and Wootton, he'd also taken definite pleasure in seeing both men summarily dismissed. Courtesy of the past days, he'd already felt protective toward Jacqueline—an instinctive protectiveness he'd excused, telling himself he would feel the same for any pretty maid.

Yet what he'd felt through the recent encounters had been far more intense. More specific, more focused.

More dangerous and deadly.

Part of him would have been only too happy to have drawn his sword on either man.

Neither, of course, had warranted such force; Jacqueline had dismissed one, and he the other, without resorting to anything beyond words and, in his case, presence.

Still, some darker part of him wished it had been otherwise.

Yet the most disturbing aspect of feeling so on edge was that he couldn't recall ever reacting so strongly—not over a lady or anything else —before.

He sincerely hoped he and Jacqueline would encounter no more of her would-be suitors; he hoped the idiots would notice him with her and have the sense to draw back. The last thing he wanted was to cause a scene, yet if they persisted in troubling her, he suspected he would.

The clock on the tower of the village church tolled the hour—midday had arrived.

With relief in sight, he turned to the three women. "Ladies—shall we repair to the inn to enjoy our luncheon?" He'd bespoken a private room at the inn before they'd started wandering the stalls.

Elinor beamed at him. "Thank you, dear. I confess I will be grateful to rest my feet."

With a quite genuine smile in return, he ushered the three ahead of him to the inn at one corner of the square.

He moved to enter the inn first, but a quick glance around revealed no likely causes of interruption. He stepped back and waved the ladies in, then spoke to the innkeeper, who had seen them and came hurrying up. The man beamed and bowed them to the private parlor set aside for their use.

The meal passed uneventfully. Richard relaxed at the head of the small table and listened to the three women exchange comments and observations on all they'd seen, with Elinor and Mrs. Patrick essentially reporting to Jacqueline. He was left with the impression that the guardian of Nimway Hall kept watch over the local population, even those who lived beyond her pale.

At the end of the meal, he ushered the ladies out into the tap and paused to settle the account with the innkeeper, adding several coins in thanks for the man's swift service and the excellent food.

In a group, the ladies had ambled to the inn's front door. As Richard rejoined them, bringing up the rear, Jacqueline led the way out.

Jacqueline had taken only a single step over the inn's threshold when a strong arm collected her, and she was bodily swept to the side. Perforce, she stepped off the inn's stoop—it was that or fall—but she immediately dug in her heels, halted before the front wall, and swung to face her accoster.

"Miss Tregarth."

Shocked, she found herself staring at Sir Peregrine Wallace's dissipated countenance.

"My apologies, my dear lady, but I'm delighted to have a chance to speak with you." His body shielded her from the inn's doorway. He smiled ingratiatingly at her, his handsome but dissolute face the picture of neighborly helpfulness. "I realize, of course, that you now have water in your lake, but with the lake being so distant from your farms on the Levels, I strongly suspect you'll find that ferrying water from it will simply not serve. However, the lake on my farm, Windmill Farm, is on the same level as your farms and mill. Much easier for water to be carted across, you see?"

Sir Peregrine's brown eyes glittered with expectant triumph.

Jacqueline drew in a tight, furious breath.

"And I understand"—Sir Peregrine's expression turned commiserating—"that your stream is nearly dry."

She caught and clung to her temper; her gaze on Sir Peregrine's face, she fought to keep her expression unreadable. She, Hugh, Richard, and Elinor had agreed they had insufficient evidence to make an accusation against Sir Peregrine, but perhaps if she encouraged him to explain, he might say enough to reveal his involvement in the dastardly scheme. Reining in her anger, she clasped her hands at her waist and, lowering her gaze yet watching his face from beneath her lashes, murmured, "Well, sir, as to that..." She let her words fade and waited, willing him to misinterpret and speak further.

Sir Peregrine swallowed her show of meekness whole and smiled as if all was progressing as he wished. "Indeed, my dear Miss Tregarth, there's nothing to fear in being frank with me. Nothing at all." He waited until she raised her gaze and again met his eyes, then went on, "I fully comprehend how anxious you must be, what with your guardian helpless to lift the weighty burden of the estate from your shoulders. I assure you, my dear, that all I wish is to see your farms prosper, and if, in time, you come to see me as a friend on whom it's safe to lean, I would be more than happy to fulfill such a role." He held her gaze and pointedly said, "You have my deepest regard."

Clearly, he intended to make her indebted to him, then offer his hand in marriage.

She allowed her lips to curve. Resolutely.

Sir Peregrine blinked.

"I'm unsure, sir, from whom you got your news." She kept her tone even, her accents cool and matter-of-fact. "However, our stream is now running strongly. We discovered that some blackguard"—she paused to let the word sink in, her eyes steady on his—"had created a cunning set of tunnels that diverted the waters of our stream. Rest assured that the damage has been fully repaired and the stream returned to its customary flow. And as the area in which the diversion was constructed lies within Balesboro Wood and is thus a part of the Hall estate, my people will be keeping a close eye on the stream and all who approach it from now on."

Sir Peregrine's face had fallen; the change was almost comical. He stared at her, then when she arched her brows, pointedly inviting a response, he stuttered, "T-Tunnels? I'm sh-shocked. Quite shocked."

He was, too, and then chagrin crept into his eyes.

She couldn't stop hers from narrowing. "What's more, Sir Peregrine, two nights ago, we had a disturbance at the Hall. In the small hours. A would-be burglar who was surprisingly clumsy—he fell over the furniture and was forced to flee." Her gaze unrelentingly fixed on his face, she firmed her chin and asked, "You wouldn't happen to know anything about that, would you?"

His eyes flew wide, and he recoiled. "What? No!"

Tense and ready to go to Jacqueline's aid, Richard watched the scene play out from his position in the doorway of the inn. Elinor and Mrs. Patrick stood a little to the side—out of his way—both bending sternly disapproving looks on Wallace's back.

Wallace tried to come about, drawing himself up and, judging by his tone, adopting a wounded expression. "Of course I don't know anything about any intruder. I don't know why you might imagine—"

Wallace rattled on, but from the stony look on Jacqueline's face and the way she folded her arms across her chest, not to mention the increasingly belligerent gleam in her eyes, Wallace would have been wiser to save his breath.

Jacqueline let Sir Peregrine run on. Had she harbored any doubts that he was the guilty party—both over the diversion and the attempted break-in—those doubts had been well and truly laid to rest. His tone, the restlessness of his hands, and the calculating look in his eyes as he desperately tried to find some way to overcome her resistance and gain her favor all screamed his guilt.

Indeed, he sank himself deeper in her estimation with every word that fell from his untrustworthy lips. Blackguard, she had called him, and blackguard he was; she was beyond convinced of that.

From the corner of her eye, she could see Richard, standing quietly just out of Sir Peregrine's line of sight.

Why couldn't her suitors—any of her suitors—be like Richard Montague?

He was kind, considerate of others, willing to step in and help anyone regardless of their station. He understood her and her position, understood how to support her without trying to wrest control. He was, in Elinor's old-fashioned way of gauging such things, a worthy man.

If only he were her suitor...

The thought made her blink. It effortlessly distracted her from Sir Peregrine—still pleading his case before her—and sent her mind careening over all the moments she'd shared with Richard over the past days...

She'd sensed a certain kinship—that of a kindred spirit—but at no time had he given her any reason to imagine he was interested in her in a more personal way.

He was a guest, a supporter; he might be a friend. He'd never stepped over that invisible line...except for those frissons of reaction she felt when he lifted her to and from her saddle, as he had made a point of doing as often as he could, but she had no grounds to believe he felt any physical attraction at all.

Then again, he was an experienced gentleman; that she did not doubt. He was also deeply honorable, and as a guest in her house...he would feel constrained by that, wouldn't he?

Richard saw Jacqueline's expression blank, saw her thoughts turn inward. He had no idea what had caused the change—nothing Wallace had said seemed likely to have evoked it. But Wallace saw it, too, and perhaps unsurprisingly, interpreted it as a sign that she was softening toward him.

Richard could see only a sliver of Wallace's face, but the man's relief showed clearly in the line of his shoulders.

Then Wallace reached for Jacqueline's arm—just as she snapped back to the moment.

"My dear Miss Tregarth, come. Walk with me and—"

Jacqueline's eyes spat sparks. "Don't touch me."

Again, Wallace recoiled, this time in response to the ice-cold fury in Jacqueline's face.

Her gaze skewered him, and her tone resonant with authority, she stated, "I have nothing further I wish to say to you." She lowered her arms and tipped up her head. "Kindly allow me to pass."

Richard saw the corner of Wallace's lips tighten. Sensed he was debating refusing to yield.

Enough. Richard stepped out of the inn's doorway and off the step—deliberately jostling Wallace with his shoulder.

Wallace glanced his way, a scowl descending as he opened his lips to protest.

Richard trapped Wallace's gaze, held it mercilessly, and let all he truly was—his father's son—fill his eyes. Slowly, with a deliberation that was a statement in itself, he took the last step that set him at Jacqueline's side. "Richard Montague." The words rang with challenge and undisguised menace; he wished he could use his title and cow the man still further, but he bit down on the impulse and instead, with deadly calm, said, "I believe the lady wishes to pass."

Color rising, Wallace blustered, "I say, I know Miss T—"

"Surely, sir"—Richard shifted his hand to the hilt of his sword—"you are not going to be such a churl as to insist I put you aside." His tone made it blatantly clear he was very willing to do so and, more, would relish the doing.

Wallace paled, but something—desperation?—stiffened his spine and kept him where he was. He moistened his lips and demanded, "Who are you to threaten me? You're a stranger in these parts."

Richard smiled intently, the gesture designed to be anything but reassuring. "I make you no threats, Wallace. Merely a promise. I hold myself a friend of the lady's"—pointedly, Richard looked past Wallace at the witnesses behind him and amended—"all the ladies, and I believe, sir, that you need to step aside."

Wallace glanced behind and was surprised to find Elinor and Mrs. Patrick, both with severe expressions on their faces, within hearing distance.

Still, the man vacillated for a second more before, reluctantly, stepping back.

Frostily, Jacqueline inclined her head and stalked past him.

Richard moved with her—forcing Wallace to take another step back. With a glance, Richard gathered Elinor and Mrs. Patrick and calmly ushered the three ladies ahead of him along the side of the marketplace toward where they'd left their horses.

He didn't bother looking back at Wallace; he could feel the man's gaze boring into his back.

Of the three of Jacqueline's suitors he'd thus far met, he would rate Wallace the most dangerous. And he was perfectly certain the man wouldn't desist. Given he'd gone to the extent of diverting her stream, Wallace was clearly prepared to act to bring about his desired end.

Richard's buoyant sense of satisfaction over having hobbled Wallace's heavy-handed approach to Jacqueline lasted until they came within sight of the horses.

Then reality reared its head.

What am I doing?

What right did he have to pass judgment on Jacqueline's suitors—to decide who was suitable and who didn't deserve her?

He was merely a guest—it wasn't his place.

Something inside him stubbornly insisted: *Yes, it was.*

Jacqueline's words of the previous day echoed through his mind. *Everyone likes to have a purpose.*

And on the heels of that, his unvoiced response replayed: *If one had a purpose, one had a reason for living. So what was his?*

What was his purpose in being there? In being?

He went through the motions of settling the three women—Elinor and Mrs. Patrick in the trap and Jacqueline on her mare—by rote. Then he mounted the gelding, and with his mind sunk in his thoughts, he escorted his small party onto the lane that would return them to Nimway Hall.

Sir Peregrine Wallace stormed away from the inn, away from the market-place. His face a mask of black temper, uncaring of whom he shouldered out of his way, he strode to where he'd left his horse in Morgan's care.

The sight of his loyal henchman gave Sir Peregrine pause.

His temper cooled, chilled by unnerving realization. He needed to marry Jacqueline Tregarth. There was no other way to achieve his ends.

He joined Morgan and, with a curt nod, accepted the reins of his rawboned hack. "They found the tunnels and filled them in. So now, not only has Miss Tregarth a lake full of water, but their blasted stream is running strongly again."

Morgan blinked in his usual dour way. After a moment, he asked, "Do you want me to go and set up the tunnels again?"

Sir Peregrine thought, then shook his head. "No—that's over with." After several moments of further cogitation, he said, "There's a gentleman who I gather is visiting—a family friend. He was by her side just now. From his accent, he might well be from London. I don't want to do anything to signal my interest in the Hall, not while he's about." Sir Peregrine focused on Morgan. "Find out who the fellow is, where he's staying, and when he's likely to leave."

Morgan nodded.

Sir Peregrine grasped his saddle and mounted. Gathering the reins, he looked down at Morgan. "Meanwhile, I've plans to make. Once our interfering gentleman departs, I want to be ready to act." Sir Peregrine nodded in dismissal. "Come and tell me what you learn. I'll be at Lydford."

Morgan tugged his forelock. He stood and watched Sir Peregrine ride away, then turned and lumbered toward the marketplace.

Throughout the uneventful ride back to Nimway Hall, with Jacqueline and Richard on their mounts trotting in the wake of the trap, Jacqueline's mind remained obsessed with the notion—the vision—of Richard Montague as her husband.

No matter how determinedly she tried to turn her mind away from the fascinating prospect, her thoughts slid back to contemplating the possibility to the exclusion of virtually all else around her. Given her position as guardian of Nimway Hall, it was difficult to discount the fact that Richard had, indeed, been trapped by her wood, apparently in spite of his hunter's skills. The stories telling of the destiny of those thus trapped might be old, but were they anchored in reality, as many such stories were?

And if that was true…?

Impossible to stop herself from glancing his way, from thinking and considering and wondering.

What if he truly was her love—the man drawn to the Hall by some fated force, the man destined to stand by her side?

She knew she was attracted to him—the leap of her senses whenever they touched was impossible to deny—yet she had no grounds to believe he was equally attracted to her. That didn't mean he might not be, only that he was better than she at concealing such reactions.

And if, moreover, he was holding back and resisting giving her any sign because he was a guest under her roof—what then? How could she learn the truth of what might already exist between them enough to gauge its potential?

The conundrum had her frowning.

The crunch of gravel under their horses' hooves drew her back to her surroundings. Nimway Hall rose before them, the sun glinting off the leaded panes of its many windows.

As she and Richard trotted behind the trap around the drive and into the forecourt, she was still at a loss as to how she might learn what she was now convinced she needed to know.

Young Willie came running from the stable, with Hopkins not far behind.

Jacqueline drew the mare up at the edge of the lawn.

Richard halted the gelding a few paces away and dismounted with his customary fluid grace, then with a smile on his face, he came to lift her down.

Still absorbed with her thoughts, she hadn't been quick enough to free her boots from the stirrups and slide down without his assistance. Steeling herself against what she knew would come, she freed her feet and gathered her skirt.

His smile widening, he reached up and fastened his hands about her waist. He gripped, lifted her, and swung her down—

Her heavy skirt snagged on the saddle.

The unexpected tug unbalanced them both.

She gasped, her eyes flying wide.

His expression hardened as he juggled her, shifting his hold.

They tipped—instinctively, he snatched her closer.

He staggered, hugging her to him as they toppled, tumbled, and fell in an ungraceful tangle on the grass.

She landed atop him, her breasts plastered to his chest, her skirt trapping his legs. She heard his breath expel in an "Oof!"

For one superb second, safety, security, warmth, and comfort engulfed her, then she realized her elbow had jammed into his stomach, causing that oof, and she squirmed to free her arm—

And froze.

As the reality of what was causing the ridge of solid pressure against her stomach impinged on her mind.

Heat rose to her cheeks. Without daring to meet his eyes, she babbled, "I'm so sorry! The train of my habit…"

Even as she wriggled, trying to shift off him, the wretched train held her in place.

"Hold still."

She froze again. He sounded as if he'd spoken through gritted teeth.

He shifted his legs, releasing the train that had got trapped beneath them, then his hands firmed about her waist, and he lifted her up and to the side.

She scrambled and got her feet beneath her. He released her, then sat up.

Barely breathing, from beneath her lashes, she watched as he rolled away from her, then, slowly, stood.

He resettled his coat, then turned to face her and offered his hand. "My apologies—I should have checked your skirt was free."

"No, no." She placed her gloved hand in his and allowed him to draw her upright. "It was entirely my fault."

It had been no one's fault, but she couldn't deny the incident had been most…fortuitous. Breathless and giddy she might be, but she now knew the answer to one of her questions. Richard Montague was attracted to her in very much the same way as she was to him.

She busied herself shaking out, then smoothing down her skirts.

Elinor had halted the trap by the steps. She and Mrs. Patrick clambered down and hurried over, but by then Jacqueline and Richard were back on their feet. "Are you all right, dear?" Elinor inquired.

Jacqueline summoned a reassuring smile. "Just a tumble." From beneath her lashes, she glanced at Richard. "No harm done."

His gaze on Elinor, he inclined his head. "A moment of clumsiness, I regret to say."

Did he regret it? There was a note in his voice that made Jacqueline wonder.

Cloaking the stiffness that had afflicted him as best he could, Richard waved Jacqueline on, then fell in alongside her as they followed Elinor and Mrs. Patrick across the forecourt, up the steps, and into the great hall.

He fought to keep his features impassive, to conceal the dismay washing through him. Courtesy of a decade and more of ducking the attentions of over-amorous young ladies, his instincts were exceedingly well honed in detecting that critical moment when a young lady decided to view him as husband material.

Logically, rationally, he wasn't sure Jacqueline Tregarth had made such a decision—her train might have got caught beneath her saddle on its own.

Yet his instincts were pricking, sharp and insistent.

The questions he'd asked himself the previous day rang again in his mind. What was his purpose?

More immediately, what was he doing there—at Nimway Hall?

Sir Peregrine Wallace entered his house in Lydford via the front door. Located just outside the village, the house was a neat, unpretentious gentleman's residence built earlier in the century—nothing on the scale of Nimway Hall and completely lacking in history.

Sir Peregrine tossed his riding gloves onto the hall table and, still smarting over the failure of his attempt to lure Jacqueline Tregarth under his thumb, strode for the comfort of the brandy decanter in the study.

Summoned by his footsteps ringing on the hall tiles, his valet, Higson, popped his head around the servants' door as Sir Peregrine walked past. "Letter came for you, sir. I've left it on your desk."

Sir Peregrine grunted, but paused to close the study door before crossing to the desk and lifting the folded parchment from the salver there. Sir Peregrine squinted at the writing, then straightened. "Dashwood."

Reinvigorated, his expression transforming to one of hopeful eagerness, Sir Peregrine set down the letter, crossed to the tantalus, and poured a good two fingers of his best brandy into a crystal glass. Glass in hand, he returned to the desk, picked up the letter and his letter knife, then crossed to sink into the well-padded armchair angled before the empty hearth.

Late-afternoon sunshine streamed through the window, affording Sir Peregrine ample light. After placing the glass of brandy on the small table by his elbow, he gripped the letter knife, broke the letter's seal, and, his heart beating a trifle faster, spread open the two sheets.

As he read, his lips lifted, then he grinned. "Excellent!"

It had been a mere two days since he'd dispatched his offer to Sir Francis. That the leader of the Order of the Knights of St. Francis had replied so expeditiously suggested that Sir Peregrine had, at last, found the perfect treasure with which to beguile his way into the upper echelons of the order. Indeed, if all went as planned, he rather thought he would be able to lay claim to the position at Sir Francis's side.

After fortifying himself with a mouthful of brandy, Sir Peregrine returned to the letter.

Dashwood wrote in glowing and laudatory vein, urging Sir Peregrine on and assuring him most earnestly that, should he succeed in securing Nimway Hall—built atop the hallowed cave of the mystical sorceress, Nimue—and further, laid his hands on the ancient orb he'd spied in the residence, which surely must be the fabled orb that had once formed the head of Merlin's staff and was said to hold a powerful spell, then Sir Peregrine would be assured of a place of honor in the annals of the order, second only to Sir Francis himself.

Sir Peregrine paused to savor another mouthful of brandy and imagine that result—precisely what he'd hoped for when he'd first realized the significance of the local tall tales of the Hall.

After several moments of staring into space, he sipped again, then returned his gaze to the letter and read on.

Sir Francis wrote that Sir Peregrine should send him word the instant he gained possession, so that the order might put in train arrangements to suitably celebrate with an orgy of truly extraordinary extent. Even if Sir Peregrine's claim to the Hall was via implied possession consequent on a betrothal, that, Sir Francis declared, would be enough for the order's purposes.

Sir Peregrine turned the sheet, following Sir Francis's scrawl. He smiled with satisfaction as he read Sir Francis's assurances that the entire order would be waiting with bated breath to hear news of Sir Peregrine's success, especially if he was able to seize the prize in time for the summer solstice, which—Sir Francis noted—as Sir Peregrine knew, would be marked by the order with a week-long orgy of the senses, commencing on the solstice.

Sir Peregrine blinked, then glanced at the ornate calendar sitting on the mantelpiece. It was only the tenth of June; he had time enough to lure Jacqueline Tregarth into his clutches.

Reassured, he went back to the letter to read the last two lines. He did, then, staring at the page, he sat up and softly cursed.

Sir Francis Dashwood, Grand Master of the Order of the Knights of St. Francis, had written that, regardless of whether Sir Peregrine had succeeded in seizing the goal by that time, Sir Francis would visit him at Lydford, arriving toward the end of the coming week. Sir Francis had added that Sir Peregrine would not be surprised to learn that Sir Francis wished to gaze upon the wonder of Nimway Hall, and the orb, himself. And, of course, to celebrate Sir Peregrine's imminent rise through the order's ranks.

"Damn!" Sir Peregrine lowered the letter and stared unseeing across the room.

By the end of next week...

Until he managed to bend Jacqueline Tregarth to his will, he wouldn't be able to allow Sir Francis the run of Nimway Hall, much less allow the founder of the order to claim the orb—which, he knew, was precisely what Dashwood was hoping to do during his impending visit.

The incident in the marketplace replayed in Sir Peregrine's mind.

He might have erred in his estimation of how long it would take him to charm Jacqueline Tregarth. Indeed, charm had never seemed to have much effect on the wretched woman.

Which simply underscored the sense in setting charm aside and bringing other forces to bear.

By the end of next week...

Sir Peregrine glanced at the letter, then set it aside. He wouldn't write and put Sir Francis off; such a move would definitely not improve—and might even scupper—his chances of securing the position he was determined to claim, the one by Sir Francis's side in all the order's rituals.

Slumping back in the chair, Sir Peregrine sipped, then drained the brandy from his glass.

Once the interfering gentleman was no longer by Jacqueline Tregarth's side and no one else who could wield a sword was there to defend her, Sir Peregrine would seize the moment. It was his to seize, after all.

There were well-known and well-used ways of forcing reluctant ladies to front the altar.

As soon as Morgan brought word of the gentleman's departure, Sir Peregrine would act.

He would plot, plan, and be ready to seize and secure his future the instant Jacqueline Tregarth was once more effectively alone at Nimway Hall.

CHAPTER 8

*H*ow did young ladies encourage gentlemen?

Jacqueline had no clue. She'd never wanted to do such a thing before.

So she dallied in the drawing room until, as had happened on the previous nights since Richard had arrived at the Hall, he and she started up the stairs side by side.

Cruickshank was doing the rounds of the ground floor, checking that all the doors and windows had been locked. Ever since the break-in, he'd been extra vigilant.

A candelabra on the central table in the hall cast flickering light over the walls as, holding her skirts raised, Jacqueline climbed. Cruickshank would douse the candles downstairs. The single large candle in its ornate stick that sat on the side table in the gallery opposite the head of the stairs cast enough light to guide Jacqueline and Richard to their rooms; when, eventually, Cruickshank followed them upstairs, he would take the candlestick with him to light his way up the next flight to the staff quarters above.

Not having to juggle a candlestick as well as manage her skirts was a definite boon…

Inwardly cursing, she wrestled her skittering thoughts back to the problem at hand. How was she to encourage Richard? How to convey and make clear to him that she would welcome his advances if he chose to make them—if he felt that way inclined?

The gallery loomed ahead. The end of the stairs was nigh.

She frowned in earnest, raking through her mind to find some form of words with which to at least allude to the subject, to indicate—

Her toe hit the top step, and she pitched forward—

Before she could gasp, she sensed Richard beside her, swooping, then a muscled arm wrapped about her waist, and she was abruptly hauled upright.

She tilted toward him—was pulled even nearer—and found herself locked in his arms.

Once more with her breasts pressed to his coat, cradled against the warm hardness of his chest. But this time, they were on their feet.

She looked up. Their faces were only inches apart. The flickering light of the candle played softly over one side of his face, revealing the austere planes of his cheeks beneath his sharply delineated cheekbones.

His eyes, the bright hazel wreathed in shadow, trapped hers. Gazes locked, they stared at each other, their breaths mingling in the dimness while hunger rose, powerful and potent, a tangible entity claiming the air between them.

She stared into the sharp hazel gaze of a predator.

Her heart sped, galloping faster and faster. Her lungs seized, denying her breath.

As every sense she possessed stretched and reached for him.

Passion flowered, a need she'd never experienced before. Desire bloomed and seduced her.

She felt heat rise and spread beneath her skin, urging her on, needy and wanting. Instinctively, she moistened her lips—and saw his gaze deflect, releasing her eyes to follow the passage of the tip of her tongue over the lower curve...

Emboldened, she lowered her gaze. To his mouth.

His lips were edged in shadow, infinitely intriguing...infinitely tempting.

She drew in a shallow breath, then tensed and stretched upward—

He stiffened.

She looked up, surprised. His hooded lids had fallen, screening his eyes.

Then his arms eased—slowly but smoothly releasing her. Before she could stagger, he closed his hands about her upper arms.

He gripped and, for one instant, stilled, but then she saw his jaw set, and with his lips now a thin line, he stepped back, simultaneously setting her on her feet.

Away from him.

His hands fell from her. His rejection could not have been clearer.

Struck to the heart, her blood cooling as if he'd plunged her into ice, she dragged in a breath. "I'm…thank you." After a second, she added, "Again. I seem to be making a habit of stumbling…"

What was she saying? Both falls had been accidents.

She reached for a shawl she wasn't wearing, then realized, straightened, and clinging to what dignity remained to her, inclined her head. "Again, thank you. I will bid you—"

"I meant to mention it before." He'd edged even farther back; the candlelight barely touched his face. He clasped his hands behind his back; standing rigid and somehow distant, with quite terrible politeness, he went on, "I believe my horse will be recovered enough to ride on…if not tomorrow, then certainly, the day after. I've enjoyed my time at Nimway Hall immensely and wish to convey my deepest gratitude to you and the household for the welcome you've shown me—a stranger lost in your wood. However, despite the pleasure I've found here, others will be wondering where I've got to. I must ride on."

Despite the cauldron of feelings roiling inside her—embarrassment, hurt, disappointment, and self-directed anger among them—she nevertheless thought, on a spurt of irritation, that obviously his stay hadn't been so very pleasant that he would consider remaining forever.

Metaphorically pulling the shreds of her dignity more tightly about her, she forced herself to—however stiffly—incline her head. "Of course." Her voice was low; despite her best efforts, temper edged her tone. "We cannot—and would not wish to—keep you."

An outright lie, but at least she'd got the words out.

With a fractional inclination of her head, she turned away. "Goodnight, sir."

She didn't look back but, head high, walked to her door, opened it, went inside, and carefully let the latch fall.

Only then did she allow the tremors that had been building inside to surface. She slumped back against the door and closed her eyes.

She breathed in, out, and waited for the maelstrom of her raging emotions to subside.

Once it had—only once it had—she drew in a deep breath and opened her eyes.

Her gaze fell on the orb. It sat on her dressing table; she hadn't moved it since it had appeared there. Yet even though the moonlight was falling full upon it, the moonstone seemed curiously dull. More milky, less translucent, and with not a hint of a glow.

She humphed and pushed away from the door.

Without allowing herself to think—without allowing her still-surging emotions to capture her again—she walked to the open window and looked out. The view was to the north. She could see the lake, its waters shimmering under the moon's light, its edge marked by the dark shadows of trees, and on the distant horizon, silhouetted against the night sky, pale and somehow infinitely lonely, stood the Tor.

Had Nimue once stood somewhere near, on the Hall's lands, and looked out on a moonlit summer night—at the Tor, at the lake and the wood—and wondered about life and love?

Jacqueline stood for long minutes and grappled with the reality of rejection.

Of the pain of offering and being deemed unworthy, of being turned away from.

It hurt.

As the minutes ticked by, she sensed the ancient peace of the Hall rise around her, wrapping comfortingly about her, an all-but-palpable presence in the dark.

Held, supported, she took her courage in her hands and looked inward —to where the hurt resided. As if it was a physical wound, she examined it. Acknowledged it.

Admitted to herself that the slash had scored her heart.

Only now that the prospect of a future with Richard Montague had been denied—had been shown to be an unattainable dream—did she finally understand, did she finally comprehend how deeply the hope and the promise of what she'd sensed she might have with him by her side had burrowed into her soul.

"I don't know as I would advise it, sir." Ned Ostley, his gaze on the pink line that was barely detectable along the edge of the pad of Malcolm the Great's hoof, pursed his lips and shook his head. "Could flare up again."

"Perhaps tomorrow," Hopkins put in placatingly, his gaze on Richard's frowning face.

Ostley patted Malcolm's glossy neck. "You won't want to risk this fellow."

Malcolm fixed his large eye on Richard as if to echo that sentiment; normally, after being idle for days, the horse would be fractious and wanting a run. Instead, the look in that dark eye spoke of peace and contentment and a disinclination to be disturbed.

Richard clenched his jaw. His hands gripping his hips, he drew in a deeper breath and tried to quell, or at least contain, the impulse urging him to flee.

Now, before anything more could occur between him and Jacqueline.

A decade and more of running from the advances of—in some cases, extremely inventive—young ladies had created a self-protective drive that gave no quarter. He could barely think through the alarm flooding his brain.

"Very well." He forced out the words; there seemed little else he could say. "Tomorrow, then." He looked at Malcolm. "But we will have to leave then."

The horse snorted and looked away.

"So," Hopkins said, turning to walk up the stable aisle beside Richard, "I suppose you'll be going to the fair with Miss Jacqueline and the others, then, and I should saddle up the gelding along with Miss Jacqueline's mare?"

And that, Richard suspected, was the real—or at least, another major —reason Ostley and Hopkins didn't want him to leave. They'd heard through the household grapevine of their mistress's difficulties with her would-be suitors the day before and that Richard had come to her aid. The pair—indeed, the whole household—would be infinitely happier if he accompanied Jacqueline to the fair.

If he had to remain at the Hall for another day, he would be happier with that arrangement, too. Regardless of his intention to flee her presence, the thought of her being prey to unwelcome attentions twisted something inside him.

He nodded. "Yes. Given I need to kick my heels for another day, visiting the fair"—*even with your mistress*—"will fill the time."

A fair was an eminently public venue; as long as he resisted all attempts to create a private interlude—and heaven knew, he was experienced enough to have no qualms on that score—then acting as Jacqueline's friendly protector for one more day shouldn't pose any real risk.

He'd gone out to the stable early, hoping to get away as soon as the household was fully awake. With escape denied him, he parted from Hopkins in the stable yard and headed for the breakfast parlor.

From the instant Jacqueline joined him there, he remained on guard, but after that awkward scene the previous night, she'd clearly taken his intentions to heart; if anything, it was she who maintained a certain distance between them.

A distance, he now realized, that had not been there before, even at their first meeting.

Regardless, he could hardly cavil, and two hours later, as he walked by her side onto the fairground, he told himself he was glad of her understanding.

The field in which the fair was set up was located to the west of the village of West Pennard. The village lay on the road between Shepton Mallet and Glastonbury, so was easy to reach for all those interested in the fleeces, woolen cloth, leather, horn, and associated products displayed on the fifty-odd stalls that ringed the field. In between the farmers' stalls were those of blacksmiths, farriers, and similar trades offering tools and equipment of interest to the farmers.

The stalls were arranged around the periphery of the field, while in the center, holding pens were filled with animals of various sorts, but mostly with sheep and lambs.

Jacqueline strolled the fair, circling past the stalls, nodding and exchanging greetings with the locals whose paths she crossed and pausing at the stalls of the Hall's farmers to smile and speak encouragingly. She was determined to appear untroubled and unconcerned, to behave as she usually did, even though, inside, she was—still—railing against the fate that had sent Richard Montague riding into Balesboro Wood.

She felt more helpless than she'd ever felt before. Helplessness over fixing something that was wrong wasn't an emotion she was accustomed to feeling, and it raked at her with sharpened claws. She wanted to reach for him, to shake him and force him to look at and appreciate what she could now so clearly see—what she was convinced could be theirs—the strength, the security, and the satisfaction that a union between them would bring to them both. To see how right such a marriage would be.

From where her unwavering belief drew its strength, she couldn't have said, yet that did not diminish her absolute certainty in the least. She'd known him for only a matter of days, yet she now knew—beyond question—that he was hers. The one chosen to stand by her side.

The one ensnared by Balesboro Wood and sent to the Hall and her.

She wanted to speak of it, to give voice to her certainty and try to persuade him—

But she couldn't.

The same powerful, irrefutable certainty that told her he was her rightful mate also insisted that only if he came to her, cleaved to her, of his own free will, with his own understanding—his own certainty— would they be able to claim what could be theirs.

She wanted to act, but there was no point in even trying.

The critical decision, in this instance, did not lie with her.

She slanted a sharp glance at Richard's face, handsome and austere, his expression outwardly easy, yet to her educated eye, closed against all comers.

The fact he was pacing beside her was no help at all. While maintaining her outward calm, she was forced to constantly battle her senses' obsession with him. But he'd made it clear that it was only the need to allow his horse another day to recover from the inflammation that had affected the beast's hoof that was keeping him there, so her senses would soon have nothing to focus on. Metaphorically gritting her teeth, she forced herself to ignore his presence and concentrate on why she was there—the business of the fair.

If he and she were meant to be...

Despite the clamor of her emotions, it seemed she would have to place her trust in Fate and those higher powers said to guide the lives of such as she, the guardians of Nimway Hall.

A tug on her sleeve had her turning to find Elinor pointing to a nearby stall.

"There's some very nice woolen lace over there."

Jacqueline accompanied Elinor to the stall; to her relief, no one else seemed to have noticed the distant stiffness that had sprung up between her and Richard.

"Miss Tregarth! Well met, my dear lady!"

Jacqueline swung around to behold Lord Wootton bearing down upon her. His cheeks were ruddy, his fine, pale, not to say wispy hair covered by an over-large wig, he came striding past the stalls, his protuberant gaze, as usual, fixed on her.

She couldn't help it; she glanced at Richard—only to find he was already strolling to resume his place by her side.

Instinctive protectiveness had spurred Richard into motion. Nevertheless, he was glad of Jacqueline's wordless appeal; it silenced the niggling voice inside him that demanded to know by what right he was stepping in and how he could be certain Jacqueline wished him to. Her look gave him the license he craved.

His gaze locked on the approaching lord, he halted close by Jacqueline's side, deliberately placing himself within the field of Wootton's tunnel vision.

Wootton blinked, and his feet slowed. His eyes widened as his gaze dwelled on Richard, then Wootton visibly swallowed.

He couldn't turn away without being obvious; perforce, he came forward, but in a much less forceful manner. He made Jacqueline a leg, and she curtsied.

"Sir." With one hand, she indicated Richard. "I believe you met Mr. Montague yesterday."

Richard exchanged a stiff bow with his lordship.

Straightening, Wootton glanced briefly at Richard's face, then, with increasing nervousness, looked at Jacqueline. "I…er, hope you enjoy your day about the stalls, Miss Tregarth. You and your party." Wootton had noticed Elinor, who, after purchasing some lace, had turned and joined them; he bowed to her. Straightening, he tugged his coat down, then gripped the lapels as if for reassurance. His eyes shifted, as if he wasn't sure where to look. "I…ah…must get on. A pleasure, as always. If you'll excuse me?" He bowed again.

"Yes, of course." Jacqueline inclined her head graciously.

Richard coolly half bowed.

Beside them, Elinor watched his lordship depart. A frown tangling her fine brows, she shook her head. "I'm so glad you've never wished to look in that direction, my dear. He really wouldn't do."

Richard glanced at Jacqueline—as she glanced at him, amusement glinting in her eyes. The sight soothed something inside him; he felt his lips curve and looked away.

To survey the crowd, his hand resting lightly on the hilt of his sword.

He might not approve of the unreasoning, unrelenting pressure to protect Jacqueline that had, apparently, taken root in his soul, and he definitely didn't like being helpless to deny it, yet the satisfaction that warmed him over accomplishing such a simple task as discouraging Wootton was undeniable.

Given he would be leaving on the morrow, he might as well accept the role his instincts urged on him and enjoy the small pleasures of the day.

He strolled beside Jacqueline, idly listening to her exchanges with her people as well as to various discussions and negotiations with farmers from farther afield.

Once again, he saw how tirelessly she worked to advance her farmers' various causes; with a word here, a suggestion there, she was instrumental in sending a significant amount of business their way.

At one point, Richard glimpsed Sir Peregrine Wallace standing between two stalls at the edge of the field. Jacqueline had halted to speak with a stallholder; beside her, Richard stared at Wallace—until Wallace saw him.

Across the intervening yards, with warning and challenge in his eyes, he held Wallace's gaze—until Wallace broke the contact. Wallace looked aside, then stepped into the flow of fairgoers and walked away.

Thereafter, Richard kept his eyes peeled; he—his instincts—did not trust Wallace, not even as far as he could throw him.

Five minutes later, Jacqueline and Elinor were busy investigating the offerings of a weaver from the north. Richard moved to the end of the stall the better to scan the shifting throng now packed between the stalls and the central animal pens. Almost immediately, his gaze was drawn to a personable gentleman with light-brown hair neatly tied back in a queue. The man's appearance was a touch above most others Richard had seen thereabouts, but in a subtle way—he was well dressed, well turned out, his clothes of good quality and well chosen to make the most of his otherwise average stature. His features were good, the cast of his countenance pleasing.

The gentleman's gaze was fixed on Jacqueline.

Richard glanced her way, just as she and Elinor parted from the weaver and turned to continue their stroll.

His senses locked on Jacqueline, Richard knew the instant she noticed the approaching gentleman; her eyes flared—not with pleasure—and she stiffened. She halted.

Even more alarming, Elinor also saw the gentleman and, halting, too, all but visibly bristled—like a frosty hedgehog.

Richard looked back at the gentleman, swiftly closing on his target, but the man was all smiles and nicely judged charm as he came to a halt before the two ladies and swept them both elegant bows.

"Miss Tregarth—Jacqueline, if I may presume on our long acquaintance. And Miss Swinford. It's a pleasure to see you again, ma'am."

Jacqueline rose from her instinctive curtsy and, before Elinor could speak, coldly stated, "Mr. Marbury." She was certainly not going to call him David. This was the man who had broken her heart when she'd been young and still naive enough to think that any gentleman who wanted to marry her must at least feel affection for her. Clasping her hands before her, she raised her head and met his eyes with all the icy disdain she could muster. "I trust we see you well, sir."

Marbury smiled—reminding her just how easy it had been to trust him. To trust in his glib assurances. If she hadn't heard the truth of his view of her from his own lips, she would never have seen through his polished façade. "You perceive me in the pink of health, my dear Jacqueline. I don't need to inquire of you or Miss Swinford—I can see that you both are prospering in every way." Marbury's gaze locked on Jacqueline's face. "You remain as beautiful as ever, Jacqueline—indeed, with no fear of contradiction, I believe I can state that, over the past years, your beauty has only grown more pronounced."

The compliment was delivered with a smiling expression designed to induce any young lady to lap up his words with a giddy sigh.

Coldly, she arched her brows. "Indeed, sir? But what brings you to the fair? I had not thought your interests ran to sheep." She was no longer a young maid to be cozened by charm.

Marbury's smile didn't falter. "As you say, my interests are rather less bucolic." He swung around, angling so that he put himself more definitely beside her. His gaze scanning the fairground, he went on, "I admit that I never understood, much less do I share, your liking for country life." He lowered his voice. "However, I understand you are still unwed, fair Jacqueline. Consequently, given we so nearly tied the knot years ago, I wondered if, now you are older and no doubt less susceptible to missish sentiment, we might, perhaps, reassess the prospects of a joint future." He returned his gaze to her face; although his expression remained pleasant, his eyes had grown harder. "Being a lady alone, coping with the business of an estate, makes you a target for the unscrupulous, my dear. You should really think about that."

Fury burned, cold and crystalline, inside her. She held Marbury's gaze, her own gaze level and direct. She was aware of Richard, two paces away at the end of the stall, watching, listening—waiting to ascertain whether Marbury, outwardly more suitable than any other of her would-be suitors, was a gentleman whose company she might wish to entertain.

But at Marbury's last words, Richard's features had hardened, and he'd tensed, but she was no longer the young girl she once had been. More, she was honestly incredulous that, given the manner of their parting, Marbury was yet so conceited he believed that he could return and cozen her into marrying him and losing control of Nimway Hall and all that went with it. "Mr. Marbury, allow me to assure you that I have absolutely no interest whatever in joining my future with yours or in linking myself in any way with you."

Marbury's assured composure cracked. His features tightened, and his tone was edged with contempt as he replied, "My dear Jacqueline, you fail to comprehend—"

"Sadly, sir, it appears to be you who lack comprehension."

A frown marred Marbury's handsome countenance, and he reached for her arm.

Deftly, she swung aside, preventing him from touching her. Her gaze flicked Richard's way to find him closing the short distance to her side; she returned her gaze to Marbury and, with a graceful gesture, indicated Richard. "Mr. Marbury, I don't believe you've met Mr. Montague."

Plainly taken aback, Marbury blinked at Richard; a hint of unease flashed through his eyes before his face hardened.

Richard met Marbury's coldly irritated gaze with one of arrogant dismissal. With specious politeness, he half bowed. "Sir."

Lips tight, Marbury was forced to return the courtesy. As he straightened, his gaze flicked to Jacqueline.

Richard spoke before Marbury could. "My dear, time is passing"—he gave full rein to his London drawl—"and I regret to say that if you wish to call on all your farmers, we'd best be moving on."

"Indeed."

Smoothly, he offered his arm; equally smoothly, Jacqueline reached for it. Something primitive inside him calmed at the touch of her hand on his sleeve, the weight as it settled there.

Dripping aloof superiority, he directed a brief nod Marbury's way. "Sir. A pleasure." A glib and customary phrase; in this case, the words were patently meaningless.

With a glance, Richard gathered Elinor, who, judging by her bright eyes, was pleased and entirely approving of his actions. With his head arrogantly high—ignoring Marbury as if he had already disappeared from their view—Richard steered Jacqueline on.

Until Marbury had reached for her arm, Richard had been trapped by indecision as he'd weighed up what his instincts were urging against the observations of his rational mind. Marbury appeared significantly more acceptable than Jacqueline's other suitors. As Richard was leaving the next day, and as Jacqueline was definitely not his in any way—given he was refusing to lay claim to her—what right had he to interfere with Marbury's suit?

Thus had spoken his rational mind. His instincts had paid not the slightest heed.

All they had seen was Marbury's over-glib utterances and Jacqueline's icy reaction; there was, transparently, some past history between them.

Then Marbury had tried to touch her—to coerce her—and that had been that. Jacqueline turning to him had simply confirmed that he'd been right to step in.

He might not be the marrying sort, but he was definitely the protective sort, and at least in his mind, he'd accepted the title of Jacqueline's protector for that day.

They halted before another stall, and with a soft "Thank you," Jacqueline drew her hand from his sleeve.

He squelched the impulse to reach out, snare her hand, and return it to that soothing spot. Instead, he waited patiently while she and Elinor chatted and exchanged news with one of the Hall's farmwives. But when Jacqueline rejoined him and, with Elinor trailing behind, they walked on side by side, he noticed a frown lurking in her eyes. He seriously doubted the frown had been occasioned by the farmwife, who had been a jolly sort, excited and content with her day thus far, and it hadn't been there before Marbury had accosted her.

He studied what he could see of her face and wondered...

She sensed his gaze, glanced up, and briefly met his eyes...then she grimaced and faced forward. After another moment of silent strolling, she offered, "Marbury was...the only one of my suitors I...actually entertained. Years ago. He was first in the procession." Her tone had turned cynical and bitter.

When she said nothing more, he quietly observed, "You didn't accept him."

"No." Her lips tightened. "But I very nearly did. I very nearly walked, all unknowing, into his snare. If it hadn't been for a...twist of fate, I would have." She paused, then drew breath and went on, "One day, months after he'd first started courting me, we'd arranged to meet in Wells. Elinor and I were to meet him outside the cathedral. We were fifteen minutes early. I left Elinor outside on a bench in the sun and went into the cathedral—I'm quite partial to the quiet of the chapels."

She paused.

Sensing the tension gripping her, this time, he held his tongue and waited.

"I was seated in one of the side chapels, head bowed, still and silent, when I heard two gentlemen walk in. They sat in a pew in the nave, closer to the front doors, so I couldn't see them, and they couldn't see me." A ghost of a smile touched her lips. "The one place in which one should never whisper secrets is a church—such buildings are designed to amplify sound. The pair weren't talking loudly, yet I heard every word. It was David—Marbury—and one of his friends. And the friend asked David how things were going with me."

She huffed cynically—whether at her younger self or at Marbury, Richard couldn't tell. She went on, "The long and the short of it was that, courtesy of his openness with his friend, I learned that the only genuine interest Marbury had lay not in me but in my lands. All the rest was fabrication, a deliberate ruse to pull the wool over my innocent and gullible eyes." Her tone changed, growing harder. "Once I'd heard enough—more than enough—I rose and walked out of the chapel and into the nave. He saw me approaching. The look on his face... If I'd needed any assurance that all I'd heard was true, his expression provided it. Of course, he recovered and tried to tell me I'd misheard or misinterpreted... I just kept walking."

She shrugged, then glanced at him. "In hindsight, I should probably have thanked Marbury for the lesson in reality. It was he who taught me that, when it comes to offering for my hand, the first and really only thing gentlemen are after is my land. Primarily, the farms."

He said nothing; there was nothing he could say. With respect to the would-be suitors he'd met, her assessment was correct. Yet her tale reminded him of the incident in his past—his own "coming of age," as he thought of it. And the moment made him feel even closer to her, linked by another similar experience. "First disillusionments always hurt the most."

The words had slipped from his lips without conscious thought.

Diverted from her own musings, she shot him a quizzical glance.

He didn't meet her eyes but, his lips twisting in a self-deprecatory grimace, admitted, "There was a young lady who, a long time ago, taught me a similar lesson. Even though she's no doubt married now, if I met her today, I would still cut her dead."

Jacqueline's lips quirked upward. Her expression lightened, and she tipped her head his way, then faced forward. "Sadly, I don't go about sufficiently in society to cross Marbury's path, and even if I did, in the country, I suspect the impact of cutting someone dead would simply not be the same."

With a soft laugh, he inclined his head, and they walked on side by side.

Encouraged by the moment of unexpected empathy, he set himself the challenge of banishing Marbury from her mind. He was tall enough to see over most heads; he kept watch for distracting and amusing incidents to point out to her—like the geese someone had brought to sell that were sticking their heads out through the woven withies of their enclosure and snapping at the ankles of unwary passersby, making people jump and dodge, creating a minor pocket of mayhem. Then there was the ram who, far from appearing the least interested in ewes, had fallen asleep.

She laughed at both sights, leaving Richard with a warm glow in the center of his chest.

Jacqueline continued on her duty-bound route around the fairground, feeling increasingly…if not precisely happy, then settled. Accepting of her lot in life. Richard was intent on leaving in the morning, and there was nothing she could do—or indeed, should do—to change his mind. So she might as well make the most of the day and enjoy his company; letting go of any hope for more, she accepted Fate's decree and did.

She drew him to the stall she always visited to buy pasties for lunch. She, he, and Elinor stood to one side looking over the milling throng and munching their way through the crisp pastries filled with succulent meat.

Afterward, she insisted on doing one final round of the Hall's farmers' stalls. She suspected the day had proved a prosperous one for all her people, but from what they had seen, the farmers with livestock to sell had done especially well.

"And," she told Richard, "Higgs found four more of those black sheep. He might just have enough for Martha to generate sufficient black yarn for Mrs. Higgs to use as a definite color. She'll be thrilled, if so."

Richard smiled and nodded. Thus were the small pleasures of country life. To his mind, they easily surpassed the more showy pleasures of life in the capital.

He ambled at Jacqueline's heels as she and Elinor led the way on their final circuit. At last, the ladies were ready to depart, and after glancing back to make sure Richard was close behind, the pair turned through the gap in the ropes that led to the area where the horses had been tethered under the eyes of several grooms hired by the fair's organizers.

Some sixth sense tickled Richard's nape as he made to follow in Jacqueline and Elinor's wake. Unobtrusively, he paused beside the gap in the ropes and swiftly glanced around.

The watcher was standing in the shadows between two stalls. Richard let his gaze move unheedingly on as if he was merely taking a last look at the fair before leaving and hadn't spotted the man at all. Large and heavy-set, the man wasn't a gentleman.

Richard turned and lengthened his stride to catch up with Jacqueline. The unknown man had looked vaguely familiar, but Richard couldn't remember ever speaking to him; he couldn't place him.

There was no mounting block in the paddock. Earlier, in her own stable yard, Jacqueline had avoided Richard's help by using the mounting block there, and when they'd arrived, she'd slid down from her saddle without assistance.

Now, he walked to where she waited by her mare's side. Without making any fuss, she steeled herself, and he did the same, and he grasped her waist and hoisted her up, then set her gently in her saddle.

For an instant—one fleeting instant—their eyes met and held. His hands remained about her waist as his gaze and hers...

He fell into her, and she fell into him, and in that single instant of perfect clarity, both knew and acknowledged their connection—that spark of physical recognition that had linked them from first sight and which had only grown stronger over the past days.

Then, still trapped in each other's gazes, they both drew breath, and he forced his hands to ease and drew them from her.

Her expression impassive, she inclined her head and reached for her reins, and he walked on to where Elinor waited to be helped into the trap.

With Elinor settled, the reins firm in her old hands, Richard swung up to the saddle on the chestnut's back. He and Jacqueline waved Elinor ahead, then fell in behind, ambling.

As they left the fairground, alert and on guard, Richard glanced sharply to the side and caught the briefest glimpse of the heavyset man slipping away through the crowd.

Richard frowned, dredging his memory. Could the man be the one he'd seen in the wood with Wallace? What had his name been...Morgan?

They reached the lane that would take them south, and Elinor smartly turned the trap for the Hall. She set the cob trotting, then glanced back at

Richard. "Hopkins told me you plan to leave tomorrow, Richard—is that correct?"

The question jerked him from contemplating the reason Wallace might have set his man to watch them—and focused him instead on the prospect of his tomorrow. He'd expected to feel eager, keen to move on. Instead, he felt...

He forced himself to say, "Yes, that's right. My horse's hoof will be healed, and I need to be on my way."

"So someone is waiting for you?" Elinor called back.

Not as she meant it. "My uncle," he replied.

"Ah—that's right!" Elinor nodded. "I'd forgotten."

As they traveled through the gentle countryside, past fields and, eventually, into the wood around Nimway Hall, Richard ruthlessly suppressed the unexpected resistance surging within him. He couldn't stay—that was impossible, and he knew it. Jacqueline had—clearly and transparently—started to hope, and it wouldn't be fair to lead her on by dallying longer.

He was who he was. And she was who she was. It was her duty to marry a man of sufficient wealth and position to protect the Hall—she'd said it herself, that being the guardian of the Hall meant protecting the Hall was her highest priority.

If she learned his true identity, she would feel even more bound to make a bid to snare him, true affection or not.

He wasn't about to risk that by staying; leaving was definitely the right thing to do for him and for her.

From all he'd gleaned of her past and all he knew of himself, acceding to a marriage based on considerations other than true and abiding affection would trap them both in their worst nightmare.

Over dinner, Hugh inquired as to Malcolm the Great's recovery.

Richard seized the moment; he related his latest findings—on their return from the fair, he'd dallied in the stable to check on Malcolm—and grasped the opportunity to reiterate his intention of taking his leave of the household come morning.

Hugh harrumphed, his jowls shaking. His expression said he was disappointed, but he didn't argue. After a moment, he huffed, "I'll miss having you to talk with."

A somewhat strained silence descended, then Elinor glanced across the table. "I daresay Richard has his uncle and his life to return to. Indeed, after London, being forced to remain here for...what has it been? Six days? Well," Elinor continued, "it must have seemed quite strange, isolated and quiet as we are."

His time there had been a blessed relief. Richard held the words back and, instead, inclined his head in silent acknowledgment.

"So it's back to the fray." Hugh took up the refrain, then frowned. "But I thought you were headed to the bishop's household." Hugh arched his brows. "Not much of an entertaining nature there, I'd warrant. Not for such as yourself, at least."

Richard had been heading to his uncle for safety; entertainment had been the last thing on his mind. "That's true enough," he admitted. He couldn't think of anything more to add and was grateful when Cruickshank appeared to remove the plates.

At Jacqueline's signal, they all rose. Richard glanced at Cruickshank; the butler briefly caught his eye, then busied himself dealing with the covers.

Richard circled the table to take hold of the handles of Hugh's chair. As he had for the past nights, Richard steered the older man in the wake of the ladies.

The wheels rattled softly over the hall tiles. Both footmen passed them, their expressions downcast.

Inwardly, Richard frowned. He absolved everyone of deliberately trying to darken the atmosphere of the usually serene household, yet there was no denying the news of his leaving appeared to have cast a pall over all.

Their time in the drawing room dragged. Where, before, they'd tossed comments back and forth and then settled comfortably to read, tonight, they struggled to find anything to say, and comfort seemed in short supply.

Her gaze on her stitching, Elinor finally remarked, "I expect, Richard dear, that after your visit in Wells, you'll be heading back to your accustomed life. Back to London—or, given it's summer, are you expected somewhere else?"

He'd left a veritable stack of invitations to house parties on his desk in London; he was absolutely certain he wouldn't be accepting any of them. Finally allowing himself to think of what, exactly, he intended to do after spending a few days, at least, with his uncle, after several seconds, he slowly shook his head. "I really don't know. I doubt I'll want to return to

London, not in this season, but I have no other plans…" Quickly, he added, "At present. There might be a summons from the family waiting for me with my uncle."

He doubted it, but the last thing he wanted was for Elinor to voice the thought he was sure had just passed through her head and invite him to return to the Hall. He couldn't do that—not to himself or Jacqueline. Through long experience, he'd learned that a clean break was best.

Elinor glanced at Jacqueline, then returned her gaze to her embroidery.

Surreptitiously—warily—Richard followed Elinor's gaze. Jacqueline appeared absorbed in her embroidery, but he felt certain she'd heard every syllable of their exchange. Neither by word nor expression did she evince any reaction.

He returned his gaze to the book he'd balanced, open, on his knees. And pretended to read.

Freddie came and, after Hugh had extracted a promise that Richard would not leave without breakfast and bidding them all goodbye, Hugh consented to be wheeled to his bed.

Elinor sighed, then set her needle in her work and started to fold it up.

Jacqueline glanced up, then did the same.

Finally, it was time for them to retire. Elinor climbed the stairs, and Richard, with Jacqueline beside him, followed more slowly.

They reached the first landing, and Jacqueline drew breath and said, "Although I'll see you tomorrow, of course, I wanted to personally—and formally—thank you for all you've done for the household and estate while here. All the considerable help you've rendered us." Through the flickering shadows cast by the candles ahead and below them, she met his eyes. "On behalf of Nimway Hall and all those on the estate, I thank you most sincerely for all your assistance, and I hope you've enjoyed your time with us."

It felt strange and stilted to revert to formality with her, but he inclined his head and replied, "It was my pleasure to be able to render that assistance, to be in a position such that I could help both you and your people. And I have, indeed, enjoyed my days here." *More than I suspect I will appreciate until I'm far distant.*

With those unspoken words echoing in his head, he glanced up and saw that Elinor had paused at the head of the stairs. Briefly, she met his eyes, and he could almost see the question on her lips: If he had enjoyed himself, why was he leaving?

Elinor held his gaze for an instant more, then, confusion in her face, she turned and headed along the gallery toward her room.

Leaving Jacqueline and Richard to step into the gallery, more or less alone.

At the point where they would part ways—she to go one way to her room while he headed down the corridor to his—they both halted.

Paused.

Through the soft shadows, their eyes met, their gazes held.

And both remembered with crystal-edged clarity the moment they'd shared the previous night.

Like a cloud of suppressed need, the compulsion of that moment swelled and engulfed them—even more intense than twenty-four hours before.

For one finite instant, he wanted nothing more than to take one step forward, sweep her into his arms, and taste her lips.

Taste her—a prelude to learning all he now hungered to know of her.

The impulse was so strong, so insistent, he trembled and almost gave in.

But it couldn't be. He knew that.

Slowly, he forced his lungs to expand, to draw in much-needed air. To clear his head so he could remember his resolution.

He had to leave. He couldn't remain.

No matter the temptation.

He straightened, raising his head.

As if she could read his decision in his eyes, she held his gaze for an instant more, then smoothly yet rigidly, she inclined her head. "Goodnight."

She turned and moved toward her chamber.

He stood, helpless in the face of his own reality. His fists slowly clenching, he watched her go—watched her walk into her room and close the door.

CHAPTER 9

*R*ichard's departure from Nimway Hall was a great deal more awkward than his arrival.

Breakfast proved to be a desultory affair. Even with Elinor there— she'd come down especially to see him off—they still struggled to find anything to say.

He'd been up since dawn and had been out to the stable to check on Malcolm the Great, then he'd sought out Crawley, and they'd walked to the lake and discussed in detail how to create a controllable tunnel system to link the lake to the stream. The solution had come to Richard in the small hours, and he hadn't wanted to leave without passing on his insight.

Before breakfast, he'd taken his packed saddlebags to the stable. Consequently, when, immediately after they'd risen from the breakfast table, he walked out of the great hall and into the sunshine, Hopkins was holding Malcolm the Great, saddled and ready to ride.

Jacqueline, Elinor, and Hugh in his chair with Freddie propelling him followed Richard onto the front porch. Even as he turned to take his formal leave of them, he saw others hurrying from the depths of the hall.

In short order, the entire household had assembled, from Cruickshank and Mrs. Patrick to Young Willie, who came loping around from the stable.

They all lined up across the porch.

Clinging to his easy expression, Richard ran his gaze over them all— and felt an odd tug at the way they all looked back at him. Trusting.

Certain. As if they had unwavering confidence in him always doing what was best for them.

He told himself they weren't wrong, that leaving was the best thing he could do.

For Jacqueline, the household, and all those on the Nimway Hall estate.

Slinking away would have been so much easier.

Turning to Elinor and Hugh, Richard clung to the formal observances and the standard phrases of farewell.

Both replied, but he sensed their hearts were not in their words.

Then he turned to Jacqueline.

What to say?

Giving in to compulsion, he bowed low—a full court bow, one he accorded very few. Straightening, he held out his hand.

Faintly surprised, she surrendered her fingers to his clasp.

He captured her gaze, raised her fingers to his lips, and pressed a kiss —a faint echo of the kiss he had held back from giving her in the gallery in the shadows of the night—to the backs of her fingers.

He released her and swept her a last bow.

Then he turned and, pulling on his riding gloves, descended the steps.

Hopkins held Malcolm steady, and Richard swung up to the saddle. He settled and gathered the reins, then he looked one last time at the household of Nimway Hall—at Jacqueline in their center, the heart of the house—then he raised his hand in a salute, dug in his heels, and sent Malcolm into a quick trot.

He rode away from Nimway Hall and refused to let himself look back.

Jacqueline watched him go. She couldn't think. She could barely breathe through the emotion gripping her.

The trees closed around his dwindling figure, the shadows swallowed him, and then he was gone.

She felt hollow inside, as if in leaving he'd taken some vital part of her with him. She didn't want to think what that part was; he'd gone, and that was that. She had a household to run; she couldn't afford to turn maudlin.

Around her, the others shifted, then turned and, softly murmuring, quit the porch, Elinor and Hugh making for the parlor while the staff returned to their duties.

She needed to return to her duties, too, yet she allowed herself a moment. To stare after him and grieve for what might have been.

The backs of her fingers still tingled with warmth as if they'd been marked in some significant way.

At some point over the past days, she'd started to wonder, and then to believe, that Richard Montague was the one—that as the stories foretold, Fate had snared him in Balesboro Wood and sent him to her. Sent him to be her one, her husband, the man who would stand beside her, her champion in her role as guardian of the Hall.

It hadn't been so—that hadn't come to be.

She'd read the signs wrongly. Perhaps because, in her heart, she knew that she needed him—the man who would willingly be hers—the man who would be happy to stand beside her and defend the Hall, its lands, and its people.

In her bones, she'd felt that Richard Montague could be that man, but he hadn't been willing, and only a man willing to be her true partner could fill the role. Could help her shoulder the burden.

A burden she'd been born to which she nevertheless consciously embraced with her whole heart and soul.

This was her place, and Richard had wanted no part of it.

At least he'd been honest. She needed to respect that, accept that, and be content.

And wait.

With a sigh, she refocused on the now-empty drive, then turned and went inside.

The shadows of the great hall engulfed her. She didn't look back, so she didn't see the bushes along the drive shake.

Grinning, Morgan rose from his crouch, turned, and crept away from the Nimway Hall drive, making his way deeper into the wood.

The farther he went, the harder he grinned. His sturdy cob would carry him to Lydford in no time at all, and then...he felt certain his demanding master would be well pleased.

Richard cantered steadily through Balesboro Wood. He was following the same track he, Jacqueline, and Elinor had used the previous day. He kept his wits about him, determined that, this time, he wouldn't get lost.

Finding himself forced to return to Nimway Hall—lost again—would be beyond embarrassing.

The trees closed in on both sides, draping pleasantly cool shadows over the track. Birdcalls drifted down from the canopies, but little else stirred; the area was, indeed, isolated, and few people, it seemed, used this track.

Head up, eyes trained forward, he fought to keep his mind on his destination—tried to recall the streets of Wells and the route to the bishop's palace, thought of his uncle, of the particular cognac he might have in his library decanter...anything rather than what he was riding away from.

To no avail. Regardless of where he tried to send his thoughts, they circled back to Nimway Hall, to the household there, to Jacqueline.

To the settled feeling that had engulfed him there, the subtle sense of belonging he now recognized—now that he was leaving it behind.

A small crack had opened within him as he'd turned north out of the drive, and with every yard he traveled, that crack widened, revealing a chasm of nothingness, of deadening despair. On top of that, his instincts were pricking him, increasingly insistently.

Then the trees started to thin, and the track ahead lay awash with sunshine as it led on through open fields, and that chasm yawned and ached with loneliness and a yearning denied, and the clamor of his instincts rose to a shriek.

What am I doing?

Malcolm's stride broke, then the big dappled gray unaccountably jibbed. Richard swore and looked down, wrestling for control as the powerful horse fought the bit, wrenching to the side.

Richard glimpsed the branch just before it hit.

Thwack!

His eyes flew wide as he was swept from his saddle. He landed on his back, and his breath *whooshed* from him.

Jacqueline met with Mrs. Patrick for their usual morning meeting, but with the wrench of Richard's leaving dragging at her, it was difficult to concentrate on mundane household matters. Once the housekeeper, who had done her best to mask her sympathy and underlying confusion over Richard's departure, bustled back to her domain, rather than joining Hugh and Elinor in the parlor—and weathering their unvoiced sympathy, too—Jacqueline snatched up a shawl, swung it around her shoulders, and headed for the side door.

She slipped out of the house and strode determinedly for the lake. If anyone asked, she was surveying the prospects for connecting the lake and the stream. In reality, she needed time alone with no one else about—no one who looked to her for guidance—so she could grapple with her unruly emotions, think things through, and search for guidance herself.

On reaching the path of beaten earth that circled the rim of the lake, she drew her shawl more tightly about her shoulders, folded her arms across her chest, fixed her gaze on the path before her feet, and started walking.

Only then did she lift the lid on the cauldron of her seething emotions. A sense of loss struck her, potent and poignant. It was followed by a deadening feeling of emptiness, of dullness and despair. A vista of never-ending loneliness swam into focus, one lacking all warmth, all joy, all life.

Lacking love.

She tried to turn her mind from the prospect and look further into the future instead. But the future, nebulous though it was, appeared bleak and cold. Empty as well.

As if something that should have been there had been taken away.

She supposed it had.

She was a quarter of the way around the lake when it struck her. Her lips eased, and she almost smiled.

Affirmation, in a way; perhaps she could take some solace from that. Clearly, she hadn't been wrong in thinking she had fallen in love with, was still in love with, and would probably always love Richard Montague.

Only love could end like this—could leave such a soul-deep emptiness behind.

Over the past days, her heart had made its choice. It had chosen Richard Montague.

She paced on, considering the implications of that; she had a strong suspicion that for her, that choice was irreversible and immutable—set in stone.

"So," she murmured, "where does that leave me?"

Where did it leave Nimway Hall?

She'd reached the far end of the lake, the northernmost point. There, the trees crowded close to the path, the way overhung by reaching branches, the air beneath dim and cool.

She was halfway through the shadowed stretch when a sound penetrated her absorption. She raised her head—and sensed movement behind her. She whirled.

Black cloth fell over her face.

She gasped and clutched at the fabric—a black cloth bag?—but it was yanked firmly down over her head.

Rough hands seized her.

She opened her mouth to scream, and a band slapped across her face, pressing between her lips—she shut them, but the band cinched tight, anchoring the black material firmly over her lips, gagging her, almost smothering her.

She fought to break free, but there were at least two men, possibly three, and it was far too late.

They'd used her shawl to tie her arms to her sides. She felt a rough rope tighten about her ankles, then she was lifted, hoisted like a sack over a man's burly shoulder.

The man started walking.

Her heart thundering in her ears, Jacqueline was certain he wasn't carrying her to the Hall but into the trees and away.

Richard must have lost consciousness—when he realized he was lying on his back to one side of the track with his eyes closed, he had no idea how much time had elapsed.

His wits had been rattled by the fall. His thoughts were still careening, dizzyingly swirling through his head.

With effort, he raised his lids. The sun striking through the canopy blinded him, and he quickly shut his eyes again.

And as sometimes happened in that curious space between sleeping and waking, between conscious and unconscious minds, the answer to the last question he'd asked floated up from the morass of his churning thoughts.

I'm fleeing as I always do whenever a lady makes advances toward me.

Whenever a lady indicates she has feelings for me, given those feelings are invariably occasioned by my wealth and station and are never truly about me, then it's time for me to go. To run. Because nothing good comes of staying—I know that.

So I'm running from Jacqueline because she might want me.

Pain lanced through his head. His brain seemed to seize; he winced. Moving slowly, he sat up, raised his hands to his head, and massaged his temples.

There was something wrong about those thoughts. Even in his stunned state, he knew it.

Perhaps *because* of his stunned state…

He drew in a slow breath and tried to bring order to his disordered mind.

I love Jacqueline. Yes, yes, I've been trying not to think that, but I've known it for days—why else do I feel so compelled to protect her?

And she'd started to look at me as if she might feel a reciprocal emotion, but as always, there's the question of how much my wealth and station contribute to that…

His eyes flew wide. "My God."

He might have been staring at the deity's face for the wonder that filled him. Several seconds passed, then, as if even now he could barely credit it, he whispered, "She doesn't know."

Abruptly, he straightened, all effects of his accident disregarded. "I didn't tell anyone." He looked around and saw Malcolm the Great cropping grass two yards away. "They think I'm Richard Montague, unremarkable gentleman of London."

Hope of a kind he'd never felt before surged through him—and still, the wonder lingered.

He scrambled to his feet, walked to Malcolm, and caught the trailing reins. Then he paused, for one instant uncertain of the wisdom of placing his trust in the surging tide of happiness, of sheer joy, that was welling from the very depths of his soul.

Then he filled his lungs and, giving up all attempts to keep that joy from his face, stated, "She loves me. *Me.* Just me."

He gripped the stirrup, slid his boot home, and swung up to the saddle.

Malcolm the Great had already been facing back toward the Hall. The horse was no fool.

Richard laughed, tapped his heels to the big horse's flanks, and grinned as Malcolm stretched his legs and, unresisting, headed back the way they'd come.

"What a fool I've been." He should never have left. It hadn't been instinct prodding him to flee but too-well-remembered fear.

How he would explain his return he didn't know. "I'll think of something once I'm there."

Nimway Hall was where he was supposed to be. Remembering the household's parting looks, he suspected everyone there already accepted that.

Exactly what his role would be might not yet be clear, but if Jacqueline truly wanted him and would forgive him for being an idiot and leaving, he felt sure he and she would work it all out.

Somewhat to his surprise, his instincts were still clamoring, urging him to get back to the Hall.

To get back to Jacqueline's side.

He frowned. She hadn't mentioned leaving the Hall that day, yet...

With a mental shrug, he loosened the reins and urged Malcolm the Great into a gallop.

The way forward was clear, and on multiple counts, the sooner he got back to Nimway Hall, the better.

Malcolm the Great thundered up the Nimway Hall drive. The horse had his head down and was all but racing, huge hooves flinging gravel as he charged along.

Richard was nonplussed. He hadn't urged the horse into such a show; the beast seemed infected by a need to get back to the Hall with all possible speed. Richard wasn't arguing—his instincts were urging much the same thing—but he was thankful when Malcolm eased the pace as they rounded the last bend in the drive.

The Hall came into view.

Chaos reigned in the forecourt.

Richard's heart leapt into his throat. His instincts spiked; an unfamiliar fear surged, then gripped and pierced like an eagle's claw.

The front door stood wide. Hugh was on the porch, in his chair, attempting to direct the men and women rushing inside and out. As Malcolm slowed further, Richard saw boys hurrying from the stable, while another larger party was returning at a jog around the other side of the house, most likely from the lake.

On reaching the forecourt, Richard hauled Malcolm to a halt, flung himself from the saddle, and vaulted up the steps.

Everyone saw him and slowed.

Hugh scowled ferociously, but the anxiety lacing his words gave his disapproval the lie. "Thank God you're back!"

Richard scanned the figures rushing out of the house; a chill touched his soul. "Where's Jacqueline?"

"That's the question, ain't it?" Hugh waved at the staff gathering about. "We've been searching for her everywhere."

"What happened?" Richard didn't try to mute the command in his voice.

Pale, Hugh dragged in a breath. "Seems that after her regular meeting with Mrs. Patrick, Jacqueline went off to walk about the lake. Elinor was in the parlor and saw her go. That was near an hour ago. After a while, Elinor got anxious, so she sent one of the boys after Jacqueline, but the lad couldn't find her." Hugh's expression fell into grim lines. "That's when we started searching."

Richard looked at Cruickshank; the butler had come to stand behind Hugh's chair.

Understanding Richard's unvoiced question, Cruickshank reported, "We've searched everywhere in the house, sir, and called all the while. Miss Jacqueline isn't inside."

Richard nodded and directed a commanding look at Young Willie.

The lad hurried to say, "We've searched everywhere around the stable, sir. The mistress's mare is still in her stall, and no other horse is missing. No sign she took a horse nor was anywhere near there."

Richard turned to look at Crawley as he came lumbering up with Hopkins and Ned Ostley, with Crawley's lads at their backs.

"We found her footprints on the lake path." Crawley braced his hands on his knees and hauled in a breath. "They were clearest in that spot at the far end, where the path's shaded and the ground stays damp." Grim-faced, Crawley met Richard's eyes. "Lots of her footprints—and lots of others, besides. Men. Big men in boots."

A collective gasp of horror went up from Elinor, Mrs. Patrick, and the maids who had streamed out of the house to join those on the porch.

Richard felt cold, iron-willed calm settle about him. "How many?"

"Three." It was Hopkins, looking wild enough to chew nails, who answered. "Three big blackguards. They carried her off through the trees a-ways to where they had horses waiting on one of the littler paths."

"Two horses hitched to a small closed coach." Ned Ostley spoke with certainty. The farrier met Richard's gaze and went on, "And I can tell you the horses were shod by Jem Smith in Lydford. There's a tiny mark he puts on all his shoes, and we could see it clearly where the horses had walked."

"Lydford." Virtually everyone else had stiffened when Ostley mentioned the place. Richard scanned the now-anxious-yet-furious faces. "Who lives there?"

"That damned blighter, Wallace!" Hugh looked close to apoplectic. "The family house—the one he inherited from his father, who was a damned sight better man—is there. A red-brick house at this end of the village, on a lane just off the village street." Hugh huffed, his color fading. "The family used to be honorable—nice people—but if half the tales told are true, this latest sprig is anything but. And if he's taken Jacqueline, he's a black-hearted scoundrel through and through!"

"He's got Jacqueline?" Elinor sounded faint. She pressed a hand to her chest.

Richard tried to sound reassuring, but his voice was a growl as he replied, "Not for long."

Hugh reached up and patted Elinor's hand where it gripped the back of his chair. "Don't fret—Richard will get her back."

Richard nodded decisively. "I will." It was a vow. Regardless of whether Jacqueline loved him or not, he loved her, and he would do whatever it took—even fight to the death—to return her unharmed to the Hall. He looked around at the men of Nimway Hall. "Who's with me?"

A chorus of "Me!" and "I'll come!" rolled back at him.

Men and boys rushed toward the stable.

In less than five minutes—minutes Richard spent learning everything Hugh could tell him about Wallace's house—a small mounted army of men, youths, and boys had gathered in the forecourt.

Richard walked down the steps, grabbed Malcolm's reins, and swung himself into the saddle. He beckoned Hopkins, Ostley, and Crawley to ride at the head of the group with him, then turned Malcolm's head down the drive and simply said, "Let's go."

With a clatter of hooves that echoed back off the house, they set out for Lydford.

CHAPTER 10

*R*ichard was thankful the men had come with him—they were locals, well known and well liked. As soon as their company had turned onto the lane to Lydford that Ostley and Hopkins were sure the coach must have taken, the men and lads had asked anyone they'd seen—farmers in their fields, two laborers working on a bridge, three women walking out visiting—and quickly confirmed that a small black coach had indeed passed that way within the past half hour.

They weren't that far behind.

Richard didn't let himself think of what Jacqueline might be going through; that would have been too distracting. Instead, he reminded himself that she was no meek, milk-and-water miss; she would stand up to Wallace well enough—long enough—for Richard and her men to reach her.

Without prompting, two of the farmers and one of the women they'd spoken with had named the coach they'd seen as belonging to Sir Peregrine Wallace, so as they neared Lydford, they were certain as to where they needed to go.

Crawley waved, attracting Richard's attention and signaling him to call a halt.

With a potent mix of fury and impatience pounding through his veins, Richard wanted to rage on, but knew well enough to listen to the locals. He slowed Malcolm and drew him to a halt. The others followed his lead and milled about.

"The lane to Wallace's place is just a bit along on the right." Hopkins brought his horse alongside Malcolm.

"Aye," Crawley said, "but I'm thinking we'd do best to get to the house under cover of the wood rather than clatter up his drive and alert not just him but those three blackguards of his as well."

Richard nodded curtly. "Surprise would serve us best."

Crawley outlined what he had in mind, and Hopkins, Ostley, and Richard agreed. With Crawley—a huntsman in his spare time—in the lead, they walked their horses off the lane and through the wood to a natural clearing not far on. They left the horses there with two of the boys and set off on foot. After a hundred yards, Crawley signaled for quiet, and they crept on.

The upper story and roof of a red-brick house loomed ahead.

They left the wood and continued on through an overgrown shrubbery. Eventually, Crawley paused and crouched beside an archway cut into a high hedge. Looking over Crawley's shoulder, Richard saw the side wall of the house mere yards away, across a poorly scythed stretch of lawn.

There were few windows that faced that way, and all had their curtains closed.

Richard smiled intently, clapped Crawley on the shoulder, and moved past him. Fleet-footed and silent, Richard crossed the lawn and flattened himself against the side wall beside the window of the room at the front corner of the house.

In a house of this size and style, that room should be the drawing room—the room the master of the house would use to entertain guests. No matter his ultimate intent, Richard would wager Wallace would first speak with Jacqueline in that room.

He knew he'd guessed correctly when Jacqueline's voice, her tone harsh and condemnatory, reached him clearly through the glass.

His heart leapt, then her words registered, and relief sluiced through him.

They'd got there in time.

"You're not listening, Sir Peregrine." Jacqueline's speech was rigidly controlled. "No matter what idiocy you've convinced yourself will come to pass—no matter any brilliant plan to compromise me—I will not consent to marry you!"

"Of course you will." Wallace sounded completely assured. "After spending a night in my house alone with me, no young lady of your station would be allowed to refuse my hand offered in marriage." The clink of crystal reached through the window. "It won't be up to you. Tregarth's your guardian—he'll see sense. So will your vaporous chaperon. They'll force you to it—you'll see. Cheers!"

A pause ensued, then Jacqueline—by the sound of her voice, she stood closer to the window, but facing the room and, presumably, Wallace —spoke. "I say again, Sir Peregrine—you are not listening." Her voice had lowered; power of a sort thrummed beneath her words. "I am the guardian of Nimway Hall—the deed to the Hall and all its lands is wholly in my keeping. I do not hold those rights by whim of my great-uncle or anyone else. I hold them by virtue of who I am."

"Virtue!" Sir Peregrine chuckled. "Yes, indeed—that's just what I've been saying. It's your virtue that will be the deciding point."

"You're a numbskull if you believe such semantics will gain you anything! My virtue is neither here nor there. In order for any man to become my husband—and through me, exert any control at all over the Hall, its lands, and its people—*I* have to agree. Before God, witnesses, and an altar, *I have to agree.* And I can assure you that, regardless of anything you think to do to me, I will *never* marry you!" Her voice had escalated to a reined shout. "And for your information, regardless means in no circumstances whatsoever!"

A slight pause ensued, then Wallace responded, his tone not quite so cocksure, "You've lived too isolated—you don't understand how ploys such as this work. Simply by me letting it be known that you've spent the night here, under my roof, with me in residence at the same time, you will be ruined." Wallace's voice strengthened. "That's the way society works, and, my dear Jacqueline, there's nothing you can do to change that. I don't even have to lay a hand on you, and truth be told, I've never been attracted to women with tempers—too much effort to tame. But that's of no moment—just by being here, you will be ruined, and my desired outcome, namely marriage to you, is therefore assured."

Somewhere deeper in the room, a chair squeaked. Richard sensed that Wallace was sitting while Jacqueline was on her feet, possibly pacing, closer to the window.

Apparently convinced by his own arguments, more eagerly, Wallace went on, "I have it all planned. It's entirely straightforward. Now that I have you here, the best thing you can do is to accept the inevitable with good grace—no need for any tantrums and tears. I assure you such behavior will have no impact on what will, ultimately, occur. Once you accept that I hold the upper hand, you can save your reputation from even the faintest slur by agreeing to marry me immediately."

Richard frowned, wondering how…

After a pause—no doubt a gloating one—Wallace went on, "I have a special license and a priest in my pocket." In more persuasive vein, he continued, "Just say the word, and we can be married within the hour— no fuss, no whispers, no slurs on your good name."

"You are still not listening." Jacqueline's tone had hardened, her voice conveying adamantine resolution. "I don't care what plans you've made. The notion of marrying a man like you curdles my stomach. No matter your actions, one fact remains: You cannot marry me without my agreement. And regardless of what you stoop to do, I will never, ever, agree to marry you."

Silence greeted that declaration.

Alarm flaring, Richard turned to the men plastered as he was against the wall and, by signaling with his hands and mouthing orders, explained what he wanted done.

Suddenly, in the drawing room, Wallace spat, "It's that damned man, Montague—isn't it?" His voice had taken on an ugly edge. Richard felt certain Wallace had come to his feet. His voice drew nearer, as if he was approaching the window—stalking closer to Jacqueline. "I saw the way you looked at him. So the wretch got in first, did he? Did he turn your head and make you fall in love with him?" Abruptly, Wallace sounded a lot closer. His tone was sneering as he said, "He did, didn't he?"

"Let me go, you fiend!"

"No—why should I? You're in my house, in my power. Entirely in my control." A scuffle sounded. "Oh-ho! Don't like that, heh? But yes, you're now mine to do with as I please." Wallace's tone had turned vicious.

Timing was everything. Richard held the men poised and waited— there were bound to be other men inside, not just Wallace. Richard wanted the master well and truly distracted before he launched their attack.

"You say you don't care what I stoop to, so let's put that to the test, shall we?" Wallace was all but slavering. "Let's see how proud you are afterward."

His face hard, Richard gave the signal, sending most of the men scurrying past him and around to the front of the house, while the stronger, heavier men circled to the rear door.

Wallace ground out, "Montague left you and rode away, you silly bitch! He got what he wanted, so there's no need to feel shy about sharing yourself around—"

A resounding slap echoed through the room.

Now standing pressed against the wall beside the window, Richard breathed, "Come on—come *on*."

Inside Sir Peregrine's drawing room, beyond furious, Jacqueline wrenched and tugged, fighting to free her wrist from Sir Peregrine's tight grip.

He was staring at her, momentarily shocked by her slap, the imprint of her fingers and palm showing white against his pink cheek, but his hold on her wrist hadn't slackened in the least.

She couldn't break free.

Abruptly, she stopped struggling and went on the attack instead. Stepping toward him, glaring directly into his face, she stated through furiously clenched teeth, "It's none of your business who I love—you're not fit to even say the word!"

Instinctively, she knew she needed Wallace furious—furious and not thinking clearly, then he would make mistakes. In the circumstances, she was perfectly prepared to clout him senseless with the bronze semi-nude figurine she could see on a side table, but she had to get a hand on the statue first.

She glowered into his face and belligerently rolled on, "And yes, Montague might not have valued what I had to give, and yes, he's gone, but, you blithering idiot, that doesn't mean I'll stop loving him—that's not how love works! And even if I did eventually look elsewhere, I would never lower my standards to the point of accepting a proposal from the likes of you! You are unquestionably the very worst of a batch of unsuitable suitors—I wouldn't accept you were death in the balance!"

Under her unrelenting onslaught, Wallace had paled, but now his light-brown eyes glittered, cruelty and malice swirling in their depths. "That can be arranged, my dear. But first, if you like it rough…"

Wallace yanked her wrist up, jerking her against him.

She couldn't help her gasp, and her eyes flew wide. She struggled to step back, but his other arm banded her waist, and then he tipped back his head and laughed.

"Oh yes—glorious." He looked down, into her face; his eyes, gleaming maniacally, trapped hers. "Rough as you like, my dear—I'm only too happy to oblige!" Abruptly, he swung around and bent her back over the edge of another side table. His face had contorted into a mask of lasciviousness. His gaze lowered to her breasts, heaving beneath her tight bodice. "Oh yes, indeed—I guarantee you won't find me lacking in that regard. And once I'm finished with you—with breaking you in and instructing you—you'll be only too happy to spread your legs for my friends as well. Dashwood will enjoy using you—he's especially partial to the hoity ones brought to kneel before him."

Under her now openly horrified gaze, Wallace licked his thick lips, then he glanced up and met her eyes...

She fell into his gaze, and suddenly, she couldn't breathe as revulsion rose up and choked her.

She'd misjudged. Panic lent her desperate strength; she forced her lungs to fill and, eyes closing, *screamed*!

Wallace laughed. "Yes, *yes*! It only adds to the pleasure!"

Hammering fell on the front door, heavy and insistent.

She and Wallace both jerked and looked toward the drawing room door—Wallace with surprise, she with leaping hope.

Wallace glanced back at her and saw her expression, and his slavering smile returned. "Whoever they are, it'll do you no good. My staff know to deny all comers at moments like this. They know I like my privacy."

The blackguard bent her farther back. Her gaze locked with his, with her free hand, she groped behind her, hoping to find something on the table she might use as a weapon, but nothing met her questing fingertips; it seemed this table was bare—

To her right, the side window shattered behind the curtain, then came the sound of the sash being shoved upward, and the curtain was ripped aside.

Even as she and Wallace blinked, Richard Montague sat on the sill, then swung his long legs into the room. His face a grim mask promising all manner of retribution, he planted his feet on the boards and stood, his sword, blade naked, in his hand.

Jacqueline's heart soared. She'd never in her life seen such a welcome sight.

Such a promising sight in so many ways.

Noise erupted on the other side of the drawing room door.

After one swift, comprehensive glance that seemed to have taken in every inch of her, Richard's gaze had fixed on Wallace. Slowly, Richard smiled. Chillingly. He stepped forward, swishing his sword side to side through the air. "It appears, Wallace, that you require a lesson in manners. Unhand the lady, sirrah."

Wallace had frozen, but although his grip on her had slackened, his body still trapped hers against the table—she couldn't move until he did.

Then the drawing room door crashed open, startling Wallace so much he swiveled to stare—locking her against him as he did.

She gritted her teeth and peeked around Wallace. Crawley and Ostley filled the doorway, and she glimpsed other Hall men behind them.

Crawley took in the scene in a searching glance, then he tipped a salute to Richard. "All present and accounted for out here, sir."

"Thank you." Richard's gaze had returned to Wallace. "Close the door."

Crawley and Ostley backed out, and the door shut with a definite *click*.

Jacqueline felt Wallace's chest expand as he hauled in a huge breath, then he flung her away—toward the wall—and lunged for the sword he'd left propped against the side of the fireplace.

Her back hit the wall—the front wall of the house—and Jacqueline steadied. She watched as Wallace, the sword's hilt in his hand, turned with a snarl to face Richard. With a dramatic flourish, Wallace unsheathed the sword. He flung the sheath to the side and sliced the blade through the air. "I warn you, Montague, I'm considered something of a master with this blade." Wallace swished the steel side to side, then cocked a brow at Richard. "You sure you don't want to put that down? We could share her, if you like."

Richard stilled. Fleetingly, something primal passed through his eyes, then his lips curved mockingly. "That's not why I'm here. I have a lesson to administer, if you recall. But as for your claim to mastery..." Crooking the fingers of his left hand, he beckoned Wallace on. "Let's put that to the test, shall we?"

Gracefully, Richard straightened and presented the formal salute.

Facing him, several paces away, Wallace barely performed the salute before launching himself at Richard in a furious attack.

Jacqueline's heart leapt to her throat, and her breath caught, but apparently, Richard had foreseen the attack; before Wallace struck, Richard was already moving and fluidly countered. Then, with seemingly effortless grace, one hand raised behind him in the classic swordsman's stance, his feet shifting as if in a dance, Richard struck back.

They were much of a height, with Wallace possibly an inch taller; while Richard appeared more athletic, more muscular and powerful, Wallace probably had the longer reach.

For the next minute, the flash of steel back and forth was too fast for Jacqueline to follow.

Was Wallace truly a master with the blade? Was he toying with Richard—or was it the other way about?

The next minute of slashing and ringing steel left her in no doubt. If Wallace was a master, then Richard Montague was a past master; Richard was making Wallace look awkward and frequently off balance.

Then, without any warning Jacqueline detected, Richard launched a flurry of slashing strokes—and when, on a gasp, Wallace stumbled back, he was blinking, and a slash down one cheek was trickling blood.

Richard's lesson didn't end there. If anything, the engagement became more rigidly defined, more completely under his control.

Soon, Wallace was panting. He fell back, giving ground. He was now sporting several slashes—on his face, on his hands, and even on his arms, blood seeping through slashes in his sleeves—and was starting to look panicked. He hadn't once got past Richard's guard.

"Who the devil are you?" Wallace edged back another step. "You're not just some landless gentleman wandering past."

Jacqueline looked at Richard. She'd grown increasingly sure of the same thing; there was an absolute confidence at the core of Richard Montague that his skill with the sword was only underscoring.

The ends of Richard's lips lifted, his half smile mockingly intent. "Whoever said I was a landless gentleman?" He raised his sword in a taunting gesture. "But never mind who I am—we're here to determine who you are, Wallace. Or should I say"—Richard's voice lowered —"*what* you are, given you count Dashwood among your cronies."

Mention of the infamous Sir Francis Dashwood seemed to fire something in Wallace. Teeth gritted, he launched another, this time clearly desperate, attack.

Jacqueline's hands flew to her face. She pressed her fingers to her lips to hold back her helpless squeak as she looked on in near panic.

The blades were a flurry of shining steel. Both men were moving and circling so swiftly, striking with such vigor, it was difficult to follow—

Straightening, almost contemptuously, Richard batted aside Wallace's blade, then, in a fluid movement that had him rising on his toes, sliced viciously, diagonally, across Wallace's chest.

Winded, Wallace snarled soundlessly. He stumbled back and bumped into the other side table, half folding over it. His face contorted beyond recognition, he seized the statue Jacqueline had seen and swung back—

"Look out!" she screamed.

She needn't have worried. Richard had guessed. He was already moving when Wallace struck, attempting to brain him.

Having viciously struck nothing but air, Wallace teetered, then started to flail, trying to catch his balance. The tip of his sword caught Richard's left sleeve and ripped.

Already past Wallace, Richard stepped inside the man's guard and, with the hilt of his sword, administered a distinctly ungentle tap to Wallace's head. Even from the other side of the room, Jacqueline heard the *thunk*, then Wallace's eyes rolled up, his limbs went limp, and he collapsed in a heap on the floor.

For an instant, Jacqueline stared at Wallace, then she raised her gaze to Richard.

Her savior.

Panting slightly, he stood looking down at Wallace, his fallen foe. Then, slowly, Richard raised his head and looked at her.

Jacqueline all but flew across the room—flew into the arms that opened and gathered her in. For a split second, she gloried in his warmth and strength, then she pulled back, and her gaze locked on his left forearm. "Oh God—he cut you! There's blood oozing through your sleeve!"

"Hmm?" Richard released her and glanced at the slash. He flexed his arm, then shook his head. "It's barely a flesh wound. It'll stop in a moment." He returned his gaze to her face—to her beloved countenance —and caught her eyes. "Are you all right?"

The only question that mattered.

"Me?" She frowned, her attention diverting once more to his injured forearm. "Yes, of course." Then the true meaning of his question registered, and she looked up and met his eyes. "Nothing happened. You arrived in time."

Then something like wonder stole across her face. Her lips softened; her fascinating blue-green eyes shone. "You came back."

He grunted and looked down at Wallace. "Obviously, I should never have left." He nudged Wallace with the toe of one boot, but the man didn't stir. "I saw his man watching us—me—at the fair yesterday.

Wallace must have set a watch, waiting for me to leave the Hall and ride on before he made his move." He frowned. "To have acted so quickly after I left suggests he was in a hurry."

From the corner of his eye, Richard saw the door carefully opening. He ignored it. He stepped to the side, placed his sword on the table, then he reached for Jacqueline's hands; taking one in each of his, he drew her fully to face him. Away from the crumpled heap that was Wallace.

Standing before her, Richard looked into her face, into her lovely eyes —eyes that were wide and clear and that had always seen him for the man he truly was. He raised first one hand, then the other, to his lips. "I was a fool to leave you—even for a moment. I won't make that mistake again. Because, in the end, I couldn't leave—I didn't truly want to. My heart was, and always will be, with you."

She'd stopped breathing. So had he. Or so it felt.

Time stood still.

Then, lost in her eyes, he drew in a shuddering breath and took the final plunge. "Wallace was correct in stating that I'm no landless gentleman wandering past. My full name is Richard Edward Montague Devries. I'm the second son of the Marquess of Harwich. I'm rich beyond reckoning and stand to inherit more—I have an estate in Lincolnshire and am like to have another in Oxfordshire soon. By all society's standards, I'm overly eligible, but until these last days, in all my years of being on the town, in society, I've found no lady to love. No lady I could love who would return the favor and love me back. I've been a lost soul for years, drifting aimlessly, but when I walked up the Nimway Hall drive and passed into your great hall, I found my anchor. My port in life's storm." He held her gaze and simply said, "I found you. And I hope and pray that you will accept my love and will love me back. Yet regardless of whether you do or not, I am yours, now and for eternity."

Her eyes—those glorious eyes—had filled with tears. Happy tears; he was experienced enough to know that.

Emboldened by the sight, with her hands still clasped in his, he went down on one knee and voiced the question he'd thought he would never want to ask. "Jacqueline Tregarth, will you do me the honor of marrying me?"

Her eyes remained locked with his while, slowly, her lips curved, then she smiled—transcendent joy lighting her face. "Yes, of course—I would be honored to marry you." Her voice was husky with emotion, yet her words rang strong and true. She pressed his fingers. "Not because you are

Lord Richard Devries, well connected, I'm sure, and wealthy beyond compare, but because you are the man I and my people have come to admire and trust, to love and to cherish, and because, today, you turned back and came home and came for me."

"When you need me, I will always be there—I will always stand as your protector."

"And that," Jacqueline said, "is as it should be."

Misty-eyed, she smiled into his eyes, certain to her soul that this— their union—was meant, fated.

Then she pulled on his hands, tugging him up, and he rose. She released his hands, flung her arms about his neck, and lifted her face for his kiss.

Richard didn't think but simply responded to her cue, bent his head, and set his lips to hers.

In a kiss that should have been a mere formality, an acknowledgment of their betrothed state, but which, instead, from the first brush of their lips, blossomed into a physical echo of their vow—burgeoning with promise, passion, and meaning.

With contentment and a profound sense of rightness; all rose in a great, irresistible wave and washed through them. Swamping all relief, replacing all anxiety with the shining prospect of their future.

This is *as it should be.*

The realization thrummed through him, a certainty that struck through his heart and anchored him as nothing else ever had, and as her fingers rose and caressed his cheek and her lips moved beneath his in wordless invitation, he angled his head, parted her lips, and unerringly steered the kiss into deeper waters.

Waters he knew well, but to which she was unaccustomed. Nevertheless, her hand metaphorically in his, she took to the play as one born to the role—the role of being his bride. His wife. His lady.

Eventually, reluctantly, he drew back, if for no other reason than to allow them both to catch their breaths and steady their giddy heads.

When their lips parted and he raised his head, she looked up at him, her customary serenity infused with a golden joy he hoped to see for the rest of his life. Would work for the rest of his life to see.

He looked into her eyes and saw therein the same expectation he felt rising within, a heady sense of anticipation founded on the sure knowledge that they had seized and secured an indescribably precious prize.

A creak and a tentative knock on the doorframe had them both looking that way.

To see the doorway crowded with her men all sporting beaming faces. Clearly, they did not need to explain their new relationship.

Nevertheless, buoyed by a feeling of irresistible pride, Richard turned to face the men, raised Jacqueline's hand, and formally declared, "Your mistress has done me the honor of agreeing to be my wife." He glanced at Jacqueline and caught her eyes. "And I solemnly swear to stand beside the guardian of Nimway Hall for the rest of our lives."

The men cheered, clapped, and slapped backs. There could be no doubt the news was welcome.

Then Crawley led the others in. They bowed to Jacqueline and Richard, then peered inquisitively at the still-slumped and insensible form of Sir Peregrine Wallace.

"Now, that is a sight to behold," Crawley said. "Mr. Hugh always said he was a bad'un."

"So what do we do with him?" Hopkins, along with Ostley, stood staring down at Wallace.

Richard realized that wasn't a straightforward question. Wallace was a neighboring landowner, and, moreover, any charges brought against him would involve the local magistrate, and the news would spread throughout the local area. "I think," he said, his gaze resting on Wallace, "that we should consider carefully the best way to deal with our villain— the way that will suit us best."

"Sir—m'lord." Billy Brakes hovered by the doorway; the boy's use of Richard's title confirmed that the men had, indeed, heard all of Richard's earlier declaration. "Mrs. Pickles—she's the housekeeper here—wants to know if you and Miss Jacqueline would like a pot of tea."

Richard blinked, then looked at Cruickshank.

"The Pickles," Cruickshank explained, "worked as butler and house-keeper for Sir Peregrine's parents. They stayed on, but they've been very unhappy with their young master. They don't approve of his outlandish interests or his association with thugs like Morgan."

Richard glanced at Crawley and Hopkins and arched a brow. "Where is Morgan?"

Hopkins grinned, immensely satisfied. "He and his two friends— meaning Higson, Wallace's valet, and Jenner, the groom—are tied up nice and tight in the stable."

Jacqueline looked at Billy Brakes. "Our thanks to Mrs. Pickles, Billy, and yes, we would like some tea." She looked at Richard. "Obviously, deciding how to deal appropriately with Wallace and his men is going to take some time."

Richard inclined his head. He guided Jacqueline to a small sofa, then waved the men to find what seats they might. "As to that, I rather think…"

~

After considerable discussion, led by Richard and Jacqueline but freely contributed to by the assembled Hall men, with their best way forward defined, all agreed that Richard—Lord Richard—was the most appropriate person to interrogate Wallace.

"I"—Jacqueline glanced at her men, gathered around, then returned her gaze to Richard—"trust you and your instincts to secure the best outcome for Nimway Hall."

The men all rumbled in assent.

Richard inclined his head, accepting the commission; inside, he felt honored by their confidence.

With all decided, they set their stage and elected to rouse Sir Peregrine, still unconscious, via the application of a jug of cold water.

Jacqueline claimed the right to administer the treatment and did so with relish.

Wallace spluttered and coughed, then struggled up on one elbow; they'd left him lying where he'd fallen, slumped in front of a sideboard.

Shaking water from his face, he opened one bleary eye and looked around. Then he shifted, wincing, and dragged himself up to prop his shoulders against the sideboard.

Finally, he squinted at his accusers. They'd moved two armchairs to face him; Richard and Jacqueline sat regally enthroned while the men of the Hall stood in a semicircle around them. All stared in condemnation at Wallace.

Eventually, Wallace brought his gaze to Richard. Weakly, Wallace waved. "Can't I at least sit?" His tone was one step away from a whine.

"No." Richard's tone, in contrast, was adamantine. "We wouldn't want you to get ideas above your station. You surrendered all claim to civilized treatment when you kidnapped Miss Tregarth. Be thankful we haven't tied you up or visited any physical punishment on you. Yet."

Wallace blinked. His expression suggested the reality of his predicament was starting to sink in. His pallor worsened, turning sickly. He focused on Richard. "We're gentlemen, Montague—surely we can come to some...ah, agreement—some arrangement—over this"—he waved weakly—"contretemps."

Jacqueline uttered a derisive sound that made her opinion of Wallace's suggestion clear.

His lips quirking, Richard glanced at her, then looked back at Wallace. He regarded Wallace steadily for long enough to make the worm squirm, then, in contemplative tone, said, "I doubt Miss Tregarth or her people consider your transgressions a mere contretemps." He paused and, voice strengthening, observed, "I know I don't. And, incidentally, the name is Devries. Lord Richard Devries."

Wallace blinked, then his brain caught up with the information, and his eyes widened. He looked at Richard with increasing horror as full realization of the power of the man into whose hands he'd fallen—the man of whom he'd made an enemy—registered. Throughout the length and breadth of England, the name of Devries was synonymous with political and social power.

Richard allowed a cold smile to curve his lips. "Indeed. Now that we understand each other...as to any arrangement, that will depend on how helpful you prove to be. How eager to make appropriate amends."

Now as pale as an over-bleached sheet, Wallace shifted and, in a strangled voice, offered, "Whatever you wish. Anything I can do..."

Unimpressed, Richard sat back and steepled his fingers before his face. "You can start by explaining your connection to Dashwood."

Isolated though Nimway Hall was, Jacqueline and all the Hall men had nevertheless heard of Sir Francis Dashwood, his followers, and their licentious proclivities.

Wallace hurried to comply. Strand by strand, thread by thread, Richard drew out the details of Wallace's association with the notorious libertine. When Wallace recounted his plan to volunteer Nimway Hall as the perfect site for Dashwood's "entertainments"—his Order's orgies—explaining that the Hall's putative connection with Nimue and Merlin, and the orb itself, made the site, in the eyes of such as Wallace and Dashwood, beyond perfect for such use, Wallace effectively rendered Jacqueline and her men speechless.

Although it was the first Richard had heard of Wallace's true motive, his real reason for wanting to gain control of Nimway Hall, Richard wasn't quite so surprised; as soon as Wallace had mentioned Dashwood,

Richard had started to wonder if Wallace's connection with Dashwood—and the Hall's history—was behind Wallace's drive to seize the Hall. And the orb.

That the Hall's site, the orb, and the associated legends had been responsible for Jacqueline, the household, and the Hall itself being targeted by such as Dashwood for defilement was understandably deeply shocking. It was also a call to arms, a threat to which all there—other than Wallace—responded.

Before any of the Hall men could act on that feeling, Richard reasserted control and embarked on an inquisition designed to extract all the incidental information Wallace possessed of Dashwood's activities and of the structure and the members of his Order of the Knights of St. Francis.

While Dashwood skirted the bounds of law-abiding society, his activities were closely watched by those in power. While the others in Wallace's drawing room might not understand the significance of much of what Wallace revealed, Richard did and knew his father and his uncle, the bishop, would be glad of the intelligence.

"Very well." Finally satisfied he'd wrung all he could from Wallace on that topic, Richard moved on to his next stipulation. "The deed to the property north of the Hall estate—Windmill Farm. How did you acquire that?"

Wallace shifted, his gaze falling. "In a card game."

"A game that was rigged to ensure you won?" Richard asked.

Judging by the shifting of Wallace's eyes, he debated lying, but then raised one shoulder. "I needed it to be able to offer assistance to the Hall once the stream ran dry…"

"Indeed." Richard paused, then inquired, "Who did you win the deed from, and what happened to them?"

Wallace mumbled, "It was Percy Lydford. As for what happened to him, I haven't the faintest idea."

When he volunteered nothing more, Crawley growled, "Percy Lydford was a nice young man—local family, as the name suggests. He'd only just come into his inheritance. He wasn't no farmer himself, no more'n his father before him. Merchants of sorts, they were—the farm's always been run by the Wilsons."

"It still is," Wallace somewhat defiantly put in.

"So you preyed on this local young man and cheated him of his inheritance." Richard paused, then observed, "You certainly haven't been endearing yourself to those 'round about, have you?"

When, unsurprisingly, Wallace made no reply, Richard continued, "So where is Percy Lydford now?"

Again, Wallace shrugged.

"Last I heard," Ned Ostley said, "he'd moved to Bath to see what work he could find with the merchants there."

"I see." His gaze resting on Wallace, Richard tapped his chin with his steepled fingers. "I believe, Wallace, that it will be necessary for you to track down Percy Lydford, confess your cheating ways, and offer him cash to the tune of the worth of Windmill Farm."

Wallace frowned.

Imperturbably, Richard went on, "The sum will be determined by Miss Tregarth in consultation with others. In order for you to satisfy me that you have discharged this part of your penance, you will obtain a written statement from Percy Lydford that he has received the stated amount from your hand. I will give you a month to complete that task."

Wallace glanced up.

Before he could make any comment, Richard smoothly rolled on, "And in recompense for the trouble you have caused Miss Tregarth and the household and tenants of Nimway Hall, you will make over the deed to Windmill Farm to Miss Tregarth and the Hall estate. As you so rightly concluded, access to the spring located on that farm will insure the Hall estate against any future water shortages."

Wallace wanted to argue, to protest and refuse, but the reality of Richard's power held him back. After several moments of inner wrestling, Wallace peevishly shrugged. "Easy come, easy go."

"And that, Wallace, is a maxim you would do well to take to heart." Richard kept his tone even, but took a leaf from his father's book and allowed menace to ride just beneath his outwardly urbane surface. "Any further action of any nature whatsoever by you or any associated with you against Miss Tregarth or the Nimway Hall estate will result in a great deal of noise being made about your...tendencies...in the hearing of those guaranteed to make it their business to hunt you down and mete out appropriate punishment. Your morals, of course, will be shown to be questionable, as will your reliability—your ability to keep your counsel and even your word... There won't, I promise you, be any place—any corner, nook, or cranny—left for you in society. Not even in Dashwood's circle."

Wallace read the truth of that threat in Richard's eyes. Slowly, Wallace's face set. Then he sat up, clearly intending to get to his feet.

Instantly, the Hall men tensed, bristling.

Wallace froze, then slowly subsided. In a voice devoid of emotion, he said, "The deed's in my lockbox."

"Which is where?" Richard asked.

"In the study," Wallace sullenly replied.

"Excellent. You and I will repair there, and while you're executing the transfer, which, of course, must be done formally, I'll take sworn statements from your staff and all others in the house to the effect that Miss Tregarth took no harm whatsoever while she traveled in your coach and during the few short minutes she was alone with you here, in the drawing room." Richard smiled. "I'm sure Mrs. Pickles had her ear to the panel and can testify to that."

Richard watched as the very last glimmer of cunning that had lived in Wallace's eyes faded and died, and all fight—all hope—fled.

Satisfied that he'd spiked the last of Wallace's potential weapons, Richard rose. He looked down at Wallace, once again slumped against the sideboard. And finally allowed his contempt to show. "Get on your feet, you cur, and let's make a start on putting everything you disrupted back to rights."

Wallace glanced up, briefly, then he looked down and, somewhat unsteadily, hauled himself to his feet.

Richard waved Wallace to precede him out of the door, through which Hopkins and several of the other men had already gone, no doubt to ensure Wallace had no chance to escape.

After one swift glance at Jacqueline, who responded with a look of outright disgust, Wallace turned to the door and, his feet dragging, went out.

Richard paused to catch Jacqueline's eye. "Do you want to join us?"

She thought, then shook her head. "No. The less I see of him, the better."

Richard nodded. "Leave him to me. Why don't you have another cup of tea? This shouldn't take long."

Jacqueline found herself smiling. "Send in Mrs. Pickles—I'm sure she could do with someone to confide in."

"Good thinking." Richard tipped her a salute and went out.

Jacqueline watched him go, then relaxed into the chair.

She looked inward, assessing, then she smiled and settled to wait for her protector to put all right, and her husband-to-be to return to her.

An hour later, Jacqueline walked by Richard's side through the shrubbery and the adjoining woods to the clearing where they'd left their horses. Behind them, the Hall's men trudged and talked. All, it seemed, were well satisfied with the outcome Richard had wrought.

There would be no scandal, and there would be no further threat—not to her, the Hall, or the orb.

And they'd come away with the deed to Windmill Farm, which appeased the natural demand for recompense, for the villain to pay.

Of particular note, at least to her, was that, amid the crafting and signing over of the deed to the farm, Richard had thought to send one of the lads running to the boys left to mind the horses, dispatching one boy to ride hard for the Hall, bearing news of her rescue, that she was well and unharmed, and that their party would return to the Hall shortly.

She smiled to herself. As she'd already noted, Lord Richard Devries was a thoughtful man.

He was also observant and insightful; he hadn't bothered wasting breath suggesting she ride back to the Hall in Wallace's coach. Just the thought sent a shiver down her spine; she'd hated those moments of being sightless and helpless, rocking away to she'd known not where.

They reached the clearing, and Richard led her to his huge dappled gray, Malcolm the Great. The horse lifted his head and looked around inquiringly. Richard stroked the horse's neck. "You could ride before or behind me."

She smiled. "Before."

He lifted her to the saddle and held her steady while she crooked her knee around the low pommel and arranged her skirts. He released her, glanced around to ensure the other men were mounting up without issue, then set his boot in the stirrup, swung up, and settled across the horse's broad back behind her.

As his arms came around her, caging and protecting her, and he gathered the reins, she felt her smile spontaneously deepen. She felt utterly safe and totally captured at the same time.

Richard walked Malcolm the Great out of the wood. When they reached the lane, and Richard turned north, toward the Hall, and at his urging, the big gelding lengthened his stride, Jacqueline relaxed against the warm chest at her back and, finally, allowed herself to sigh.

With relief, with pleasure, and a sense of going forward. Of finally moving on into the next stage of her life—of having it open up before her.

The steady, heavy clop of the gelding's hooves and the rumbling thunder of her men riding behind underscored the feeling.

When they reached the outskirts of Balesboro Wood, she directed Richard down a narrow bridle path. "It's significantly faster this way."

He softly humphed, his breath wafting her hair. "We'll see."

Sometime later, after he'd instinctively—without any sign whatever from her—taken the correct turning for the Hall, he murmured, "I've noticed that whenever I'm riding with you, I don't get lost—I don't *feel* lost. Not as I did when I first wandered into this wood. And earlier today, when I rode back to the Hall... I didn't think of it then—I was just focused on getting back—but I didn't once take a wrong turn or even pause to think which way to go."

She smiled and made no comment.

They came to another fork in the path. "Don't tell me," he murmured. And, as before, even though it wasn't at all obvious which path was the correct one, he unerringly went the right way.

After a moment, she laid a hand on his sleeve and softly said, "If you don't fight it, you will always find your way back to the Hall."

Richard felt her touch, felt the reality of her observation settle like a benediction on him, and finally, let go.

Of all resistance to the legends of Nimway Hall.

He relaxed and rode on, allowing Malcolm the Great—or whatever was steering him—to find his way, tacking from one bridle path to the next as they passed beneath the towering trees of Balesboro Wood.

And as he'd expected, without let or hindrance, he led their small procession to the door of Nimway Hall.

CHAPTER 11

heir return to the Hall was triumphant, and the news of their betrothal sent the entire household into alt.

Congratulations and good wishes rained down on their heads.

Richard suggested, and Jacqueline readily agreed, that in light of the many who had a right to know the full tale of Wallace's perfidy and the true nature of the threat that had been leveled at Nimway Hall, a general gathering in the great hall was in order.

Everyone leapt on the idea, and summonses were gladly run to the farms and the cottages.

Three hours later, as dusk took hold, all the people of Nimway Hall—men, women, and children—gathered in the great hall.

At Jacqueline's nod, Richard commenced their retelling at the point where, lost in the wood, he'd come across a then-unknown gentleman and his accomplice discussing a diversion of the stream. That information immediately fixed the attention of everyone there. Richard continued, relating Wallace's subsequent offer of water and his attempt to seize the orb—which Jacqueline had, once again, brought down to the great hall and placed on the mantelpiece there for all to see that the Hall's good luck charm was still with them.

Eventually, Jacqueline took up the tale, describing her kidnapping and the gist of her moments with Wallace at his house.

Rumblings among those gathered suggested it was as well that they hadn't sought to bring Wallace back as a prisoner. But then Jacqueline described Richard's arrival and that of the other men, and the consequent vanquishing of Sir Peregrine Wallace and the comprehensive overturning of all his plans, and her eloquent descriptions returned the smiles to every face.

Richard concluded by outlining the penance they had enforced on Wallace and hinted at the retribution that would ensue should Wallace again step over any line with respect to the denizens of the Hall, and relief and resurgent happiness flowed through the assembled crowd.

Then Hugh cleared his throat and, in ringing accents, announced that as Jacqueline's guardian, he was pleased to announce her betrothal to Lord Richard Devries, known to the assembled throng as Richard Montague.

Although the news of their betrothal had already filtered through the crowd, hearing it officially declared as well as learning Richard's family name—one even those in deepest Somerset recognized—set the seal on the resultant celebrations.

As Richard stood beside Jacqueline, a mug of ale in his hand, and smiled and laughed at the many toasts proposed in their name, he felt more at home than he ever had in his life.

Eventually, the celebration wound down, and people headed off to find their beds.

As had become their habit, with the Hall settling into its accustomed peace about them, Richard and Jacqueline were the last to climb the stairs. Tonight, Elinor had gone ahead. Cruickshank, too, had repaired to his room, leaving the great hall already wreathed in shadows.

With only each other to think of, hand in hand, Richard and Jacqueline stepped into the gallery. The single candlestick sat on the side table, waiting to light their way.

In the shaft of moonlight filtering through the gallery windows, Jacqueline paused and studied Richard's face. When he arched his brows, inviting her question, she softly asked, "What made you turn back?"

He held her gaze for a long moment, then in the same quiet tone, replied, "To understand that, you need to know why I left."

She tipped her head, inviting his confidence—confident he would accept.

Lips twisting in faint self-mockery, Richard reached for her hands; he took one in each of his, then met her gaze. "This is my story—the most important parts, the start and the end of my relevant past. Long ago, when I was barely twenty, I almost fell victim to a young lady who had set her sights on my money and my title. That was all she was interested in, but she was skilled at dissembling, and I believed I was in love with her and she with me. I learned my error, but only just in time. From that day forward, I learned to avoid young ladies who showed any interest in me as a husband."

Understanding glimmered in her eyes.

"But it wasn't only that that sent me fleeing from here." Briefly, he recounted the response of the ton's matchmakers to his great-aunt's declaration and described his recent escape from being kidnapped and forced into offering for some lady's hand.

"Good Lord!" Through the shadows, she stared at him. "I would never have imagined a gentleman might be pursued in such a way." She paused, then added, "Exactly as I have been."

Wryly, he inclined his head. "In many ways, my experience of would-be suitors has mirrored yours." After a moment, he went on, "So when you showed interest in me, I…didn't stop to think—I simply reacted. As I invariably have through the years—as I'd long ago learned I must in order to live life as I wished it, by my own choice."

She smiled commiseratingly and gripped his fingers. "I triggered a reaction that was too deeply ingrained for you to shrug aside."

He nodded.

"So what brought you back?"

He held her gaze for an instant, then confessed, "Your wood. It brought me to you, and it turned me back—via a branch to the head."

She blinked, then struggled to keep her lips straight. "Really?"

He grimaced. "Malcolm the Great jibbed and distracted me, and I ran into a branch. I fell from my saddle and was jolted enough to set my wits spinning. When they settled…I realized what I'd done." His eyes found hers through the dimness. "That this time, in you, I had finally found a lady *I* loved, one who might, possibly, love me back. And I saw that I was fleeing from what might prove to be my one and only chance to create the sort of life I truly wanted." Holding her gaze, he raised her fingers to his lips, first one hand, then the other. Then he drew breath and stated, "Finally, I saw things clearly. That a life with you, by your side, is my heart's one true desire."

Jacqueline smiled, letting the emotions welling inside her invest the gesture. "I'm glad you came back. Even had Wallace not seized me, my heart would have sung simply to see you return—I love you so much.

More than I'd imagined could be. And yet with every day that passes and I learn more of you, I only love you more."

He held her gaze, his expression serious, yet filled with hope. "I've heard it said that love is a journey during which one learns more and feels more intensely with every passing season. I pray our love will be like that, forever growing. I'm sure there'll be challenges, yet..."

Her voice clear and strong, she took up the creed. "Yet as long as we're together—meeting life side by side—come what may, as we did today, we'll meet every challenge and triumph."

His lips curved. He raised one of her hands and pressed a lingering kiss to her knuckles. "Come what may. Into the future as lord and lady, side by side."

Eagerness unfurled inside her. She curled her fingers and gripped his. Holding his gaze, she let her certainty speak for her. "Our future, my lord, starts now. Tonight."

He searched her eyes as if to confirm her meaning. When she only looked more eager, his lips curved, then he murmured, "I feel compelled to ask—are you sure?"

"Yes." Her voice had grown husky, her tone sultry. Allowing her expression to underscore her answer, she released one of his hands and, still gripping the other, her eyes locked with his, tugged and stepped toward her door. "Come."

For a second longer, Richard searched her eyes, her face, then he leaned to the side, blew out the candle, and went—finally, after all his years of resisting, he surrendered and followed an unmarried young lady into her bedchamber.

There, the moonlight fell in soft swaths across the polished boards, reaching to shed a gentle radiance upon and about her bed.

He closed the door behind him and heard the latch click. Signaling, for him, an end and also a beginning.

Jacqueline walked to the clear space before the bed; when she halted and swung to face him, the moonlight paid homage to her beauty.

As he walked toward her, he catalogued anew the silver gilt of her hair, the delicate lines of her features. Her eyes, those glorious eyes that had fascinated him from the first, that had reached into him—to his soul —and touched, caressed, were wreathed in shadows and mystery.

He halted before her, and she tilted her head. Then she stretched up, her hands rising to his shoulders as he grasped her waist and drew her nearer. Drew her to him. She came up on her toes as he bent his head, and their lips met.

In a kiss of exultation. Of triumph.

Their lips melded and matched, then he traced her lower lip with the tip of his tongue, and she opened for him. Bold and confident, he slid his tongue between the soft contours and settled to explore. To learn and to entice, to engage her senses.

She followed eagerly, with an innocent abandon—an implicit trust—that touched and tamed him. That gave him the strength to ignore the primitive urge her transparent surrender evoked and, instead, devote himself to her pleasure. To ensuring it above all else.

Jacqueline found her wits whirling and inwardly marveled. So this was what giddy delight felt like.

Assiduously, she set herself to follow his lead, eager to learn the paths, to explore any and all byways.

Along the road to passion. To the fulfillment of their desires.

There was no impediment. This was meant to be. She'd waited for years for him to come to her, and now that he was there, acknowledged as her betrothed before her people, accepted by all, she was eager to take the next step—to pass through the veil of sensual innocence and explore what lay beyond.

With him. In truth, she couldn't imagine taking this path if it wasn't him in whose arms she stood. He was the key to unlocking the door of passion for her.

When his hands shifted, palms and fingers gliding over her curves, up to feather over her bodice, over the swells of her breasts, setting the sensitive skin exposed above her neckline prickling, she caught her breath on a rush of desire.

She knew it was desire, that anticipation that sharpened her senses and set her nerves on edge. That triggered the compulsion to kiss him more fiercely, to return his escalating ardor in full measure. His palms settled over her breasts, and her breath suspended. His hands weighed, then his fingers shifted and firmed, seeking and finding the tightened buds of her nipples beneath the fine brocade of her bodice. His fingertips gripped, squeezed—dexterous and deliberate—and sensation streaked through her, and she gasped through the kiss.

Immediately, he soothed her, drew back, and let her sparking nerves relax, but when, wordlessly through their kiss, she pushed for more, he repeated the exercise, his touch, this time, more forceful, the result commensurately more potent.

Within seconds, she felt drunk—drunk on the pleasurable sensations his clever fingers evoked and stoked.

Richard couldn't get enough of the woman in his arms. A goddess who was his and his alone to worship, to his senses, she personified all he desired. Her lips moving beneath his entranced and captivated; the delights of the succulent haven of her mouth lured him in and trapped him. In that moment, he knew nothing more than his flaring need to be her lover, to make her his and give himself to her.

To that end, he set about educating her senses and appeasing his own.

The firm curves of her breasts, even shielded by the fabric of her bodice, filled his hands as if sculpted exclusively for him. Her response to even the lightest of caresses spurred him on.

Spurred him to send one hand sliding down, over her stomach, over her hip, to caress the globes of her derriere, smoothing and molding the silks of her gown, learning the shape, tracing the curves, then splaying his hand and possessing.

Beneath his other palm, her heart leapt; so did his as he drew her nearer, angling her hips to his. Wanting her to sense all she did to him, to know and understand.

Her hands slid to frame his face; she gripped, holding him to the kiss as his tongue plundered and his hands closed and held, then he eased his grip and, with both hands, gently kneaded, and she made a soft sound in her throat.

Under the circumstances, disrobing wasn't an act to be hurried. There was no need to rush. Unlacing her bodice took time and skill. When he tugged the last lace free and the material sagged, she drew back from the kiss—pushed back.

Curious, he allowed it. Watched as, her lips swollen, her fine skin faintly flushed, her expression passion-blank, she swiftly stripped the sleeves from her arms, then tossed the embroidered bodice away.

Leaving only the fine ivory silk of her chemise to screen her breasts from his hungry gaze.

His fingers had already shifted to the laces securing her skirt and petticoats. Impatient, she waited only until he'd unpicked the knots before she eased out the drawstring and wriggled and pushed both skirts and petticoats down her legs.

Her long, slender, shapely legs.

His mouth watered, but then she stepped from the mound of silk and linen directly to him, and with her luscious lips now firm, she grasped the sides of his coat, spread them wide, and tried to push the coat off his shoulders.

He chuckled and obliged, shedding the garment. By the time he'd drawn his arms from the sleeves, letting the coat crumple to the floor behind him, she was working her way down the large mother-of-pearl buttons of his waistcoat.

Jacqueline was determined to get her hands on the wide muscles of his chest. Determined to see what, to that point, she'd only imagined and feast her eyes on him. Although the night air was cool, warmth had risen beneath her skin, a delicious flush that left her breathless and hungry for more, eager to find the ways to fan the flames higher, to wallow and burn.

On walking into the room, she'd set aside all inhibitions, knowing beyond question that instinct, and he, would guide her. Now, instinct assured her that her most urgent and immediate needs would be met once she'd rid him of his clothes. She applied herself to that task with unrestrained fervor.

His lips curved; he seemed faintly amused, but also approving as he shrugged out of his waistcoat. She unraveled the knot of his cravat, dragged the long length from about his throat, and flung it aside, then focused on the ties of his shirt; she had them undone in seconds, then he stepped back and drew the billowing linen off over his head.

She barely waited until he straightened to set her hands, fingers splayed, to his chest. To the wondrous expanse of taut skin stretched over hard muscle. To the crinkly dark hair that adorned the splendor. Heat and welcoming warmth reached for her; sweeping her hands across his torso, she exalted and filled her senses. Her lids lowered as she drank in the reality, and his arms slowly closed about her, drawing her in, drawing her to him.

Richard quelled a shudder provoked by her questing touch and compounded by the evocative caress of her silk chemise over his bare chest. Those sensory delights were followed by the firm pressure of her breasts, screened by that single, flimsy layer. Torture of a sort, a suggestive, seductive teasing of his senses. Instinctively, she moved against him, side to side, settling, then pressing closer yet as she lifted her face—and he bent his head, found her lips with his, and whirled them and their now-clamoring senses back into the sensual fire.

The flames rose, desire fanning the embers of passion into a blaze, then into an all-consuming conflagration.

She was country-born; unlike naive, town-born innocents, she knew what was to follow. More, she was increasingly explicit in her eagerness to embrace the experience. Her lips and tongue engaged with his, flagrantly demanding. Her hands caressed, blatantly explored, then gripped and urged him on.

His control grew thin as her hot, greedy hands reached between them and closed about his iron-hard staff.

Possessing. Wanting.

Needing.

They turned to the bed. Her chemise floated to the floor. With all modesty long gone, between them, they dispensed with his boots and breeches and, in a heated breathless rush, fell onto the sheets.

Hands reached and found, and they drew each other closer, rolling body to body. Skin met naked skin—and a jolt of pure sensation lanced through them both.

Beneath him, she stilled, eyes closed, her breath, soft pants, washing over his cheek.

His body—his every muscle—tensed as he held against the roar of his instincts.

Then her hands clutched again, and her lips found his, and he fell into her kiss, into the moment—into the passion that rose and rushed through them and swept them into the age-old dance.

Jacqueline's senses had imploded the instant their naked bodies had met, skin to skin. As if the sensual impact had been too great for her mind to encompass—not in that instant, not at first. Yet within seconds, her mind had caught up, and now, the rest of the world fell away as sensation flooded her, overwhelming her wits, tightening her nerves, and smothering her senses. Taking them—and her—over.

She gasped and clung, then flung herself headlong into the fire, into the beckoning cornucopia of sensual delights. She caught his lips with hers and kissed him ferociously, returning his ardent kiss with one even more fiery. She swallowed a moan as his palm, slightly roughened, closed about one breast. He kneaded, the possessive act underscored by his heavy body lying over hers, his weight pinning her to the sheet. Then, with his fingertips, he circled her nipple, teasing her senses; in wordless reaction, she sank her fingertips into the long muscles of his back, and he closed his fingers about her aching nipple—tight, tighter—and she arched beneath him as fire lanced through her, streaking down her veins to pool deep, a glowing furnace at her core.

She stroked his back, glorying in the long planes, the pliable, powerful strength of him. She reached farther, her fingertips skating over the upper swells of his buttocks.

He shifted and repeated his previous ministrations on her other breast —reducing her to wantonly writhing, breath bated, her heart thudding to an escalating rhythm.

A rhythm of want and need that only built as, between them, desire rose, a tangible entity, and stretched and flexed its claws.

It gripped, hard, and drove them on.

Her legs tangled with his. Driven to sensual distraction by the abrasion of her already sensitized skin by the wiry hair that dusted his, she arched and shifted and pressed herself to him, using her limbs to slide and stroke and caress.

With passion swelling, her skin feeling stretched and taut with need, she focused what little wit she had left to making him as desperate as she.

The rigid rod of his erection was pressed like a burning brand to her hip; she reached down, found the fine-skinned, silky head, and with the tips of her fingers, circled the flared rim. Then she reached farther, closed her fingers about the steely length, and stroked.

From the sudden tension that streaked through him, she sensed that she'd succeeded in capturing his attention.

Emboldened, she played, and he let her. Gradually, he returned to his own agenda, with increasingly explicit caresses playing on her senses and orchestrating a symphony of pleasure that steadily, caress by caress, built toward a crescendo.

The flames rose between them, more urgent, more potent than before as desire soared and whipped them on. With breathless, gasping murmurs, both directing and imploring, with touches and caresses both gentle and firm, wanting, hungry, and consumed by need, they forged on.

With deft, experienced touches, Richard built her desire and fanned her passions and readied her. She writhed beneath him, clutched, encouraged, flagrantly demanded, and ultimately, opened for him. Flowered for him.

The petals guarding her entrance were swollen and slick. Her honey scalded his probing fingers, stealing his breath, sending his need soaring. The pearl of her passion throbbed, tense and tight beneath its hood, begging for his touch. With one fingertip, he circled it and felt her nerves leap. He stroked, and she bowed beneath him, and a strangled moan escaped her lips.

He parted her folds and pushed one long finger deep.

She clutched and held him with a desperation to rival his own.

He refocused on their kiss, plundering evocatively, recapturing her attention, then he stroked, and beneath him, she trembled and quaked.

Jacqueline wanted him inside her with a certainty impossible to mistake and with a fervor impossible to deny, to hold back from.

She gripped, tugged, pulled back from the all-consuming kiss long enough to whisper, "Now. *Please...*"

Instantly, he moved over her, his heavy legs parting hers, his hips settling between her spread thighs. She felt the smooth head of his erection part her folds, and she tipped her head back into the pillow as expectation gripped, but then he recaptured her lips, kissed her with utterly rapacious ferocity, and ripped her senses and wits away.

With one sharp thrust, he breached her. The pain was nothing more than a brief sting, then the sudden intrusion of his body into hers swamped her mind. Heavy and alien, yet oh-so-welcome, his erection stretched her and impressed the reality of their joining on her body, on her senses, in myriad ways. He'd frozen, head bowed, the muscles of his arms locked and quivering as he held his chest above hers, giving her time to absorb and accept the undeniably novel, elementally intimate sensations.

Then, powerful and sure, he forged deeper.

Barely clinging to sanity—when had joining with a woman ever been this intense?—Richard eased the hold he'd clamped upon his most primal urges and nudged deeper yet, into the molten embrace of her body, forging in until he was sheathed to the hilt. Until she'd taken all of him and held him deep within her.

Then he showed her how to dance, how to drive their senses on. She was an avidly eager pupil; all too soon, she was demanding he dispense with every last rein and allow passion to have its way. To, between them, let desire hold uncontested sway and, unrestrained, whip them on and up passion's peak until...with their skins slick and burning, their hands locked, fingers clutching, with eyes closed, with her breath coming in sharp pants and him with his head bowed, chest heaving, their bodies merged to an unrelenting beat in the last desperate rush toward completion.

And then they were there.

Ecstasy struck, the tension gripping them snapped, and they were flung into the void.

Their senses fractured—shattered, fragmented. Glory rained upon them and flared inside, scintillatingly brilliant and bright. Senses awash, overloaded, they clung to each other as ecstasy's starburst blinded their minds.

Leaving one shining truth illuminated—clear to their senses, obvious to their minds, and anchored in their souls.

Linking them, fusing them, binding them for all time.

Gradually, the brilliance faded, and a different type of pleasure rolled in. Filling them, buoying them, soothing their senses.

Steeping them in its indescribable beauty before letting oblivion take them.

Eventually, the possibility that he was crushing the lady he had vowed to protect penetrated Richard's mind. Wracked more profoundly than he could ever remember being, he stirred and raised his head enough to look down at her face.

Her features were relaxed, but a faint smile—a richly satiated expression—curved her lips.

He softly humphed, yet the sight sent smug satisfaction flowing through him. He dipped his head, brushed his lips across hers, then lifted from her.

She stirred and made a protesting sound that cut off when he settled in the bed beside her.

Despite the loss of Richard's oddly comforting weight, Jacqueline remained enfolded by, engulfed in, a blissful warmth unlike anything she'd ever known could be. Pleasure still coursed beneath her skin; her senses seemed to glow, her nerves were softly humming, and satiation flowed like the very finest wine through her veins.

She'd had no idea it was possible to feel so thoroughly and deeply pleasured, much less so completely possessed. Nor to feel so certain that, in return, she'd pleasured and possessed him to the same degree.

The sensations of when they'd joined still echoed through her mind. The mutuality of the giving and taking, the true meaning of being intimate, had been so much more powerful than she'd imagined.

Content didn't come close to what she felt. Euphoric, buoyed by a sense of rightness so profound there were no appropriate words with which to do it justice.

Him and her—together was how he and she were meant to be. Their joining that night had been the next step along their road. Their futures were one, their paths forward the same, irrevocably intertwined. Their fates were merged, now and forever, two halves of the one coin.

She lay amid the rumpled sheets and dwelled on the prospect with quiet joy.

Richard reached down and flicked the sheet free, then drew it over them. They settled; he raised his arm, and Jacqueline shifted to lay her head on his chest—but the moon had drifted farther on its arc, and the silvery light slanting through the window struck her full in the face.

"Hmm." Eyes closed tightly against the glare, she frowned.

He smiled and nudged her. "Turn around."

She did, and he followed, spooning his larger body around the soft curves of hers. She chuckled, then sighed deeply; he felt her muscles relax.

As, still smiling, he settled his head on the pillow behind hers, he noticed a mark on the back of her left shoulder, now illuminated by the moonlight.

Gently, he touched the spot. "You have a birthmark—just here."

"Hmm? Oh, that. Yes, I know." She snuggled deeper into the mattress. "It's always been there."

Her skin was like fine porcelain; even though the mark wasn't that dark, it stood out in stark relief.

Fascinated, he traced the outline with one fingertip. Then, struck by the coincidence, he glanced across the room—at the orb sitting, once more, on her dressing table.

He stilled, staring, then murmured, "The orb. Did you have someone bring it up again?" She couldn't have brought it upstairs herself; he'd been with her from the moment she'd placed the orb on the mantelpiece in the great hall.

"No—why?" Then he felt her stiffen. Clearly, she'd opened her eyes, looked across the room, and seen what he had. "Oh." The exclamation fell softly from her lips. "There it is."

After a moment, her voice a bare whisper, she confirmed what he'd suspected. "I didn't ask anyone to bring it upstairs but…perhaps one of the maids saw it when they were clearing the hall and realized I would rather keep it here, safe, and so she brought it up." After an instant's pause, she stated, "That's what must have happened."

His "Presumably" was distinctly dry.

For half a minute, he stared at the orb—glowing with nothing more than the radiance one might expect from the moonlight caressing it—then he looked back at her birthmark. Took in the lines, the shape, once again. He hesitated, then told her, "Your birthmark is the same shape as the orb."

She stiffened rather more, then she twisted her head and looked over her shoulder. She met his eyes and searched them, confirming he wasn't inventing anything. Her lips parted on a silent exhalation. Then in a wondering tone, she said, "I've never truly seen the mark—well, even with a hand mirror, with the angle, it's just a roundish blob to me."

"It's definitely the orb." He traced the outline again. "The moonstone, its upper curve surrounded by the jagged tips of the claws, with the ornate base beneath."

She nodded fractionally, then faced forward. After several silent seconds, she relaxed into the mattress again. "I suppose that means the orb belongs to me, and I belong with it—here."

He couldn't—didn't wish to—add anything to that. He hesitated for a heartbeat, then bent his head and placed a soft kiss on the mark before lowering his head to the pillow.

A moment later, he drew her closer, cradling her back to his chest. She sighed and relaxed even more. He closed his eyes and felt sleep creep nearer.

Tomorrow, he knew, neither he nor she would mention the reappearance of the orb in her chamber. They wouldn't ask who had moved it; they wouldn't do anything to call attention to it moving.

As far as he was concerned, and he felt sure she would agree, the orb and its strange abilities was one mystery that could remain unsolved.

The orb was where it was meant to be—there, and therefore safe—and that was all he and she needed to know.

CHAPTER 12

*T*hey were married in July, with the fields green, Balesboro Wood in full leaf, and the summer sun beaming in benediction.

The ceremony was celebrated in the household chapel by no less an august personage than the Bishop of Bath and Wells. His Grace had insisted, claiming it as his right given Richard had been on his way to visit him when Cupid had struck.

That Cupid had struck was evident to all.

When, gowned in ivory silk trimmed with summer green, a circlet of white rosebuds atop her upswept hair, Jacqueline stepped into the chapel with Freddie steering Hugh in his chair beside her, the chamber was packed. People stood shoulder to shoulder on either side, all the way to the walls, leaving only a central aisle running from the door to the altar for her and her companions to pace down.

To her right, she saw her people—all the Hall's household and the tenant farmers and their families—as well as their closest neighbors all smiling fit to burst; the men bowed their heads and the women bobbed curtsies, and she beamed upon them all.

As the harpsichordist labored and the music swelled, she looked ahead, down the aisle—to where Richard, resplendent in a perfectly cut blue coat, waited. Watching. Her smile deepened with love, and she stepped out, walking with all due sobriety to his side; inside, she felt like dancing with joy, but that wouldn't do—not there, not yet.

The press of people to her left was comprised of Richard's family—

which had proved to be quite enormous—as well as several of his friends from London. His friends she'd met, but she'd yet to meet all his relatives.

Of those she had met... She hadn't been sure how his noble family would react to the news that Lord Richard Devries had chosen to ally himself with a relative nonentity who lived buried in deepest Somerset. She'd anticipated some degree of disapproval, possibly even discouragement, although Richard had smiled and assured her it wouldn't be so and that his entire family would welcome her with open arms.

He'd been right, but for reasons that, she suspected, were not quite as he'd imagined.

Nevertheless, as she walked forward to join him before the altar, she sensed the wave of sincere goodwill that rolled toward her from his side of the church.

She halted at the step before the altar, by Richard's side.

The bishop smiled benevolently upon her, then commenced the service. The formal phrases rolled through the hushed chapel, sonorous and solemn. Both Richard and she responded to the age-old questions, stating "I do" in calm, clear voices, then the bishop turned and asked Hugh whether he gave her into Richard's keeping.

After a snuffling huff, Hugh growled that he did.

Her smile one of burgeoning joy, she turned to Richard and formally bestowed her hand on him, placing her fingers across his offered palm.

The bishop beamed and continued.

Held by the love in Richard's eyes, anchored by his touch, she listened as he spoke his vows, his deep voice laden with commitment, with love and pride and hope, and she spoke her complementary vows in a clear voice that rang through the chapel.

Richard's heart swelled as his uncle pronounced them man and wife. Some of his friends at the rear of the chapel sent up a cheer—they knew of his long fight against falling victim to a marriage devoid of love, so in their eyes, this figured as his victory—then others among those on the other side of the church added their voices to the chorus.

The bishop—still smiling—looked out on his rowdy congregation, laughed, then nodded to Richard and Jacqueline. In an encouraging tone, His Grace suggested they make it official and that Richard really ought to kiss his bride.

He waited for no further invitation, but drew her into his arms. She raised her face and lifted her eyes to his. Love and more shone in their depths.

He bent his head, set his lips to hers, and felt a swell of joy rush at them from all around, a wave of emotion that surrounded him and her and held them, cradled and secure—as if Nimway Hall itself was bestowing its blessing.

Caught by a sense of fated rightness, Jacqueline kissed her husband, and he kissed her, and distantly, faint and low, at the very edge of awareness, she heard voices chanting. Not in song, not as angels might, but in the cool measured tones…of a spell?

When Richard raised his head, she opened her eyes and saw his were slightly widened; he'd heard that unearthly benediction, too.

Their gazes collided and locked, and acceptance flashed between them, then, simultaneously, they smiled, and joy suffused them.

Together, they turned and, smiling radiantly, stepped forward as man and wife to face their world.

Their well-wishers poured in from all sides, engulfing them. Congratulations were called, Richard's hand was wrung, and Jacqueline's cheek was kissed times beyond number.

Eventually, Richard's mother, a lady none present would dare gainsay, aided by Hugh and Freddie, Elinor, Cruickshank, and Mrs. Patrick, succeeded in moving the crowd down the stairs to the great hall below.

Jacqueline had barely glimpsed the preparations—she'd been banished by general decree. Now, she discovered that the hall had been draped in summer flowers and green branches, a rose-draped, leafy bower forming an arch above where she and Richard were instructed to sit, behind a table raised on the rarely used dais set before the fireplace.

Then the wedding breakfast began.

Succulent roasted meats, fishes and fowls in aspic, vegetables of all descriptions prepared in myriad ways. Pastries, breads, pies with intricately woven lids and rich, gravy-filled interiors. Haunches of venison and several stuffed pigs. All were carried in on heaped platters and were promptly devoured. Later came cheeses, nuts, and fruits in compotes, tarts, and syllabubs, each course accompanied by wine and ale.

Those in charge of the Hall's kitchen as well as the kitchens of the farms had, apparently, run amok.

Speeches and toasts punctuated the courses, and laughter echoed from the coffered ceiling.

Later, once the covers were drawn, Jacqueline moved around the room, thanking all those she knew must have contributed to the amazing feast. If she hadn't known her people, she might have thought they'd put on the show to impress their highborn guests. Instead, she wasn't surprised when Mrs. Patrick confided, "We don't see this often—our guardian being wed. Once or twice in a lifetime, if we're lucky. So we were all determined to make the most of it." The housekeeper grinned. "And we did!"

Jacqueline laughed and turned to find Richard beside her. He'd heard, and smiling as widely as she was, he nodded his thanks to Mrs. Patrick. "You and all those who helped have done Nimway Hall proud."

After parting from the delighted housekeeper, Jacqueline glanced up and met Richard's eyes. "You're very good at that—knowing just what to say."

Pleased, he shrugged. And steered her on to a group of his friends, who, he informed her, she ought to thank for aiding him to escape the last violent attempt on his honor, thus allowing him to flee London and subsequently find his way there. "To Balesboro Wood and Nimway Hall and you."

Their eyes met, love and a connection born of the partnership they'd already forged shining, then they looked ahead, and she said, "I do, indeed, owe your friends my heartfelt thanks."

Smiling, she looped her arm in his and set off to speak with the friends in question.

She was now entirely at ease among his set—family, connections, friends, and all—thanks, in large part, to his mother.

A formidable lady of determined character, the Marchioness of Harwich had arrived within a week of Richard dispatching to his parents' Essex home the news of his betrothal. Not having anticipated such a rapid response, Richard had ridden to Wells to speak with his uncle, and Jacqueline had been busy in the kitchen garden when she'd been summoned with the news that a grand carriage had come bowling up the drive. Consequently, she'd found herself meeting her prospective mother-in-law with her sleeves rolled up and, it had turned out, a smudge on her cheek.

Realizing at the last minute—as she'd walked into the great hall—who her unexpected visitor must be, she'd frozen, uncertain.

The marchioness had turned from studying the coat of arms above the mantelpiece, taken one long look at her, then arched a finely drawn brow. "Blood turnip?"

Jacqueline had blinked. "I was just pulling some, yes." She'd frowned. "How did you know?"

The marchioness had pointed. "That smudge on your cheek. Not the right color for blood, really, and it's the season, isn't it? I pulled our first crop a few days before I left."

Stunned, Jacqueline had stared. "You garden? Yourself?"

The marchioness had grinned. "Why, yes. It gets me out of the house and away from all those wanting me to make decisions." Her hazel eyes, very like Richard's, had twinkled. "I run away and hide amid the vegetables whenever my steward gets too pushy."

That had been the start of a relationship the like of which Jacqueline had never imagined. She'd learned that, with Richard's father so deeply mired in running the country and therefore often absent from home, his mother ran the family's vast estates, much as Jacqueline ran the Hall. They'd bonded over that and over Richard.

After a day of observing Jacqueline and her son, as Jacqueline and the marchioness had strolled around the lake, the marchioness had confided, "The truth is, my dear, that while Richard enjoys the puzzle of understanding people and identifying what drives them—an innocent yet highly useful skill for any of our station, and one both I and my husband have encouraged and at which Richard quite excels—the one person he, time and again, fails woefully to correctly perceive, especially as to what drives him, is, of course, himself."

The marchioness had met Jacqueline's eyes, the comprehension of a mother very clear in hers. "He needs to be needed, you see. Not just in the simple sense, but for all he can give. You"—the marchioness had looked ahead and waved at the house, then toward the fields on the Levels below—"and all this, all that is Nimway Hall, have offered him that—a position that will take and use all he has to offer—and for that, my dear, you have my eternal gratitude."

In similar vein, when Richard's father had arrived, only the day before the wedding, he'd beamed delightedly at Jacqueline, patted her hand in avuncular fashion, and thanked her most sincerely for giving his second son the right sort of place to put down his roots.

Richard's great-aunt Dulcimea—she who had recently declared him her heir—had been even more forthright, declaring to Jacqueline in the strident tones of one partially deaf that the entire family was simply thrilled that their wandering sheep had finally found a home with a loving wife who wasn't averse to putting him to use.

Overhearing the comment, the marchioness had added that, indeed, Jacqueline should not be backward in requesting aid of the wider Devries family whenever required. "There have to be some benefits to my husband being forever at court."

To the household's and those on the wider estate's abiding surprise, Richard's family and friends had proved to be as easygoing and lacking in arrogance as he. His cousins had ridden out with Richard to help when Higgs had lost a fence, and when Richard had mentioned to his friends his idea of linking the lake to the stream via a series of ponds fitted with sluice gates, the group had declared that, before they departed, they would construct the system as a wedding gift, not just for Richard and Jacqueline but for Nimway Hall.

Everyone who had come for their wedding had been prepared to enjoy themselves and had.

Then the musicians in the gallery started playing, and the dancing began, raising the level of enjoyment yet another notch.

At one point, when Jacqueline had insisted she needed a moment to catch her breath, Richard found them glasses of punch, then steered her to where Crawley, Hopkins, and Ned Ostley were gathered in one corner of the hall.

The three men beamed and bobbed, then Ostley said, "I heard tell that Wallace closed up the Lydford house, and they say he's fled the country."

"That's excellent news." Richard smiled and raised his glass to the men. "So he won't be hanging around like an evil spirit waiting to cast a shadow over the Hall's future."

"I'll drink to that," Crawley growled, and Hopkins nodded.

Jacqueline simply continued to smile.

But when they moved away from the trio, she paused by the wall, looked out at the crowd, then glanced at Richard, who had halted beside her. "You suspected Wallace would leave the country, didn't you? That's why you didn't push more decisively to be rid of him."

He didn't try to hide his satisfaction. "It occurred to me that with friends like Dashwood, getting rid of Wallace wouldn't need further action from me. Having disappointed his mentor, had he remained, Wallace's life—at least in his eyes—would have been worthless. On the Continent, as a gentleman not well known, he might, perhaps, start afresh." He shrugged and met her eyes. "I didn't need to do more."

She studied his face, then smiled. "In personality, you seem more like your mother, but you do have some of your father's traits."

His lips twitched, but he humphed and steered her on.

Eventually, the sun slid down the western sky, and the fading light prompted the estate families and their neighbors to reluctantly take their leave.

They were followed soon after by the bulk of Richard's relatives and friends. Some were putting up at nearby inns before journeying on; others, like his great-aunt Dulcimea, were traveling back to Wells with the bishop.

Only his parents and his two closest friends were remaining at Nimway Hall, and as Richard and Jacqueline walked out with those departing, those remaining few beat a considerate retreat, leaving the great hall to the ministrations of the staff. Elinor and Hugh, escorted by Freddie, had retired earlier, all three worn out by their efforts and the unaccustomed excitement.

That left Jacqueline and Richard, once they'd waved their guests away, to turn and, hand in hand, cross the threshold and walk into the welcoming shadows of Nimway Hall effectively alone.

With smiles and thank-yous to the staff busily setting the great hall to rights, Richard led Jacqueline to the stairs. Her hand in his, feeling the strange peace of the household, that from the very first, had touched him, enfold them again, he ascended the long flight beside her. When they stepped into the gallery, he paused, and when she faced him, brows rising in query, he raised her hand to his lips and kissed the backs of her slender fingers. Holding her brilliantly shining blue-green gaze, he smiled. "I understand we have new quarters."

Since their betrothal, they'd been sharing her chamber, but he'd heard whispers and had seen Hugh, Elinor, Cruickshank, and Mrs. Patrick conferring, then the maids scurrying hither and yon on the first floor.

Jacqueline's smile—an expression of serene joy that hadn't left her face all day—brightened. "Yes, indeed." Her fingers curled about his, and she tugged. "It's this way."

She led him along a corridor into a wing down which he hadn't previously ventured. She halted before the door at its end. "This has always been the chamber of the guardian and her husband, at least in our memory." She released his hand, opened the door, and walked inside.

Richard followed. He looked around, then closed the door and walked forward to join her where she'd paused a few paces inside the door. The chamber spread to either side, spanning the width of the wing. To his right stood a massive four-poster bed hung with heavy brocade curtains presently looped back to display a thick featherbed covered with silk sheets beneath a silk-brocade counterpane. A small mountain of lace-trimmed pillows was temptingly piled at the head of the bed.

Armoires in dark wood and clothes chests were set against the walls, along with Jacqueline's dressing table, with the orb placed as Richard had last seen it, to one side of the central mirror. For a wonder, the orb hadn't been taken downstairs for the day but had, as far as he knew, remained on this level; presumably the maids had brought it there when the footmen had carried Jacqueline's dressing table in.

He glanced to his left, to where two armchairs, each with its own foot-stool, were angled before the hearth, with cushions in the same brocade as on the bed; the arrangement suggested gentle moments of relaxing exchanges, personal moments of sharing.

Jacqueline had drifted across the room. Richard raised his gaze. The chamber filled the end of the wing, and wide windows were set in all three outer walls. The window to his right looked out over the side lawn to the arm of Balesboro Wood that protected the house to the east. The window directly ahead looked toward the lake, while the window to the left framed a vista to the west, encompassing a wide view of the edge of the escarpment and the fields and farms stretching away on the Levels below. On the horizon to the northwest stood the singular outline of Glastonbury Tor.

It was to that third window that Jacqueline had gone, drawn, no doubt, to the view of her lands. He was still coming to grips with the ineffable connection she, as guardian, felt toward both lands and people, to the Hall itself, and the wood as well, and the purpose that connection bestowed was something he had already come to value.

He halted behind her and looked over her head at the lands he would help her protect. He reached forward, slid his hands about her waist, and drew her back against him. She relaxed into his hold. He bent his head and pressed a soft kiss to her temple. His voice low, he said, "My mother told me that this is my place—to stand here, beside and behind you as the husband of the guardian of Nimway Hall. I gather you explained your position to her."

Jacqueline gave a ladylike snort. "I didn't have to explain anything—she saw, listened, and learned. Your mother is an exceedingly astute lady."

He grinned. "True." He sobered. "But she was right. I feel it. To my bones, I know that this is where I was always destined to be. Marriage to any other was never in my cards. I had to find my way to your side to find my future." He pressed another kiss to her curls. "Because you embody that future, and you always will."

Jacqueline reached up with one hand and stroked his cheek. "Sweet words, husband."

"For you, always, my one and only wife."

She sighed, giving sound to the happiness that filled her soul. She turned in his hold and looked into his face, a face she'd already grown used to seeing every night and every morning and for a good part of every day. She met his gaze, then allowed a smile that held all her love to light her face. "There are no fine words I can give you in return, for there simply are no words sufficient to the task of encompassing all I feel for you. All that I see and value in you. I know you will be my and Nimway Hall's defender for the rest of your days."

His lips curved, his hazel eyes shining, affirming that truth. "I love you beyond life itself. You who have given me the life I need to live." His eyes held hers, his voice deepening as he said, "If you weren't in my life, I would be running still, evading the snares." His lips twisted wryly. "If Balesboro Wood hadn't rendered me lost—as the power inhabiting it definitely did—I wouldn't have found my way to your side. To life and love and a future filled with promise." He arched his brows. "I have to admit I don't know what to make of that. Bale means an evil force, yet for me and, I hope, for you and Nimway Hall, my getting lost in Balesboro Wood has brought nothing but good."

She tipped her head, her eyes locked with his. "Beyond the boundaries of Nimway Hall, the local people have always been suspicious and wary of…things not readily explained."

He nodded. "I have to wonder if this is one of those instances, and they used the term 'bale' as the only one they knew for an old and powerful force, despite that force not being evil."

She lightly shrugged. She studied his eyes, then softly said, "There's no point thinking too much about such things—we're not supposed to know. Life and love are abiding mysteries and will remain so, no matter the striving of mortal men."

Richard's arms were firm about her. He held her gaze, then let his lips quirk upward. "Is that your way of suggesting we've spoken enough of what led us to this point?"

She laughed. "Indeed." Over his shoulder, she scanned the room. "The household worked hard to refurnish this chamber—they polished and cleaned and painted so that all was made new for us. It's their wedding gift, intending this to be the one place that's solely ours for the rest of our days." Her gaze returned to his face, and her lips lifted, a seductively teasing light twinkling in her eyes. "I believe it's incumbent on us to appropriately lay claim to it."

He laughed and swept her into his arms. He whirled her about, then made for the bed.

They fell onto the brocade coverlet. With laughter and smiles and joyous abandon, they shed their clothes, then fell on each other—fell into each other, both surrendering, without hesitation or restraint, to the power that linked them, now and forever.

With gasps and shudders, with moans and bone-deep groans of pleasure, they worshipped at the altar of what linked them.

They now knew the ways—the pathways of love—and followed them with devotion and reverence. They took, and gave, seized, and surrendered.

Through the searing heat of passion, through the fires of desire, they rode hand in hand, body to body, heart to heart, and reached—certain and sure—for all they wanted of life. Of love.

Unchecked, desire raged, fed by them both, and passion soared, then reached its zenith, fracturing their senses, and ecstasy claimed them.

For one instant, they hung, linked by destiny and a power beyond reckoning, souls fused beyond reclaiming...and they wanted it all, together they embraced it all, then they fell.

Slowly circling through the void.

Back to earth, to the comfort of silken sheets and the soul-deep pleasure of being in each other's arms.

It seemed like, and might have been, hours before Richard stirred. Jacqueline lay boneless beneath him, deeply asleep. He lifted from her, disengaged, then slumped beside her.

For a moment, he simply lay on his back beside his sleeping wife and marveled at how his life had played out. He was, finally, whole and content—enough to know that he had never before been content at all. Yet in that moment of suspended connection with the world, the revelation that hung at the forefront of his mind was that tonight and the day that would soon dawn was and would be their true beginning.

All that had come before was their past. Tomorrow's dawn would see their future start.

Emotions far more active than contentment poured through him at the prospect—eager anticipation, determination, and a joyful happiness. A readiness to engage and make their shared life all it could possibly be.

Beyond all doubt, he had finally found his way to where he belonged.

Smiling to himself, he came up on his elbow to reach for the sheets lying tangled at their feet—and his gaze fell on the orb.

As before, it sat on Jacqueline's dressing table, placed, as it always seemed to be, in a spot where the moonlight would reach it. But now, the moon had sailed across the sky far enough for the shaft of silvery light that struck through the window to have moved well beyond the orb.

It sat on the dressing table, untouched by moonlight. And still, it glowed.

Richard stared at the unearthly radiance lighting the moonstone. Steady and sure, it was strong enough to cast faint light across the room all the way to where he and Jacqueline lay abed.

Hardly daring to breathe, he stared.

Then he forced his lungs to expand, drew in a long, deep breath, and made a mental note to have someone who understood such things examine the moonstone. It was a stone, a physical entity—there had to be some explanation.

He drew up the sheet and lay down; beneath the silk, he drew Jacqueline to him, smiling again as she murmured incoherently, then snuggled against his side.

The warmth of her body sank into his, drawing his thoughts from the orb. He closed his eyes as sleep again reached for him, and he allowed himself to sink into Morpheus's arms.

The trill of birdcall woke Jacqueline and Richard the next morn. Their new apartment lay closer to the wood than her old chamber, and as they blinked their eyes wide, they discovered the day had long ago dawned in all its glory.

Jacqueline glanced at Richard, now her husband in all ways, and met his eyes.

He smiled and lifted his head to kiss her, and for several minutes, they lay, relaxed and at peace, and swapped murmured observations from the previous day—of his family, her people, and their perfect celebration.

Both were so deeply happy, it was a wrench to yield to the beckoning of duty, yet they could hear the odd clatter and clang from downstairs.

Eventually, reluctantly, they rose.

Jacqueline headed for her armoire, beside her dressing table, then halted and stared at the dressing table's top. She frowned, then glanced at Richard. "I thought the orb was here."

His head whipped around. His gaze went beyond her, and he, too, stared at the orb-less expanse.

After a moment—a very long moment—he raised his eyes and met her gaze. "I saw it there last night—or early this morning. I can't be certain of the hour." He stepped toward her, then came to stand beside her. His fingers tangled with hers as they both stared at where the orb had been. He drew in a tight breath, then said, "When I saw it, it was glowing."

"In the moonlight?"

"No. The moon had passed. It was…glowing on its own."

After a moment, she reached out with her free hand and ran her fingers over the spot where the orb had stood.

"No one came into the room and took it," Richard murmured. "I can swear to that."

She believed him. Tentatively, she suggested, "I suppose we could hunt for it. It must be somewhere in the house, don't you think?"

"Perhaps." Richard closed his hand about hers and gently squeezed. "But I predict that, even though we might hunt high and low, we'll never find it." He released her hand, put his arm around her shoulders, drew her against him, and pressed a kiss to her temple.

She sighed and leaned into him. "I suppose that, as it did for me—for us—it'll turn up when it wants to be found."

Their evolving understanding of the orb and what its appearance and disappearance meant hung between them, unstated.

"Very likely." Hugging her to him, Richard repeated her words of the night. "There's no point thinking too much about such things—we're not supposed to know. Life and love are abiding mysteries and will remain so, no matter the striving of mortal men."

She held still, savoring the words, then turned her head and, at close quarters, met his eyes.

The look they exchanged carried acceptance and commitment.

"My lady? M'lady?" A scratching sounded at the door, then Young Willie's voice rose more certainly, "The mare's foaling. Hopkins said as you and his lordship would want to know."

Jacqueline laughed. "Thank you, Young Willie, and thank Hopkins for sending word—his lordship and I will be there shortly."

"Aye, miss—I mean, my lady."

She chuckled; her household was determined to make all due use of her new station.

As Young Willie's clattering footsteps receded, she brought her gaze back to Richard's face.

"Clearly," he said, smiling down at her, "our joint life has begun, and we need to catch up."

"Indeed." She stretched upward and lightly touched her lips to his, then drew back, and he let her go. "We'd better get dressed and go down."

Richard saw no reason to argue. Smiling, he reached for his clothes and felt a glow of expectation spread through him.

He was looking forward to the day.

To this day and all that would follow—all the days he would spend by Jacqueline's side as the defender of the guardian of Nimway Hall.

THE END

Dear Reader,

The Legend of Nimway Hall is something different—six authors telling tales-through-the-ages of generations of women in one particular family born to magic, each fated to find their one true love. I hope you've enjoyed the first in the series—*1750: Jacqueline*.

And now for the fun part—the first five volumes in the series are to be released a week apart, commencing with this book, to be followed a week later by *1794: Charlotte* by Karen Hawkins, which in turn will be followed by *1818: Isabel* by Suzanne Enoch, and *1942: Jocelyn* by Linda Needham. Expect further volumes in the series, including *1888: Alexandra* by Victoria Alexander and *1926: Maddie Rose* by Susan Andersen.

See below for descriptions of the installments to come, and plunge deeper into *The Legend of Nimway Hall* to learn more of the strange powers of Balesboro Wood, the mysterious orb, and of Nimway Hall, the house itself. Finding love was never so much fun as the unexpected twists and turns that steer, guide, and prod the descendants of Merlin and Nimue into the arms of their one true loves.

Enjoy!

Stephanie.

For alerts as new books are released, plus information on upcoming books, exclusive sweepstakes and sneak peeks into upcoming novels, sign up for Stephanie's Private Email Newsletter
http://www.stephanielaurens.com/newsletter-signup/

The ultimate source for detailed information on all Stephanie's published books, including covers, descriptions, and excerpts, is Stephanie's Website www.stephanielaurens.com

You can also follow Stephanie via her Amazon Author Page at
http://tinyurl.com/zc3e9mp

Goodreads members can follow Stephanie via her author page
https://www.goodreads.com/author/show/9241.Stephanie_Laurens

You can email Stephanie at stephanie@stephanielaurens.com

Or find her on Facebook
https://www.facebook.com/AuthorStephanieLaurens/

COMING NEXT IN THE LEGEND OF NIMWAY HALL:

The second installment
1794: CHARLOTTE by Karen Hawkins
To be released on March 22, 2018.

New York Times bestselling author Karen Hawkins writes a ravishing addition to an exciting series of romances touched by magic as old as time.

A properly raised young lady rebels against the restrictions of both society and family when she meets a dark, dangerous, and wildly passionate man as they both fight to resist their forbidden love... and the seductive pull of an ancient magic.

Miss Charlotte Harrington knows what's expected of her. Properly raised and newly reminded of her duties after the unexpected death of her far-more-perfect twin sister, Charlotte is resigned to wedding the son of a neighboring land owner and live a sedate and proper life. But Charlotte's high spirits will not be contained and she yearns deeply for a life of adventure, excitement, and love.

When wild and untamed Marco di Rossi arrives at Nimway Hall, commissioned to carve a masterpiece for the family home, he finds himself instantly drawn to the far-from-subdued Charlotte. Despite the potential ruin to his own brilliant career, he cannot resist her spirit and beauty, nor the call of the deep, wild magic that resides within a mysterious and magical orb hidden deep in the walls of the ancient house of Nimway...

A historical novel of 57,000 words interweaving romance, mystery, and magic.

AND THE LEGEND OF NIMWAY HALL CONTINUES WITH:

The third installment
1818: ISABEL by Suzanne Enoch
To be released on March 29, 2018.

New York Times bestselling author Suzanne Enoch spins a Regency-era tale at Nimway Hall, in a book series centered on a house where love and magic entwine to bring romance to all who dwell there.

A passionate, determined young lady trying to prove herself worthy of a timeless, magic-touched legacy and a steadfast gentleman looking for his own place in the world join forces to restore an abandoned estate to its former glory.

The moment Isabel de Rossi turns eighteen, she insists on taking charge of Nimway Hall, which has stood empty for the past ten years. Well-aware that all her female forebears found true love at Nimway, she can't wait to discover her own destined match. Instead she's faced with Adam Driscoll, the infuriatingly practical estate manager whose presence is a constant, insulting reminder that her own grandmother thinks she has no idea what she's doing.

Adam thought the recent offer of a position at Nimway Hall a godsend. After spending six years managing his elderly uncle's estate he is at a crossroads, facing either a dreary career in the army or the church. At Nimway he can continue working with his hands, his feet firmly on the ground and his mind on practical matters of crops, millstones, and irrigation. He revels in the chance to restore this estate to its former glory as the well-run marvel of Somerset—even though several mysterious setbacks have befallen his efforts.

The last complication he needs is a quirky, foreign-raised heiress intent on finding a magical orb and interfering with his well-laid plans; but practical Adam can't help noticing that in her presence the repairs are suddenly going well, and that the pretty mistress of the Hall is clever, amusing, and genuinely interested in improving her estate and the lives of her tenants.

Despite their conflicting sensibilities he finds it hard to resist their simmering attraction. At the same time Adam is keenly aware that the more he helps Isabel with the estate the closer he is to assisting himself out of his position—and away from her.

Despite herself, Isabel is reluctantly drawn to Adam's quiet strength and dedication, but has begun to wonder if she somehow isn't worthy of becoming the property's guardian; though she searches everywhere for evidence of magic, the famous orb—the artifact reputedly responsible for every love match made at Nimway Hall, including her own parents'—is nowhere to be found...until dreamy Lord Alton from the neighboring estate arrives and starts to pursue Isabel. The pesky orb suddenly appears, though it seems to have a preference for Adam's room.

For a young lady in need of some polish, the choice between a charming viscount and a headstrong, interfering employee should be a simple one, but magic is a stubborn thing—and the heart is even more headstrong.

The fourth installment
1942: JOCELYN by Linda Needham
To be released on April 5, 2018.

USA Today bestselling author Linda Needham brings you the fourth story in a series of romances touched by magic as old as time.

A courageous young woman is just managing to keep up with her family's vast, wartime farm when a handsome Lt. Colonel and his staff of officers take command of her home. A private war ensues between them, and the couple soon learns that resistance is futile when it comes to love in the heat of battle.

World War II has come to Nimway Hall, and with it an endless series of wartime challenges that its lady and guardian, Josie Stirling, must overcome. As passionate and courageous as each of the guardians who have come before her, Josie is fiercely determined to defend her family's ancient estate from all possible threats. But with the recent evacuation of Dunkirk and the bombs of the Blitz raining random terror all across Britain, even the once-pastoral manor farm of Nimway has become as dangerous as any battlefield.

Loved and respected by everyone in her circle of care, Josie is knee-deep in evacuee children, Land Girls, the local Home Guard, a much-reduced estate staff, two cranky tractors and her widowed father she has just rescued from the London Blitz. Her days and nights, and even her dreams are chock-full of wartime charity fund raisers, meeting the strict requirements of the Ministries of Agriculture and Food, organizing knitting circles, leading her local WVS, tending the acres of orchards, the mill, and fields of grain and defending her beloved Baleswood from the Timber Commission.

To add to her problems, not only has the military requisitioned an entire wing of Nimway Hall, they've sent the most arrogant officer in the entire army to command the unit and impose his orders on the finely-tuned workings of the estate. A man as arrogant as he is handsome. Not that Josie has time in her life to notice!

The very last post Lt. Colonel Gideon Fletchard ever wanted was to be holed up in the wilds of Somerset, in an old manor house, far from the front line. But he was seriously injured on a secret mission early in the war and has recovered just enough to command a team of Royal Engineers, commissioned to build operational bases for Churchill's new Secret Army. Once a highly respected intelligence officer, Gideon resents his demotion to the "Home Front" and has little respect for the so-called civilian army he's been assigned to recruit and train. War is waged by soldiers in the field, not by farmers and factory workers.

A sentiment the contentious lady of Nimway Hall disputes at every turn. She seems to believe that her work for the war effort is as critical as his. Though the woman's opinions are seriously wrong-headed, she is as beautiful as she is devoted to her people and he can't help admiring the firm and resourceful way she manages the estate. Can't help noticing her fiercely green eyes and the sun-blush of her cheek. Not that he should be noticing such distractions. Not now. Not with a war to win and contact to make with a secret agent named Arcturus.

As the war between the sexes heats up, so does the ancient magic of romance. Josie and Gideon may not be looking for love, but at Nimway Hall they'll soon discover that love has come looking for them.

Fourth book in the Nimway Hall series. A historical novel of 55,000 words, entwining romance, mystery and the magic of love.

Further installments will appear in due course!

COMING NEXT FROM STEPHANIE:

**The first volume in THE CAVANAUGH SIBLINGS
THE DESIGNS OF LORD RANDOLPH CAVANAUGH
To be released by MIRA on April 24, 2018**

#1 New York Times bestselling author Stephanie Laurens returns with a new series that captures the simmering desires and intrigues of early Victorians as only she can. Ryder Cavanaugh's step-siblings are determined to make their own marks in London society. Seeking fortune and passion, THE CAVANAUGHS will delight readers with their bold exploits.

An independent nobleman

Lord Randolph Cavanaugh is loyal and devoted—but only to family. To the rest of the world he's aloof and untouchable, a respected and driven entrepreneur. But Rand yearns for more in life, and when he travels to Buckinghamshire to review a recent investment, he discovers a passionate woman who will challenge his self-control...

A determined lady

Felicia Throgmorton intends to keep her family afloat. For decades, her father was consumed by his inventions and now, months after his death, with their finances in ruins, her brother insists on continuing their father's tinkering. Felicia is desperate to hold together what's left of the estate. Then she discovers she must help persuade their latest investor that her father's follies are a risk worth taking...

Together—the perfect team

Rand arrives at Throgmorton Hall to discover the invention on which he's staked his reputation has exploded, the inventor is not who he expected, and a fiercely intelligent woman now holds the key to his future success. But unflinching courage in the face of dismaying hurdles is a trait they share, and Rand and Felicia are forced to act together against ruthless foes to protect everything they hold dear.

ALSO COMING SOON:

**The sixth volume in
The Casebook of Barnaby Adair mystery-romances
THE CONFOUNDING CASE OF THE CARISBROOK
EMERALDS
To be released on June 14, 2018**

#1 NYT-bestselling author Stephanie Laurens brings you a tale of emerging and also established loves and the many facets of family, interwoven with mystery and murder.

A young lady accused of theft and the gentleman who elects himself her champion enlist the aid of Stokes, Barnaby, Penelope, and friends in pursuing justice, only to find themselves tangled in a web of inter-family tensions and secrets.

When Miss Cara Di Abaccio is accused of stealing the Carisbrook emeralds by the infamously arrogant Lady Carisbrook and marched out of her guardian's house by Scotland Yard's finest, Hugo Adair, Barnaby Adair's cousin, takes umbrage and descends on Scotland Yard, breathing fire in Cara's defense.

Hugo discovers Inspector Stokes has been assigned to the case, and after surveying the evidence thus far, Stokes calls in his big guns when it comes to dealing with investigations in the ton—namely, the Honorable Barnaby Adair and his wife, Penelope.

Soon convinced of Cara's innocence and—given Hugo's apparent tendre for Cara—the need to clear her name, Penelope and Barnaby join Stokes and his team in pursuing the emeralds and, most importantly, who stole them.

But the deeper our intrepid investigators delve into the Carisbrook household, the more certain they become that all is not as it seems. Lady Carisbrook is a harpy, Franklin Carisbrook is secretive, Julia Carisbrook is overly timid, and Lord Carisbrook, otherwise a genial and honorable gentleman, holds himself distant from his family. More, his lordship attempts to shut down the investigation. And Stokes, Barnaby, and Penelope are convinced the Carisbrooks' staff are not sharing all they know.

Meanwhile, having been appointed Cara's watchdog until the mystery is resolved, Hugo, fascinated by Cara as he's been with no other young lady, seeks to entertain and amuse her...and, increasingly intently, to discover the way to her heart. Consequently, Penelope finds herself juggling the attractions of the investigation against the demands of the Adair family for her to actively encourage the budding romance.

What would her mentors advise? On that, Penelope is crystal clear.

Regardless, aided by Griselda, Violet, and Montague and calling on contacts in business, the underworld, and ton society, Penelope, Barnaby, and Stokes battle to peel back each layer of subterfuge and, step by step, eliminate the innocent and follow the emeralds' trail...

Yet instead of becoming clearer, the veils and shadows shrouding the Carisbrooks only grow murkier...until, abruptly, our investigators find themselves facing an inexplicable death, with a potential murderer whose conviction would shake society to its back teeth.

A historical novel of 78,000 words interweaving mystery, romance, and social intrigue.

TO BE FOLLOWED BY:

**The seventh volume in
The Casebook of Barnaby Adair mystery-romances
THE MURDER AT MANDEVILLE HALL
To be released on August 16, 2018**

RECENTLY RELEASED:

**The first volume in Lady Osbaldestone's Christmas Chronicles
LADY OSBALDESTONE'S CHRISTMAS GOOSE**

A lighthearted tale of Christmas long ago with a grandmother and three of her grandchildren, one lost soul, a lady driven to distraction, a recalcitrant donkey, and a flock of determined geese.

Three years after being widowed, Therese, Lady Osbaldestone finally settles into her dower property of Hartington Manor in the village of Little Moseley in Hampshire. She is in two minds as to whether life in the small village will generate sufficient interest to keep her amused over the months when she is not in London or visiting friends around the country. But she will see.

It's December, 1810, and Therese is looking forward to her usual

Christmas with her family at Winslow Abbey, her youngest daughter, Celia's home. But then a carriage rolls up and disgorges Celia's three oldest children. Their father has contracted mumps, and their mother has sent the three—Jamie, George, and Lottie—to spend this Christmas with their grandmama in Little Moseley.

Therese has never had to manage small children, not even her own. She assumes the children will keep themselves amused, but quickly learns that what amuses three inquisitive, curious, and confident youngsters isn't compatible with village peace. Just when it seems she will have to set her mind to inventing something, she and the children learn that with only twelve days to go before Christmas, the village flock of geese has vanished.
Every household in the village is now missing the centerpiece of their Christmas feast. But how could an entire flock go missing without the slightest trace? The children are as mystified and as curious as Therese— and she seizes on the mystery as the perfect distraction for the three children as well as herself.

But while searching for the geese, she and her three helpers stumble on two locals who, it is clear, are in dire need of assistance in sorting out their lives. Never one to shy from a little matchmaking, Therese undertakes to guide Miss Eugenia Fitzgibbon into the arms of the determinedly reclusive Lord Longfellow. To her considerable surprise, she discovers that her grandchildren have inherited skills and talents from both her late husband as well as herself. And with all the customary village events held in the lead up to Christmas, she and her three helpers have opportunities galore in which to subtly nudge and steer.

Yet while their matchmaking appears to be succeeding, neither they nor anyone else have found so much as a feather from the village's geese. Larceny is ruled out; a flock of that size could not have been taken from the area without someone noticing. So where could the birds be? And with the days passing and Christmas inexorably approaching, will they find the blasted birds in time?

First in series. A novel of 60,000 words. A Christmas tale of romance and geese.

ALSO RELEASED IN 2017:

All three exciting instalments in THE DEVIL'S BROOD TRILOGY

The first volume of the Devil's Brood Trilogy
THE LADY BY HIS SIDE

A marquess in need of the right bride. An earl's daughter in search of a purpose. A betrayal that ends in murder and balloons into a threat to the realm.

Sebastian Cynster knows time is running out. If he doesn't choose a wife soon, his female relatives will line up to assist him. Yet the current debutantes do not appeal. Where is he to find the right lady to be his marchioness? Then Drake Varisey, eldest son of the Duke of Wolverstone, asks for Sebastian's aid.

Having assumed his father's mantle in protecting queen and country, Drake must go to Ireland in pursuit of a dangerous plot. But he's received an urgent missive from Lord Ennis, an Irish peer—Ennis has heard something Drake needs to know. Ennis insists Drake attends an upcoming house party at Ennis's Kent estate so Ennis can reveal his information face-to-face. Sebastian has assisted Drake before and, long ago, had a liaison with Lady Ennis. Drake insists Sebastian is just the man to be Drake's surrogate at the house party—the guests will imagine all manner of possibilities and be blind to Sebastian's true purpose. Unsurprisingly, Sebastian is reluctant, but Drake's need is real. With only more debutantes on his horizon, Sebastian allows himself to be persuaded. His first task is to inveigle Antonia Rawlings, a lady he has known all her life, to include him as her escort to the house party. Although he's seen little of Antonia in recent years, Sebastian is confident of gaining her support.

Eldest daughter of the Earl of Chillingworth, Antonia has abandoned the search for a husband and plans to use the week of the house party to decide what to do with her life. There has to be some purpose, some role, she can claim for her own. Consequently, on hearing Sebastian's request and an explanation of what lies behind it, she seizes on the call to action. Suppressing her senses' idiotic reaction to Sebastian's nearness, she agrees to be his partner-in-intrigue.

But while joining the house party proves easy, the gathering is thrown into chaos when Lord Ennis is murdered—just before he was to speak with Sebastian. Worse, Ennis's last words, gasped to Sebastian, are: *Gunpowder. Here.*
Gunpowder? And here, where? With a killer continuing to stalk the halls, side by side, Sebastian and Antonia search for answers and, all the while, the childhood connection that had always existed between them strengthens and blooms…into something so much more.

First volume in a trilogy. A historical romance with gothic overtones layered over a continuing intrigue. A full length novel of 99,000 words.

The second volume of the Devil's Brood Trilogy
AN IRRESISTIBLE ALLIANCE

A duke's second son with no responsibilities and a lady starved of the excitement her soul craves join forces to unravel a deadly, potentially catastrophic threat to the realm - that only continues to grow.

With his older brother's betrothal announced, Lord Michael Cynster is freed from the pressure of familial expectations. However, the allure of his previous hedonistic pursuits has paled. Then he learns of the mission his brother, Sebastian, and Lady Antonia Rawlings have been assisting with and volunteers to assist by hunting down the hoard of gunpowder now secreted somewhere in London.
Michael sets out to trace the carters who transported the gunpowder from Kent to London. His quest leads him to the Hendon Shipping Company, where he discovers his sole source of information is the only daughter of Jack and Kit Hendon, Miss Cleome Hendon, who although a fetchingly attractive lady, firmly holds the reins of the office in her small hands.

Cleo has fought to achieve her position in the company. Initially, managing the office was a challenge, but she now conquers all in just a few hours a week. With her three brothers all adventuring in America, she's been driven to the realization that she craves adventure, too. When Michael Cynster walks in and asks about carters, Cleo's instincts leap. She wrings from him the full tale of his mission—and offers him a bargain. She will lead him to the carters he seeks if he agrees to include her as an equal partner in the mission.

Horrified, Michael attempts to resist, but ultimately finds himself agreeing—a sequence of events he quickly learns is common around Cleo. Then she delivers on her part of the bargain, and he finds there are benefits to allowing her to continue to investigate beside him—not least being that if she's there, then he knows she's safe.

But the further they go in tracing the gunpowder, the more deaths they uncover. And when they finally locate the barrels, they find themselves tangled in a fight to the death—one that forces them to face what has grown between them, to seize and defend what they both see as their path to the greatest adventure of all. A shared life. A shared future. A shared love.

Second volume in a trilogy. A historical romance with gothic overtones layered over a continuing intrigue. A full length novel of 101,000 words.

The thrilling third and final volume in the Devil's Brood Trilogy
THE GREATEST CHALLENGE OF THEM ALL

A nobleman devoted to defending queen and country and a noblewoman wild enough to match his every step race to disrupt the plans of a malignant intelligence intent on shaking England to its very foundations.

Lord Drake Varisey, Marquess of Winchelsea, eldest son and heir of the Duke of Wolverstone, must foil a plot that threatens to shake the foundations of the realm, but the very last lady—nay, noblewoman—he needs assisting him is Lady Louisa Cynster, known throughout the ton as Lady Wild.

For the past nine years, Louisa has suspected that Drake might well be the ideal husband for her, even though he's assiduous in avoiding her. But she's now twenty-seven and enough is enough. She believes propinquity will elucidate exactly what it is that lies between them, and what better opportunity to work closely with Drake than his latest mission, with which he patently needs her help?

Unable to deny Louisa's abilities or the value of her assistance and powerless to curb her willfulness, Drake is forced to grit his teeth and acquiesce to her sticking by his side, if only to ensure her safety. But all too soon, his true feelings for her show enough for her, perspicacious as she is, to see through his denials, which she then interprets as a challenge.

Even while they gather information, tease out clues, increasingly desperately search for the missing gunpowder, and doggedly pursue the killer responsible for an ever-escalating tally of dead men, thrown together through the hours, he and she learn to trust and appreciate each other. And fed by constant exposure—and blatantly encouraged by her— their desires and hungers swell and grow…

As the barriers between them crumble, the attraction he has for so long restrained burgeons and balloons, until goaded by her near-death, it erupts, and he seizes her—only to be seized in return.

Linked irrevocably and with their wills melded and merged by passion's fire, with time running out and the evil mastermind's deadline looming, together, they focus their considerable talents and make one last push to learn the critical truths—to find the gunpowder and unmask the villain behind this far-reaching plot. Only to discover that they have significantly less time than they'd thought, that the villain's target is even more crucially fundamental to the realm than they'd imagined, and it's going to take all that Drake is—as well as all that Louisa as Lady Wild can bring to bear—to defuse the threat, capture the villain, and make all safe and right again. As they race to the ultimate confrontation, the future of all England rests on their shoulders.

Third volume in the trilogy. A historical romance with gothic overtones layered over an intrigue. A full length novel of 129,000 words.

ABOUT THE AUTHOR

#1 *New York Times* bestselling author Stephanie Laurens began writing romances as an escape from the dry world of professional science. Her hobby quickly became a career when her first novel was accepted for publication, and with entirely becoming alacrity, she gave up writing about facts in favor of writing fiction.

All Laurens's works to date are historical romances ranging from medieval times to the mid-1800s, and her settings range from Scotland to India. The majority of her works are set in the period of the British Regency. Laurens has published more than 60 works of historical romance, including 38 *New York Times* bestsellers and has sold more than 20 million print, audio, and e-books globally. All her works are continuously available in print and e-book formats in English worldwide, and have been translated into many other languages. An international bestseller, among other accolades, Laurens has received the Romance Writers of America® prestigious RITA® Award for Best Romance Novella 2008 for *The Fall of Rogue Gerrard*.

Laurens's continuing novels featuring the Cynster family are widely regarded as classics of the historical romance genre. Other series include the *Bastion Club Novels*, the *Black Cobra Quartet*, and the *Casebook of Barnaby Adair Novels*.

For information on all published novels and on upcoming releases and updates on novels yet to come, visit Stephanie's website: www.stephanielaurens.com

To sign up for Stephanie's Email Newsletter (a private list) for heads-up alerts as new books are released, exclusive sneak peeks into upcoming books, and exclusive sweepstakes contests, follow the prompts on Stephanie's Email Newsletter Sign-up Page on her website.

Stephanie lives with her husband and two cats in the hills outside

Melbourne, Australia. When she isn't writing, she's reading, and if she isn't reading, she'll be tending her garden.